Perhaps he was in the sanctuary, or in the kitchen.

No. He would probably be on their balcony. Meg felt her feet moving. She wanted to be with him. There were only two more hours.

Cease striving and know that I am God. She looked up into the darkened sky again, but there were no falling stars to even misconstrue as being signs.

I need to stop. She'd been giving in to every feeling for the last week. *You have to obey in the small things if you're ever going to obey in the crucial things.*

Sometimes the small things *are* the crucial things.

She was now at the bottom of the steps, and had two directions to choose from. One led to the balcony stairs, the other away from the lights under a secluded, scrubby palm tree where she could clearly see the stars.

Meg moved to the right.

I Will Follow

I Will Follow

Clare Cook & Bethany Patchin

PHILOKALIA BOOKS

To our Diegos, Jeff and Sam

Chapter One

Were they clouds, or mountains?

Meg squinted her eyes and pressed her forehead against the bus window. A faint, jagged blue ridge lay low on the horizon, holding steady while in the foreground the Mexican desert brush whizzed by. The landscape was beautiful and foreign, almost other-worldly. Bobbing yellow flowers were sprinkled over the ground, and here and there among them a spiky tree grew in defiance of the sand and wind. Occasionally a lone cow could be seen standing near the road, chewing on the tough underbrush. Even the cows looked totally unfamiliar—Meg was used to the plump, black-and-white Holsteins of Wisconsin. She had no idea what these animals were raised for; they were too skinny to be beef cattle and too dry to give any great amount of milk. Maybe they were just lawnmowers.

The newness of the scenery had been appealing at first, but Meg had given up her perusal of the surroundings after half-an-hour, when it had become clear that the view outside held little variety.

The mountains—or clouds—hadn't been there then. So the scenery had changed a little. A very little.

The view on the inside of the bus was interesting for different reasons.

1

As she settled back in her plush seat she stole a covert glance at her seat partner. An elderly Mexican woman rested beside her; Meg couldn't help comparing her to a little brown walnut. The only spot of color on the señora's face was a dash of bright fuchsia lipstick across her pursed mouth.

Meg wished that she was comfortable enough to at least exchange names, but she didn't feel confident in her rudimentary Spanish pronunciations. Teresa, her sister—the Spanish expert—would have no problem with it, but Meg would probably stumble on a basic *hola*. Besides, the woman probably wouldn't appreciate being bothered. She seemed to be paying little attention to Meg.

It was strange, sitting two inches away from someone without being able to carry on a basic conversation. Meg stole another look at her companion. Perhaps her name was Maria. It seemed to fit. Then again, what were the other possibilities? Meg couldn't remember more than three Spanish names.

The seat in front of Meg shifted back a few inches to reveal Teresa's eye peeking back at her through the side crack. "Hey, Nutmeg, are those mountains?"

Meg's eyes swept over the shadowy shapes again. "I think so, but I'm not sure."

"They're clouds." Will's sandy-brown bangs and blue eyes appeared over the back of the seat adjoining her sister's. He was always one to take the opposing view.

"I think I'll side with my sister on this one." Teresa's voice was muffled by her seat. "Look at how they're all concentrated in one spot."

Everyone's attention turned to the window. Meg noticed that "Maria"'s did, too. *Maybe she understands every word we're saying.* She was probably amused at the questions of the excited tourists.

"I suppose we'll find out soon enough," Meg said. They probably *were* clouds, since all of her assumptions had been wrong so far.

When she had found out that they were going to be bussed into Monterrey, her imagination had run wild. She had figured they would wind up in an old school bus that exaggerated every pothole. Chickens would flap in the aisles, babies would cry, and the hot desert wind would cover them all with a fine layer of sand.

Instead, her fingers brushed the plastic-like glass windows of a Mercedes Benz, complete with cushioned seats, a bathroom, and four small TVs. Earlier the driver had put in a bloody Spanish cowboy movie but thankfully it had ended and the televisions now aired a Mexico versus Brazil soccer game.

She had been wrong about everything concerning this part of the trip except the road. Though her father had informed her of its importance as a transportation route, it was nothing like the highways in the United States. The surface was uneven and cracked from too much sun, with stretches where the asphalt disappeared altogether and left vehicles to rumble over packed dirt. The shocks on the bus minimized their jostling, but Meg pitied the occasional automobile they passed.

Meg glanced up at the TV. The soccer game didn't look very interesting. Mexico was losing by two points—not to mention that it was all in Spanish.

Meg pulled her Bible and a pack of gum out from beneath the seat. She popped a piece into her mouth and crumpled the silver wrapper. Had Maria ever chewed gum before? Now there was an opening for an introduction.

She turned to the Hispanic woman with the pack of Big Red.

"*Para usted.*" (For you.) Although Teresa had refreshed her on a few basic phrases, the pronunciations felt heavy. Hopefully the woman wouldn't reply with a long string of Spanish. One year of *Espanol* in eighth grade did not prepare you for conversation.

The woman's eyes remained unblinking as she reached out a tiny hand and took a stick. "*Gracias.*" (Thank you.) The heavily accented word came gruffly from her lips. Was that a hint of a smile around her mouth?

"*De nada.*" (You're welcome.) Meg let out her breath. She had communicated!

"*Aqui. Para usted.*" (Here. For you.) Maria reached into a straw bag at her feet and pulled out a small cardboard box. She motioned for Meg's hand, and Meg obliged. *Chiclets*, the box read. Three pieces of multi-colored gum fell into Meg's palm.

"*Gracias.*" *I should have known*—of course they would have gum here! This was Mexico, not Africa.

3

her Bible and began to read, rubbing her upper arms for
as she did so. The temperature was plenty hot outside, but the air conditioning in the bus seemed to be on full blast. Her red tank top and light flowery cotton skirt didn't provide much protection.

A verse on the page in front of her caught her eye. It would be a good reminder for the next five weeks. Meg nudged her sister's seat with a sandaled foot and put her face up to the crack between Will and Teresa.

"Hey, Reeses, listen to this. *'Do your best to present yourself to God as one approved, a workman who does not need to be ashamed and who correctly handles the word of truth.'* It's in Second Timothy."

Teresa sat up in her seat and looked at Meg over the top of it. She crossed her arms and rested her chin on her hands. "*'A workman who does not need to be ashamed.'* Yeah, I like that."

Meg stuck in an old Big Red wrapper to mark the page. "I think I'll bring it up tonight when we're all together." She glanced at the occupants of the seats across the aisle, then raised her eyebrow slightly to send Teresa a signal.

In front of their father sat Pete Saindon and Jamie Difrisco, the last two members of their small missionary group. They were hunched down in their seats with heads bent close together. Fortunately their quiet talking was broken only by occasional laughter and not frequent kisses. The two had been practically inseparable since the moment the group had stepped on the plane at O'Hare International Airport in Chicago. Meg didn't think Jamie's hand had broken contact with Pete's since then.

Meg frowned as she watched them. What was going on in their minds right now, as they drew closer to their destination? It would be interesting to know the honest reasons for their participation in this trip. Hopefully it wasn't because of the added time they could spend in each other's company. Pete was twenty, Jamie nineteen, and they should have been a little more discreet about their attraction to each other. Then again, Pete was Pete.

An added problem was the cultural differences between the Mexican Christians and those that came down from the States. As a group they had gone over the Monterrey mission's expectations with Jeff, the youth pastor there, when he had visited Wisconsin earlier that spring. Mexican Christians were much more discreet with personal relationships, much more formal. They made it a point to remain pure before the eyes of their society and before God. Among other things, Jeff had stressed that this meant dressing modestly and keeping romantic relationships subdued in public.

Pete and Jamie had heard all of this and agreed to abide by it, albeit reluctantly. Though they weren't at the mission yet, Meg still bet that Jamie and Pete wouldn't exactly put the relationship on hold once they arrived.

Some of the rules had sounded a bit stuffy at first to Meg but the reasoning behind them was wise. Why didn't American Christians care about these things like the Mexicans did? After the meeting with Jeff, Meg had heard Jamie complaining to Teresa about having to buy new tank tops because the ones she owned were too low-cut to pass the mission's standards.

But then, how much did Meg do to keep her own witness pure? Sure, she was modest, even at home. But were her actions so different, so distinct that people knew Who she belonged to? In America, Christians were recognized by Jesus fish decals on their cars, "What Would Jesus Do?" bracelets, and T-shirts with Christian slogans.

Dear children, let us not love with words or tongue but with actions and in truth.

Will reached back between the seats and lightly swatted Meg's leg. "Red slug-bug, no returns."

"What?"

Teresa and Will both leaned together to peer at Meg through the crack and almost bumped heads. Teresa pulled away so Will could speak. "You don't play that game?"

"No."

"There's a red VW in front of us." He motioned to the windshield. "It's a race—the first person to see a Bug has to call it and tag everyone else."

"I see."

A few minutes later a blue Bug chugged up to the bus and began to pass. Before Will could win again, Teresa spoke. "Blue slug-bug, no returns!" Meg watched her hand tap Will on the shoulder, then sneak back to brush Meg's knee. "No returns."

She had aimed for Meg, but what her fingers actually made contact with was the material covering Maria's knee.

"Teresa!" Meg said in a loud whisper.

Teresa turned slowly in her seat to look at the woman. Brown eyes gazed back at her from an expressionless face.

Teresa's cheeks were pink. "*Lo siento mucho.*" (I'm very sorry.)

"It's okay." The old woman replied in heavily accented English.

"You speak English?" Meg said.

"Yes, I do." A small smile finally tipped up the corners of her mouth.

"May I ask—what's your name?"

"Yadira. Are you Christians?" Her eyes circled to include the other members in the group.

"Yes. How did you know?"

"I see young gringas wearing skirts, then I know—that is Christians. I see in Monterrey sometimes. You read Biblia. This is good."

Gringas. A slang term for female white foreigners. Jeff had repeatedly referred to their group as *gringos* during his visit.

"For you, this is first time to Monterrey. I know because you think mountains are clouds," Yadira said. She pointed a finger at the window. "Monterrey—with beautiful mountains. These I love. You will love, too."

"White slug-bug, no returns… no returns… no returns…"

"Will, I get it already." Meg turned her flushed face to Will. She had little patience for him at this point. They had been sitting for forever, having gone directly from the Mercedes to a non-air-conditioned mission van. And there were apparently a million Volkswagens in the city of Monterrey, all zooming by the puttering Dodge Ram. "Look at all the Bugs. If you keep that up…"

"What's the deal with them, anyway?" Pete piped up from the back. His question was directed to Jeff, who sat in the driver's seat. "I thought old-style Bugs were basically extinct."

"They are, in the US. But Volkswagen does big business down here— no pollution laws to worry about. They're relatively cheap, a lot of people own them."

"Why are all the windows purple?" Jamie asked.

"'They put on a tinted plastic shield, keeps the sun from fading the seat material."

The van suddenly squealed to a stop. Meg was thrown forward so that the seat belt dug into her stomach. She tightened her grip on the top of the seat in front of her, where her hands had remained clutched since they had taken off from the bus station. Now this *was* what she had expected of Monterrey traffic.

Through the cracked side window she could see a tall iron gate directly in front of them, banked on both sides by a thick concrete wall. It was covered with graffiti, the top inlaid with broken shards of colorful glass. The bottle pieces would easily keep anyone from climbing over.

This was the mission? *It looks more like a prison compound.*

"Rick, would you mind opening up for us?" Jeff fished around in the pockets of his worn jeans for the padlock key, then placed it into Meg's father's waiting hand. Jeff turned to the rest of the group after Rick shut the passenger door behind him. "We only keep this back area locked. No one's usually around back here, so we have to keep it secure. If you ever need to get in, let me or José or Diego know. The front gate is always open to whomever, except at night." He revved the engine so the van could make it up the steep incline into its parking place. As soon as they were parked Rick pulled the gate shut behind them.

"All right, everybody out!" Jeff hopped out of the front and went around to help the young men unload the back, which was stuffed full of their luggage.

Meg felt her clothes peel from the sticky seat as she stood and hopped to the cement ground. The back of her neck itched and her thick hair seemed to trap the heat. *What an annoying length.* It was short enough to fall in her face but not long enough to be able to keep in a satisfactory ponytail.

The mid-afternoon sun still beat down steadily, but at least the humidity had stayed at a relative low. The air even smelled dry and a bit dusty. Everyone at home who had been to Mexico mentioned the stench of its cities, but it didn't stink here.

The inside of the compound was much more appealing than the outside, Meg decided. The buildings and the walls were all painted the color of blueberries, though covered with a thin layer of city grime. The cement yard lacked greenery, but tucked away in the corners were small, hardy-looking palm trees. Fitting, since the mission was known as Iglesia de Elim—*Church of the Palms.*

The unfamiliar sounds of the city jarred around her, creating a symphony of discord. The falling pitch of a car horn as it sped by, the rumble of a bus's diesel engine, the Spanish rap music echoing down from the surrounding hills, the dogs barking, brakes screeching, and an occasional rooster crow all blended together to become noise. This was definitely nothing like life in rural Wisconsin.

Strangely, though, it didn't scare her. She was usually one to be afraid of change, afraid of the unknown. She wasn't a big city person. But this wasn't as threatening as she had expected it to be, although that might have something to do with all the people from home who were with her.

She turned around when Teresa and Jamie headed past her, clumsily rolling their luggage in front of them. Will was coming towards her with her suitcase. "Man, what did you pack in here? I know, it's all that make-up of yours."

Meg put a hand on her hip. "Ah, quit your whining."

"Hey, don't be pulling any of that on me, *chiquita* (little gal)." He set down her suitcase with a grin.

"Ooh, impressive. Spanish coming from Will Engle." She reached out and took her bag. It *was* heavy.

"*Pobrecita.*" (Poor little one.) Will held out a hand. "Sure you don't want me to carry that all the way to the dorms?"

"You need to take some Spanish lessons from Teresa." Meg began walking in the direction Jamie and her sister had. "And be careful of who you call *chiquita.*"

"I'm twenty-one and you're sixteen. I can call you whatever I want to."

"Almost seventeen." Twenty-two days away from it, to be exact.

"All right, *señorita.* Now hand me your bag; you look like a duck."

Meg obliged and rubbed her shoulder where the strap had been.

Will left Meg and her luggage at the entrance to the girls dorm. Meg peered into the shadows. The aluminum door and screen offered little privacy for anyone inside. She could see that Jamie and Teresa were already starting to unpack.

Once Meg had shoved her suitcase over the threshold, she stopped and pulled a few loose strands of hair out of her face. Teresa and Jamie called out hellos to her from the other end of the room, then turned back to their suitcases.

Hands on hips, Meg surveyed the shadowed room. It was plain and relatively large, but the space was filled with bunks—they were lined in rows along three of the four walls. A thin layer of dirt rested on everything and the air was stale and thick, as if the room hadn't been aired out for several months.

She walked to the far corner where Teresa and Jamie had claimed two bottom bunks. Her backpack was soon deposited on the top of the third bunk in the row. With a little sigh, Meg sank down into the padding provided on the bottom bunk, only to sit up again, coughing. A cloud of dust had risen from the foam. *We gotta air these things out.*

It could wait. She eased back once again. The dust wasn't half as thick the second time around, and it dissipated quickly. *Time for some rest.*

They had finally arrived, after all the planning. It had been in the works since Christmas, almost six months ago. Teresa had been in the middle of her sophomore year of college as a linguistics major when Will had come from next door with the suggestion that they head to Mexico for a month or so to help build a church. Teresa's degree concentration was Spanish, and she had already been to Mexico twice with an exchange program. Ever since her first trip she had talked about becoming a missionary to the Mexican people.

Meg had been flattered at the invitation to join the four college-aged friends, but she was hesitant about going until her dad, a carpenter, had asked to go along, too. And now they would be here for five weeks...

"Meg." Jamie plunked onto the foot of her own bed. "Are you awake?"

"Yeah." Meg opened her eyes. Teresa was nowhere to be seen, and Jamie was rummaging around in her backpack for something. *Did I doze for a minute?*

She sat up and almost bumped her head on the bottom of the bed above her. Someone had opened the only window in the room, but it hadn't done much good.

Jamie drew a tube of Chapstick from her bag and turned to face Meg.

"What do you say we do a little rearranging and settling in? Jeff said we could have a while to catch our breath."

"Where'd Teresa go?"

"She said she was going to go look around a little. I think she wanted to try out her Español on a native speaker."

"Yeah." Or else the usual crowd of single young men was practicing their English with Teresa. *I suppose the crowd can't be too large here at the mission.*

Jamie nodded her head towards the other end of the room. "Don't you think we should put something over the doorway?"

"You noticed it, too?"

"Yeah, right after I had pulled off my tee-shirt to change into a fresh one. Luckily this corner is far enough away that you wouldn't be able to see back here unless you were standing right at the door."

"A sheet would work, I suppose."

"Got any extra?"

Meg shook her head. "Jeff's wife probably does, though. We can ask her at supper."

"Sounds good. Oh—I know what we need to do. Want to help me air out this foam stuff?"

A minute later they had successfully removed the pads from the plywood bunks. With the mattresses slung across their shoulders, they were able to cough their way out the door and down the small flight of wooden stairs to the open courtyard.

"I bet we could grab two or three each to pile on our bunk from the other beds we aren't going to use." Meg flapped the cushions awkwardly in front of her. "Those bunks are kind of hard underneath."

"Yeah, nobody should mind—we're the only ones sleeping in there."

Five minutes later they were at it again with a second round. Meg squinted at the dust filling the air. There wasn't even a hint of a breeze to carry it away or to relieve her itchy skin. It was a good thing dusk was rapidly approaching to cool them.

"Hey, Meg."

She stopped her flapping at Teresa's voice and turned. Her sister stood there with a young Mexican man. *I knew it—one found her already.*

"Meg, this is Diego Ramirez. I've already introduced him to just about everyone else. He lives here when he's not at college in the States, and does all the odd jobs, right?" Teresa looked to Diego for his nod. "Diego, this is Meg. She's my sister."

"I can tell." Diego put out his hand for a handshake. Meg wiped her hands across the front of her skirt before sliding one into his. Instead of clasping hers straight on, he hooked his thumb with hers and slipped his remaining fingers up around the edge of her palm. He pressed lightly before returning to the normal American position and squeezing again. "A Mexican handshake." His voice was accented, though not quite as heavily as the lady on the bus's had been. "I'm glad you could come, Meg."

"Thank you." She smiled, but kept her eyes lowered to about his shoulder level. Looking people in the eye on first introduction wasn't easy for her. Shorter hair was good for one thing—it fell forward so she could hide behind it. But this guy was only a few inches taller than she was, so it was hard to avoid his eyes.

Teresa never seemed to have that awkward, shy feeling. Meg's sister pushed her impossibly long braid off of her shoulder. "I haven't quite figured out that hand thing, but I'm sure I'll get it eventually."

"I will teach you," Diego said.

Yep, and I'm sure you'll enjoy doing so.

Teresa didn't seem to want to keep him to herself, though. "You two should really get him to show you around. He's been taking me all over."

Meg nodded. Her stomach let out a growl and her hand went to her middle as if to quiet it. "Sorry—I must be hungry."

"Supper will be ready soon," Diego said. "Would you like to see the mission before we eat?"

Meg looked to Teresa. Would her sister be willing to take a second tour? Or maybe Teresa could show her around later. Diego was probably busy.

A bell interrupted them. "That is the meal bell. It will also be a wake-up call for you. Next time you hear it will be at five in the morning." Diego's voice held a teasing note.

Diego leaned back in his chair, the plate in front of him empty. Two helpings of lasagna, four slices of bread, green beans, two glasses of milk, and three cookies—*I love being home from college.*

Across from him sat Will, who was the same age as himself. Next to Will sat Pete, a tall, thin red-head with a loud voice. Both were attempting to speak Spanish with Ruth, the youngest daughter of José, the head pastor of Elim. Ruth was laughing at their questions, but that only seemed to encourage them more.

Jamie was on the other side of Pete, staying quiet. She was following the conversation closely. Pete had his arm over the seats, around her shoulders. Diego leaned across the table.

"Do you speak Spanish?"

"No." Jamie turned to look at him. "Pete does, though."

"I see." Diego's gaze swung to Pete and Ruth.

"No, really, he's very fluent—he's just having fun with her. Languages come easy for him."

"They do not come easy for me." Diego smiled. "I have been in the U.S. for three years and I've worked here at the mission with Americans for twice that long, but I often still sound like a beginner."

"So you're in seminary?"

"Bible college. I've thought about becoming a pastor but I'm still not sure."

"My dad's a pastor. Pete was thinking about doing that for a little while, but I'm glad he decided not to." She looked back at her boyfriend.

Diego glanced at her left hand. No ring. She did seem a little young for engagement, although this group was older than most who visited the mission. *Except Meg.*

Jamie leaned across Pete. "*Cuántos años tienes?*" (How old are you?)

Diego knew what Ruth's reply would be. Newly eighteen, more like Meg's age. At least he supposed so.

A few chairs away from him, she sat finishing the last of her lasagna.

13

During the meal her eyes had been busy. That was about all he had been able to see of her face; the rest had stayed hidden behind her hair. She used her eyes to learn of people, much like he did. She did not use her mouth, like Teresa.

Teresa had approached him only a few minutes after the group had arrived and immediately started a conversation. Grammatically her Spanish was almost perfect, though she spoke with a funny accent and sometimes hesitated while searching for the right word. Both of those things would change as she spent time in Mexico.

Teresa looked directly into his eyes, unlike Meg, who kept hers downcast in the way of traditional Mexican women. Here that was considered a sign of modesty, but Diego had spent enough time around American women to realize that for them, lowered eyes were only a sign of shyness or embarrassment. Or avoidance.

Teresa's long hair, which hung past the middle of her back, made her look much older than Meg. At least two years separated them. Both had the same hair color, the same look about them—light. That Scandinavian complexion which Mexican men would notice and whistle at in appreciation, when the group eventually ventured out into the city on foot. It was good that their father had come along.

His eyes drifted back to Meg, who had finished her meal and was now seated with her hands in her lap. Her expression changed, a small smile gracing her face when she looked to the doorway. Diego followed her gaze to see a familiar woman enter the sanctuary with a baby cradled against her shoulder.

Jeff stood from his seat and approached her, then asked for everyone's attention. "Everybody, this is my wife Adelaida, and our three-month-old daughter Katie. Kerryn's two, asleep in bed I hope. I'm sure she'll introduce herself tomorrow."

Adelaida nodded a greeting at the room in general, adding a quiet hello. She pulled up a folding chair at the end of the table, nearest Meg. All shyness seemed to be gone as Meg reached out to touch Katie's pudgy hand. Adela lifted Katie a few inches and held her out to Meg.

"Would you like to hold her?"

Meg nodded and her arms reached out to take the child. She situated

Katie against her with ease. Was it instinctive or practiced?

He scooted back in his chair, grabbed his plate, and headed to the counter to put his silverware in the soapy basin.

"Do you need any help with the dishes?" Diego asked Yolanda, Ruth's mother, in Spanish.

"No, no. You go on and charm the pretty señoritas."

"My charm is reserved for you alone." He patted her brown hand.

Chapter Three

Meg was unsuccessfully tickling the baby on the stomach when Diego approached her and sat down. She looked up, then quickly looked back at Katie again.

"Would you like to get the grand tour now?" He rocked on the back two legs of the chair.

Did I ever agree to take the tour? Meg didn't remember giving a yes. She hid a smile.

"No, *gracias*." She remembered hearing something about how Mexicans always encouraged foreigners with Spanish—and that they were very forgiving of mistakes. "I'm pretty tired."

"*Habla usted Español?*" (Do you speak Spanish?) He raised one eyebrow.

Meg ran her finger down Katie's nose. "*Un poquito*." (A very little.)

"I will teach you." Diego watched Katie flail her arms. "Can I take your plate?"

"Sure. Thanks."

While Diego was gone, Jeff stood up and announced that they'd have an informal worship time for anyone who felt up to it. Meg reluctantly returned Katie to her mother, then found a seat next to her dad. Pete and Jamie had disappeared.

Diego came out from the kitchen and picked up a guitar from the corner of the room. He began strumming lightly, and everyone pulled into a tighter circle. Meg closed her eyes for a moment and settled into her father's shoulder. He put his arm around her and she sighed. She would be a lot more homesick right now if he hadn't come along.

Diego led them for about twenty minutes in familiar worship tunes. His English accent was almost perfect with the songs. He had probably sung them for years, with all of the different groups who visited. Out of the corner of her eye Meg saw Pete and Jamie slip back into the room after 'Light the Fire.' Jeff initiated a closing time of silent prayer.

Their dad gave Meg and Teresa tight hugs before heading off to the men's dorm. Teresa and Jamie left the room together; Meg wandered behind, not quite ready to go to bed.

The descending darkness of night brought with it relief from the sunlight of late afternoon. While they had been inside, a breeze had finally picked up, and it lifted the ends of Meg's hair as she turned her face into it. A light haze rested over the city, but when Meg tilted her head far back she could see a few faint stars twinkling through. God was looking back down at her here the same way He could at home when she was in the middle of the meadow behind their house.

Faint strains of guitar music came from the sanctuary, accompanied by a flowing Spanish verse. Her ears strained to catch any familiar words in Diego's song. *Jehovah*—Lord. *Siempre*—always. *Gloria*—glory. *Exaltemos... su nombre*—exalt His name? The words were too fast.

She seated herself on a bench and rested her head against the wall. The cement had turned cool in the darkness.

The heavens declare the glory of God; the skies proclaim the work of his hands. Day after day they pour forth speech... Perhaps the stars were singing.

Night after night they display knowledge. There is no speech or language where their voice is not heard—or understood. Though this place, these people, were so foreign to her, God could still speak to them.

But how did she play into it? How could He use her, a culturally sheltered American? She already felt as if she stuck out like ham at a Jewish potluck, and she hadn't even been out in true Mexican society yet. The Mexicans at the mission spoke English and were used to being around

Americans—*with all of our quirks and prejudices.*

The music stopped and a minute later Diego's shadow fell through the doorway. He turned to walk up the steps but she saw him pause to peer into the night.

He asked a question in Spanish. Was it directed at her?

"It's Meg," she said. Her voice seemed to echo around the courtyard. Instead of continuing on as she hoped, he stepped towards her.

"I thought you were tired."

His words prompted a yawn from Meg. "I am." But it was such a nice night, and it was her first chance for silence all day. Unless he stayed.

He leaned against the wall and looked up at the sky for a long while, then he turned back to her.

Meg couldn't bear the silence any longer. "What is his name?" She pointed at a Siberian huskie leashed to the front gate.

"It is a girl, and her name is Beba. She is our watchdog, but she is very friendly." Though there was plenty of room on the bench, Diego seated himself on the ground. Apparently *he* wasn't tired.

"Where do Jeff and Adela live?"

"Under your dorm, on the first floor. There are two apartments—I stay in the other when I am here." He motioned to a point beyond their visibility, around the wall of the main building. "Back there is the basket-ball hoop. I like to play, but I am not very tall."

He seemed above average for Mexican height. Then again, she hadn't seen many Mexican men yet. Only José, Yolanda's husband and pastor of the Elim church, Diego, and the Mercedes bus driver, who couldn't have been taller than five feet. Meg grinned. That tiny man with the mustache had waited on the ground to assist every woman as she exited the bus. The last step was hardly six inches off the ground, but he had gallantly offered them his hand anyway. It was the thought that counted. *Are all Mexican men so gentlemanly?*

"This is your first mission trip?"

"Yes." The idea of extended missions had never really interested her. She was a homebody, and she always got homesick whenever she went anywhere away from her family. The thought of living somewhere far away for an extended time didn't sound appealing. "But at home I try to view my life as missions, too."

"Yes. At college I try to do that. There is a great need there."

"At a Christian college?"

"*Sí*. Maybe more need, in some ways." He didn't elaborate.

"I've always figured that God wants us to see wherever we are as our mission. Some of us are called to be workmen and servants at home."

"Yes, I think there can be danger in making certain activities 'Christian' and others not. But Paul does talk about apostles, people called to share the good news in other countries. You are an apostle here, in my country, and I am one in yours. It is exciting."

Exciting? *Maybe for Teresa.* When other girls had been dreaming of becoming ballerinas, she had been in the backyard with Will, building blanket forts and playing with imaginary Amazon natives. Exciting also for Will, who had spent a year in Madagascar, teaching English and doing evangelistic work. But he found joy in everything.

Diego was a missionary in America, but there was nothing foreign about America for her.

Meg felt her eyes drooping shut. "I really should hit the hay."

"Hit the hay?"

"Sorry. I meant I need to go to bed."

Diego stood when she did and they exchanged a *Buenas noches*. The streetlights cast just enough light for Meg to see her way up the girls' dorm stairs.

Jamie's and Teresa's voices filled the room as Meg went to retrieve her pajamas.

"Where were you?" Teresa's chin was propped on her curled pillow.

"Out stargazing."

Meg pulled her shirt over her head and unbuttoned her skirt. It fell in a circle at her feet and she stepped out of it.

"Diego's such a cool guy." Jamie leaned back and pushed a few black strands of hair out of her mouth.

Meg almost tripped on her skirt, but caught herself on the bunkpost.

"Even though he *is* going to be a pastor."

Why would Jamie use *even though*? Meg looked up from buttoning her long sleeveless nightgown. Jamie had never seemed to mind being a "pastor's kid" before.

"I think he'd make a great pastor." Teresa smiled. "He's a magnificent listener. I would know—he had to put up with me for the first half-hour we were here."

"I'm sure it wasn't hard for him to sit there." Meg seated herself on her bed and pulled back the sheet.

"What do you mean?"

"Come on. Every time we go anywhere new, you've always got at least one male follower to hang on your every word."

"Whatever." Teresa shook her head. "Besides, Diego's not like that."

"He's a great guitar player—and his voice…" Jamie looked at the ceiling of the bunk. Meg squirmed on her foam, trying to find a comfortable position. The sleeping bag was just too thick. Jamie continued. "I don't know, there's just something about guys with guitars, don't you think?"

"Kind of." Teresa shrugged her shoulders. "I mean, Will plays guitar."

Even the sheet felt too warm for Meg. She tossed it off her body. How did Jamie know what Diego's voice sounded like? She and Pete hadn't come back until the last song. *I don't know what the big deal is, anyway.* So he played guitar. Her dad played guitar, too, and he was probably a lot better than Diego.

Teresa hadn't *really* heard Diego sing, either. The good stuff had come after everyone left.

"Those eyes." Jamie persisted in her praise. "Like chocolate. Wow. And I love their hair down here—it's so thick and black."

"Diego's isn't soot black; I'd say it's more of a really dark brown." Meg turned so she was on her other side, facing the girls.

Teresa turned to look at Meg. "I don't know. I think he's pretty normal looking."

"I never said I thought he was cute!" Meg put up her hands in defense. "I was just commenting on his hair color."

Jamie propped herself up on one arm. "I guess it's just something about the way he treats you. He makes you feel like a *person*. But you're right, he isn't half so good-looking as Pete or Will. Will's got that grin—"

"We should probably keep it down." Teresa spoke quietly. "I think Jeff and Adela are right below us, and I'd feel terrible if we woke Katie."

The other two girls agreed. A minute later the only sound in the room was the even breathing of slumber.

Meg opened her eyes and gazed at her sleeping sister. Meg blinked twice. *Okay, I'm in Mexico.* She stretched her legs, then lifted her head to see what Jamie's alarm clock read. *4:01.* She dropped back to her pillow and held back a moan. Somewhere outside the window a rooster crowed. The city apparently woke up early. *Maybe it never sleeps.*

She swung her legs over the side of the bunk, then realized that her mouth was extremely dry. She made a face as she ran her tongue over her teeth. It had been a long time since she'd forgotten to brush them before going to bed.

Because of the lack of a water heater, her shower was very short. With clean teeth and a towel around her, she walked back to her bunk to choose her outfit for the day. There wasn't a whole lot of choices—all of four skirts and two pairs of jeans.

Jeans. *Those are going to be hot.*

The dim light coming through the window was just enough to help Meg distinguish between her tee-shirts. A song was playing in the back of her mind, faint but persistent. She couldn't quite put her finger on it.

That was it—Diego. It was one of the melodies he had sung the night before, one that was unfamiliar yet distinctive.

She stepped into her jeans. She was glad that the mission allowed them to wear pants at the work site, although a skirt would have been cooler. Pants would be much more practical for painting and whatever else the group would be doing.

The song would not go away. She began to hum, softly. *Teresa will be a bear if I wake her up this early.*

Oh, yes. Now she remembered the words. *Por toda la tierra salió tu voz, y hasta el extremo del mundo tus palabras.*

Meg stopped in the middle of pulling her shirt over her head and stared at the sea-blue material surrounding her. Where in the world had that come from?

"*Por toda la tierra salió tu voz, y hasta el extremo del mundo tus palabras.*" She whispered the phrase out loud. What in the world did it mean? Where had she learned that Spanish?

Somehow the words were connected to her dream, which was just starting to come back to her. In it they had all been at the worksite; a Mexican man had approached with five or six children to watch them build. Meg and Diego had walked over and begun to speak with them. The children had swarmed around them, their voices high and clear as they chattered. Then Diego had discussed something with her—she couldn't remember what.

Every word of every conversation had been in Spanish.

Then, somehow, she was flying home, Wisconsin home. She walked off the airplane into the welcoming arms of her family, but people from the mission were there, too: Jeff and his family, Yolanda, Diego. Her mother tried to talk to her but Meg could only reply in Spanish. She could understand every English word from her mom's mouth, but when Meg spoke Jenn Atwell only shook her head.

Meg pushed her head through the top of the shirt. Maybe it hadn't been in Spanish—maybe it had all been in English, but her mind had somehow twisted it to imply otherwise.

Then where had that phrase come from?

Meg repeated it again under her breath, the words as clear in her memory as they had been the first time she spoke them. She wanted to write them down, so she would not forget, but she had no idea how to spell them.

Another glance at the clock showed that only fifteen minutes had passed. She would not be able to go back to sleep, especially not with those words running through her head.

Meg pulled her Bible off of the top bunk and quietly slipped out of the dorm. The sounds of the city were not as cacophonous at this time of the morning. It was warm enough to make jackets unnecessary and cool enough to maintain comfort, though the pleasant temperature would not last long once the low-lying mists were burnt away. There was already a hint of desert heat in the air.

Meg decided to explore for a good place to read. The night before she had noticed steps halfway between the girls' dorm and the sanctuary; they appeared to lead up to a landing. She rounded the corner and was on the second step when she noticed a person's shadow on the wall.

Diego turned just as she tried to back away.

Chapter Four

Meg lifted her head. "Good morning."

"*Buenos días*." Diego smiled, but Meg stayed on the step, seeming hesitant to leave or stay. She had her Bible tucked under her arm. *Maybe she wants to go somewhere private.* Or maybe she had paused because she thought she was interrupting him.

He scooted over to make plenty of room for her. "Come on up."

She walked up the steps slowly and set the Bible down where his had been. She looked out across Monterrey. A waist-high wall was all that stood between them and the city spread out in front and below them. The tightly packed buildings filled the valley and spilled over into the foothills, only to disappear in the distance where a large mountain rose up.

"Does that have a name?" Meg pointed to the striking double peak.

"That is *Cerro de la Silla*—Saddle Mountain." It was a fitting name—between the two rocky outcroppings was a scooped dip in the rock. "It is one of Monterrey's famous landmarks."

Meg nodded. The early-morning fog seemed to hang between them. Diego checked his watch—the wake-up bell would not ring for another ten minutes. She seemed content to take in the view from the balcony. Though the buildings looked run-down it was still an eye-catching area;

the brilliant lilacs, yellows, oranges, reds, and whites of painted houses splashed the hillside with color.

Meg was moving her hands, clasping them together, slowly tracing an invisible line along the top of the wall, reaching up to rub her cheek. She seemed to have something more than *Cerro de la Silla* on her mind but she wasn't speaking.

"All of those houses are only a small part of Monterrey. The city spreads everywhere, it has over 5 million people." Diego's voice echoed down the stairwell. Perhaps if he chatted she would feel more comfortable around him, because she certainly looked stiff right now. "That neighborhood on the closest hill, it is one of the worst areas of the city. The police used to never go there because it was so dangerous; we call it a *barrio*, the slums. It is better now, but we still hear gunshots at night."

Her eyes searched for the places he was talking about, then went back to the mountains in the background. Diego turned to the view. A very steep main street ran down the middle of the hill, one so steep it at first appeared as if it would be impossible to drive a car up. At the very tip of the hill stood two crosses, tiny from this vantage point but over seven feet tall when viewed close up.

Beside him Meg took a deep breath. "Could you translate something for me?"

"I can try."

She spoke quickly. *"Por toda la tierra salió tu voz, y hasta el extremo del mundo tus palabras."* The words seemed to flow without effort.

Diego stared at her. He hadn't realized her vocabulary was that extensive, nor that her pronunciation was so flawless. Granted, he'd only heard a few phrases from her, but not even Jeff could speak Spanish that perfectly.

"Where did you learn it?" Perhaps Teresa had taught her.

"I don't know." Meg shrugged her shoulders. "I woke up this morning with that phrase running through my head. Last night I dreamed completely in Spanish, which might be where it was coming from."

"Say it again." He motioned with his hands for her to repeat.

She did, then asked him what it meant.

"I think it is in the Bible. Here." He set his bilingual book next to hers, opened to the Psalms, and pointed to the Spanish side. He read the words out loud in English as his finger moved. "'Their voice goes out into all the earth, their words to the ends of the world.' But that was not exactly what you said." He looked at her. "You said *tu voz* and *tus palabras*, not *su y sus.*"

"And that means?"

She truly had only rudimentary Spanish. Amazing. "*Su* means *their, tu* means *your*—so you really said, '*Your* voice goes out into all the earth, *your* words to the ends of the world.'"

"I don't get it." Meg looked at her sandals. "What Psalm is that?"

"Psalm nineteen." He began to read from the beginning of the chapter, in English. "'The heavens declare the glory of God, the skies proclaim the work of His hands—" He remembered leaning against the wall and looking up at the stars the night before. Looking at the stars so that he wouldn't be caught looking at her. He had been pleasantly surprised to find her in the shadows when he had exited the sanctuary.

"That's really bizarre—I've never learned any of those Spanish words."

"Maybe it means you are to be God's voice."

She turned towards him and raised an eyebrow. "In what way?" Meg took a step closer to look at his Bible and bent her head to follow the Spanish with her finger. He could just hear her words as she repeated them under her breath. She must have forgotten about him, or she wouldn't be standing so close. She smelled good.

He took a deep breath. "What do *you* think?"

She crossed her arms and leaned over the book, her eyes intent on the words. A small bead of water dropped off the end of her hair onto her shoulder and trickled down her arm. Diego considered brushing it off, but Meg reached up and smoothed it away with her palm. Diego tapped his fingers against his leg.

"I don't know." Her words were slow. She rubbed her forehead. "I thought it was something you were singing last night. Or something I heard Teresa reading."

"No, I sang Psalm thirty-four last night." He shifted his weight from one foot to the other. "You did not only speak grammatically correct Spanish, you pronounced the words like a native—more perfectly than I have ever heard even Jeff speak."

At his words she looked up from the page. Why had he assumed her eyes were green like Teresa's? They were blue; the sky-color around the center deepened until they were almost black at the edges. He looked past her to the mountains.

"Maybe God is trying to say something to you." Though he had her full attention, he kept his eyes on the horizon. The sun was almost entirely visible.

"Like what?"

"Maybe God wants you to come to Mexico."

"I'm already here."

"Well, maybe He's affirming that He's glad you're here."

Meg smiled. "That's kind of Him. But—I don't know—it seems like a waste of His supernatural power just for him to reassure a sixteen-year-old girl in a strange place."

Sixteen? Diego took a step back. Teresa had told him Meg was starting college in the fall. At sixteen? She sure didn't act or look like a sixteen-year-old. *Huh.* That meant she was six years younger than him.

"Well, give it time. If I were you, I would write the dream down in detail and then let it sit. The meaning might become clearer later." He glanced at his watch. "Let's go get some breakfast." He placed her Bible on top of his and tucked them both under his arm. Meg moved ahead of him and they descended the stairs. He shook his head. *Sixteen. Could have fooled me.*

Cock-a-doodle-dooooooooooo!

Meg looked up from her Bible at the sound. It was after six in the morning—the sun had been up for almost an hour. Weren't roosters supposed to welcome it in and then be quiet?

She had been right about the heat. Teresa and Jamie were fanning themselves with old church bulletins they had tucked in their Bibles. How long until the guys were ready to go?

Her stomach rumbled, the first pangs of hunger to hit for almost two hours. The dream had gotten her so psyched that she hadn't been able to eat breakfast. She would pay for it, though—lunchtime was another six hours away.

Diego had handed her her Bible after breakfast. She felt stupid having spilled so much of her dream to him.

"*Hola, señoritas.*" At the sound of a male voice all three girls looked up. A thin Mexican man stood on the outside of the gate opposite them, his wiry hands wrapped around two of the iron bars. He had a fine-boned face, short black hair, and round ears that stuck out from his head. He looked like a living cartoon character.

"You are reading Santa Biblias, no?"

Teresa was first to answer. "Yes, we are."

"You believe in God, then." *Who is this guy?*

"Yes, we do." Teresa continued, always the one to jump right in on apologetic matters.

"Why? How do you know, that there is God?"

Meg and Jamie looked sideways at each other, then back at him. On closer inspection, Meg noticed that his eyes were not the signature brown of Mexicans, like Diego's or José's—they were strikingly icy blue, like Beba the watchdog's. His skin was brown and weathered.

"Well, He's everywhere." Teresa closed her Bible. "Look at the mountains. Look at the sun. Everything has God's fingerprint on it."

"Ha, I cannot believe that." His expression was dramatic; his voice rose and fell in the Spanish rhythm. "That is foolish dreams. There is no proof."

Meg took a deep breath. Teresa was so comfortable with this—a natural. *I'm not.* Meg's words barely made it past her lips. "It's faith—believing in what you don't see."

"What is this you say?"

She repeated her sentence a little louder.

"I cannot believe that." He said it again, the same way, with the melodic accent.

Jamie also appeared to feel like sharing. "Faith is being sure of what we hope for, and certain of what we do not see. It says it clearly in here." She tapped her Bible.

"I cannot believe that." He shook his head.

"Well, if you cannot believe that, then we will pray for you," Teresa said. She stood and offered her hand.

"Oh, no, you not have to do that." His eyes crinkled at the corners, almost as if he were laughing. "Please no do that. I will see you later, then?" He shook her hand briefly then nodded and continued on his walk. The tune he whistled was familiar... Where had Meg learned that? It wasn't Mexican. It faded away before she could place it.

"I think we need to pray for him, right now." Teresa turned and seated herself back on the cement. "God can use our words, even though that guy didn't seem to hear them."

The other two girls agreed and they all bowed their heads and joined hands. A few minutes later they arose. Wherever the man was, God was following.

Meg leaned her head back against the hard metal surface of the van wall. The carpeted ceiling was only a half-foot away from her face, and every time the van went over a bump her head nearly hit the top of it. At one time the van had been a fifteen passenger, but the seats were long gone, replaced by two-by-fours balanced on overturned buckets. One of the back windows was gone and the wind blew freely through the hole, whipping their hair around and making it very hard to talk. Pete had christened the vehicle Gertrude.

"All right, everybody out." Jeff parked the van and turned it off. The whole group jumped out of her and stretched, glad to be done with the hour-long drive.

Meg took a deep breath of the air. No diesel fumes, no dust. *Beautiful.* Monterrey was intriguing, but this—this was what she was familiar with. Crickets hummed all around them; the land stretched away to the horizon with little hills or buildings. Luscious green Mexican vegetation bent in the hot wind. God seemed so much closer out here.

But for some reason this place was familiar, like a deja-vu. A squarish foundation for the church—about forty-by-twenty-feet—had already been set in the packed ground. Across the dirt road was a bright pink adobe house, with a shed beside it and a crop of some sort behind it. Thick grass grew from the house all the way to the road. Rose bushes with drooping soft blooms grew here and there in the lawn, in all shades from red to white.

The pink house, the roses, the foundation—she had been here before. Meg stilled as she recognized the scene mirrored from her dream. Every detail came into sharp focus. *Weird.*

Diego walked past with tools in hand. She could tell him about it, but he probably wouldn't want to be bothered by her yet again.

She had to tell someone, though. *Daddy.* She looked around and spotted her father's blond head above everyone else. He was unloading cement bags from the back of the van. Jeff came around the corner and raised his voice before she could approach her dad.

"Okay, gang. Before we get moving, I need to introduce you to someone." Jeff stopped and looked around. "Paco?"

"*Si,* I am here," a man's voice returned from the direction of the pink house.

What? Coming towards them was the Mexican man with no faith—the one whom Meg, Teresa, and Jamie had prayed for only an hour before. A wide grin stretched from ear to big ear and crinkled his skin all the way up to his blue eyes. Meg looked at him, confused, and then exchanged glances with the other two girls. They hadn't expected to ever see him again.

As he neared the group he looked each of the girls directly in the eyes before he turned to Jeff. Meg watched them exchange the Mexican handshake that Diego had given her on first introduction.

"Guys, this is Paco." Jeff put his hand on Paco's shoulder. "Teens that come down usually call him Taco. You can call him whichever. Paco, this is the Wisconsin group." He proceeded to introduce each of the team members, starting with Rick and Will. Paco shook their hands and never dropped his grin.

"Paco is one of the pastors of the seven sister churches Elim has started throughout the city of Monterrey," Jeff said.

Meg watched as Teresa's face reddened. They had prayed for the salvation of a pastor. *God must have been laughing so hard*—much like Paco was laughing now. "Hello, my friends." He spoke to the girls. "Nice to see you again."

"'I cannot believe *that.*'" Teresa mimicked his phrase from earlier. "You really had us going. We even prayed that God would save you someday."

"Ah, I am sorry." There was no remorse on his face. "I did not mean to fool you. But I could not resist—you were reading your Bibles. Yeff knows I am a prank."

Yeff. Meg smiled. Mexicans did pronounce "j" as a "y" sound. *So I would be Margaret Yuliana Atwell.*

Though Paco's accent was hard to grasp, his facial expressions compensated for it. He was definitely a talented actor—this morning he had played his part flawlessly. *We're going to have to get back at him.*

Her dad came up from behind and tugged on the strands of hair she had managed to pull back into a ponytail. "Muggah, want to help me carry some cement blocks over?"

Muggah. The nickname made her miss her little brother Amos all of a sudden. He had coined the term when trying to say her full name as a one-year-old, and now her whole family called her by it. "From where?" She turned and squinted up at him.

"A ways down the road."

"Sure." She fell into step with him. "Guess what."

"What?"

She proceeded to explain her dream from the night before. ". . . And when we got here I realized that this is the worksite from the dream." Meg waved her hand at the foundation, which they were walking away from. "Even the details—the dirt piles and the trees."

"You're sure?"

"Yep." Silence settled for a few steps. "What do you think it means?"

"I don't know. It's pretty neat, though."

She slipped her hand into his. "Diego said I should write it down and try to figure it out later."

"Diego?"

"Yeah. He was the first person I saw this morning so I asked him what the Spanish meant."

"I see."

33

When they were finished hauling blocks Jeff assigned Meg the task of mixing concrete-mortar powder and water. Meg headed across the street, grateful for the lighter workload—the blockpile had been a good three hundred yards from the church, and she was not used to straining her arm muscles. She lifted the edge of her teeshirt and wiped the sweat off of her forehead. Will and Pete—who had each managed *two* cement blocks per trip—were already strutting shirtless. She unwound the hose from the side of the pink house. *Ah yes, I control the water*—if they came too close they would *really* get cooled off.

Two chattering voices came from around the corner of the house. Meg looked up to discover a young girl and boy approaching her. Were those kids from her dream, too? Hispanic kids all looked the same—dark hair, dark eyes—so how could she tell? *Nah, there were six kids in my dream, and they were lighter-skinned than these guys.* These two were speaking to each other in rapid Spanish and their gazes flickered to her face periodically. It was obvious they were discussing her—Meg caught one word, *blanca.* Were they noticing her white hair or white skin?

"*Hola.*" She crouched down so that she was eye level. "*Me llamo Meg.*"

"Meg?" The little girl said it so that the G caught on her tongue. She cocked her head to the side in question.

"*Sí. Como te llamas?*"

The girl spoke a string of names—Meg was lost after the "Christiana" at the beginning. Meg turned to the boy and asked him for his name. He stayed quiet, without a smile, and looked at her with big eyes. The girl—his sister, Meg assumed—spoke for him. "Joaquin." Then Christiana asked something in Spanish—a question, if her raised eyebrows were any indication. Meg found herself at a loss. She took a guess and nodded.

Joaquin and Christiana shuffled up within inches of her and each reached out a round hand to finger her hair. They looked at each other, then broke into embarassed giggles and ran away.

Meg twisted the rusty knob to turn the hose on, then kinked it near the end and headed back to the cement pile. As she crossed the road, she noticed Diego pull up in the van.

Chapter Six

Diego hopped out of the cab and shut the door behind him—gently, because if the rusty holes in its side were any indication the hinges would fall off with the least excuse. He walked around to the back of the van and opened the twin doors, then gripped the sides of the soda crates and prepared to hoist them up.

His grip loosened as a sight to the left of the van caught his attention. He turned and watched as two Mexican children, with handfuls of freshly picked flowers, approached Meg, who was mixing mortar. The little boy tugged on her shirt, hard enough to get her to kink the hose and kneel down. The little girl went around behind Meg and smoothed her hair gently, like she would a beloved doll's, before taking a white rose and sticking it in Meg's gold hair, just behind her ear. Meg appeared to thank them, then secured the rose with a hair clip to keep it from falling, while the boy moved to her other side and added a cluster of tiny flowers behind her other ear.

She stood, and the children went to work. Two minutes later they had stuffed little flowers into every possible pocket and loophole in her jeans. She stayed quiet the whole time, obviously a little confused but enjoying the gestures. When they were finished they said something else to her, then waved and scampered back to their house.

Diego picked up the pop and headed towards her. "Would you like to come over for a Coke?"

Meg wiped her hands on her jeans. "Sure. Thanks."

"I like your garden." He nodded towards her outfit. She smiled.

He walked to the front yard and lowered the pop crate to a wheelbarrow. "Okay, everyone." They all dropped what they were doing and circled around him. "We have Coke, and we have *muchas Joya—manzana, tonronja, naranja, y ponche.*"

"Could you say those in English please?" Jamie lifted a bottle and looked at the label.

Pete interrupted before Diego could answer her. "Joya—this must be only a Mexican brand, 'cause I've never heard of it."

"'Joya' means *jewel.*" Teresa grabbed a bottle of orange.

Diego nodded and made eye contact with Jamie. "Apple, grapefruit, orange, and punch. I recommend apple, personally."

"Which one's apple?"

Diego pointed to an amber-filled bottle with a yellow logo, then headed back to the van as everyone seated themselves on the grass. When he returned they were happily guzzling the semi-warm pop.

"So, when was the first time you came down here, Jeff?" Pete rested his elbow on Jamie's knees, his empty pop bottle dangling between two fingers.

"It was seven years ago—I was nineteen. I came down with a group similar to yours. And then I met Adela, and, well, I had to come back." Jeff smiled when everyone inched closer. "I bet you girls want to hear the story just like every other female that comes down here."

"I'd like to hear it." Will took another drink of his pop.

"It's not that big of a story. I came down, like I said. Adela was fifteen–"

"Robbing the cradle, eh?" Pete grinned.

"Hey, she thought she was an old maid!" Jeff smiled. "A couple of my best friends teased me about it, but other than that there really wasn't much of a problem, since we treated each other like friends. José and Yolanda gave us their blessing by the time she was sixteen, and we followed the mission's guidelines—it's pretty strict about relationships, particularly Mexican-American ones, if anyone took the time to read the guidebook. Which—" he looked around, "I would bet none of you did."

Diego seated himself on the edge of the circle, intent on the story though he had heard it countless times before. Adela had been a year *younger* than Meg when Jeff had been interested in her?

"I went home to Pennsylvania. We wrote letters, and six months later I flew down to see her. I came back down on an internship the following summer, and we got engaged when she was seventeen. We moved back to America after the wedding—I was twenty-two and she was eighteen. We lived there while I finished college. Then we came back and we've been here ever since."

Teresa set down her empty Joya bottle. "Come on—aren't there any little romantic stories?" Will rolled his eyes at her girly question.

"Hmm… Well, I gave her lots of roses. Oh, yeah—I gave her a diamond engagement ring, but she thought it was cubic zirconium, because that's the way they do it down here. You get cubic zirconium for engagement, and a gold band for the wedding ring. She just assumed it was zirconium, and I assumed she knew it was a diamond, and we went on like that for a good month." He smiled. "Her eyes were so big when I finally explained it to her that it was a real diamond. She thought I was kidding."

Pete sighed dramatically. "I *wish* I could get away with only cubic zirconium." At Jamie's narrowed eyes, he shrugged. "Well, it's cheaper! *You* try paying for a real rock."

A sudden shriek split the air, and everyone turned as Teresa jumped up. She arched her back and tugged on the back of her shirt. "William Thaddeus!" Diego heard a few muffled snickers. She continued to hop up and down. "Get it out, get it out!" Diego saw something long and green fall out of her shirt.

Will reached over and pulled whatever it was from the grass, then stood and placed a reassuring hand on Teresa's shoulder. "Relax, it was only a lizard. See?" He extended his other hand and opened it so she could see the creature.

She knocked his hand and the lizard went flying. "You know I hate bugs."

"Reese, it wasn't a bug, it was a reptile."

"Whatever. I'm going back to work."

Everyone else followed Teresa's lead. Diego followed Meg back to the wet cement pile. "Here," he said. He pulled a package out of his shirt pocket. "I thought you would be hungry because you missed breakfast. I bought you Flups when I went for the Joya."

Her eyes widened with pleasure, then she stepped closer and peered at the pink-and-white cookies. "Is that coconut?" There was a note of displeasure in her voice.

"You don't like coconut?"

"Oh, I don't care." She smiled her thanks and tore the plastic. He watched as she plopped a whole cookie into her mouth. It was down in a second. "Those are pretty good. I couldn't even taste the coconut." She stuck two more in, so that her cheeks puffed up. She had pink and white flakes all over her lips.

He waited as she bent to fill the five gallon bucket. She got a good grip on the handle, picked it up, winced, and set it down.

"Want me to get it?" He motioned to the bucket.

"Yes, please." Her hand went to her lower back and she stretched. "Thanks."

"Any time."

At Coke break the next day, Meg looked at Christiana and Joaquin's house. It was now a bright combination of pink and blue. The old coat had been so dirty and worn that the girls had asked Jeff if they could repaint it. He had thought it a great idea—a good way to build a closer relationship with the family there, provided that they accepted the offer.

Meg preferred painting to mixing cement—painting was work with visible results. She drained the last swallows of her drink and watched Pete grab his fifth cookie from the batch Yolanda had sent along as a special snack.

"Mmm...." He finished it off in a single bite. "We made a lot of progress yesterday."

Will spoke up from the floor where he was stretched out full length. "I think it looks good. I think we got off to a good start."

"You are better builders than many." Diego wiped cookie crumbs from the corner of his mouth.

"Hey, that reminds me," Jamie said. She hopped off the temporary bench they had set up. "I've got a Bible verse for us. Just a minute, I want to read it to you." She ran to the van and returned a few seconds later with her pocket Bible. "Here. It's in Hebrews, chapter four, I think…" She paged through the Epistles. "Okay. Actually, it's in chapter three: '*For every house is built by someone, but God is the builder of everything.*' And then it says, '*Moses was faithful as a servant in all God's house, testifying to what would be said in the future. But Christ is faithful as a son over God's house. And we are his house, if we hold on to our courage and the hope of which we boast.*'" She looked up from the page. "I thought it was a neat analogy for us. 'The church is not a building,' and all that… God's building us up, and Jesus is the overseer." Jamie sat down again. "I don't know, I just thought I'd share." She seemed slightly embarrassed. Meg didn't think she was one to usually speak up in public.

"I like that," Will said. "If you find any more, bring them." He stood and stretched, and the others followed suit.

"Meg."

Meg turned. Diego beckoned her over to the van. "Can you come help me with these buckets of paint?"

"Be there in a second." Meg raised an eyebrow. She didn't know why he was asking for her strength. Jamie was the one who worked out at the YMCA.

Diego had two pails ready for her. Meg picked them up and raised them shoulder-level. Diego looked pointedly at her tensed upper arms. "Nice muscles."

She looked down at her arms. Was he being facetious? She turned her head so that Diego wouldn't be able to see her grin and began to walk away.

She was almost to the house when she felt a slimy tickling down her arm. Goosebumps spread down her back as she involuntarily turned. Diego held a dripping brush in one hand while he raised the other in defense. "They needed definition."

She snaked a hand out and grabbed the brush quickly before he could react and swiped a good stripe all the way down his nose. Then she caught herself. *Oh my. I am being such a flirt.* But wasn't he, too? *No—he's just picking on me because I'm the kid in the group.*

He grabbed the brush back and narrowed his eyes. "Tsk, tsk." Before she could step back, the ends of her pigtails were the color of the sky.

Okay, mister. "Teresa. Jamie." Her voice was loud. "Get over here." Her hair was dripping onto her shoulders.

Teresa approached from behind and seemed to quickly assess the situation. "Are you sure it's okay that we used the paint like this?" Meg asked Diego, hoping he hadn't noticed Teresa and hoping that her sister would get the hint.

"Oh, yes, we always buy extra for surprise projects."

Diego drew in his breath and his eyes widened as Teresa painted a wide stripe down his back with her soaked roller. He turned on his new foe. "Wait," he said. "There is only one me, and—" he glanced at the house in time to see Jamie making her way toward him with another brush, "three of you. This is not fair!"

Meg lowered her head to hide her grin.

"That's right—there is definitely only one you," Teresa said. "And thank goodness."

"Hey!" Pete and Will hurried over to the gathering party. "Looks like you need some help." Pete stepped towards Jamie, but she was ready for him. With two quick strokes she had paint dripping off both of his cheeks.

"I'll take care of this one." He held her arms and pinned them to her sides while he moved around to stand behind her. The others paused to see what he would do. With one arm holding her against him, he took her paintbrush and dangled it above her face.

Jamie made the mistake of relaxing her guard and looking up. Pete bent his head and rubbed his cheeks against hers, then took the brush and started dabbing paint speckles on her nose. Jamie started to giggle and gave up all resistance.

Oh, brother. This was supposed to be a fight, not an excuse for more public displays of affection. Meg turned away in time to see that Diego was now armed as well and had a determined look on his face.

Diego stopped. "Will," he asked in a normal tone, "would you like to help me?"

"I'll get this one out of the way." Will turned to block Teresa.

"Leave me alone—Diego's the one attacking my little sister." Teresa brandished her roller and moved forward, but Will pulled her back by her shirt.

Diego ignored them both and shook his head at Meg. He moved a step closer. "You ruined my most favorite shirt."

"I didn't—Teresa did." Meg took off running. She was around the first corner before anyone came after her, but by the third side she could hear Diego close behind, and knew it was almost hopeless.

It *was* hopeless. Will was casually leaning against the last side of the house waiting for her with Teresa's roller in hand. Meg slowed to think, and laughed at the determination on his face as he took on a linebacker stance. Where was her sister?

She stopped completely as two hands gripped her wrists from behind. "I was not finished with you." Diego's voice was right by her ear. Meg struggled against him, but her muscles didn't help this time. "Why don't you stop fighting? Everything will go so much easier if you do not resist." He released her arm and fingered a pigtail. "Blue hair, to match your eyes." *What a flirt!* "Will, I will hold her—you finish my painting job."

Will moved forward. "I think I'll start with her jeans. That way we won't—"Will's words stopped as his eyes followed something just behind them. Before he could speak a river of blue came streaming down around Diego's and Meg's head and shoulders. Diego let go of Meg and they both turned to see Teresa with the empty bucket raised high over her head in victory.

"Sorry, Nutmeg, but I figured you were already too blue to care." Teresa looked Diego over and grinned. Paint covered his face and streamed off his shirt and pants. Meg gave her a high five.

Will dropped his roller and stepped around Meg. "No one dumps a whole can of ministry paint on my *amigo*."

"It was only a fourth of a can, with a bunch of water added. Besides, what are you going to do about it?" Teresa lowered the can and tipped it upside down. "'Cause guess what…the paint's gone."

Chapter Seven

"I think you forgot about something." Will pointed across the road. "Cement's even better than paint."

Before she could move away, Will put one arm around Teresa's shoulder and the other behind her knees. He lifted her off the ground over-the-threshold fashion and started towards the mess of cold, gooey cement.

"It's a long ways over there. I *can* walk, you know."

"Hold still." There was no way he was going to take a chance and let go.

Teresa nodded. Will felt her shift in his arms and he looked down. Her free hand was gripping his shoulder for support, but she wasn't looking him in the eye—she was glancing back at Meg and Diego, who were wringing their shirts out.

Why wasn't she paying attention to him? She had hardly glanced at him the whole fight. Usually she retaliated immediately when he was involved. According to their mothers, they used to push each other over while fighting for favorite toys at age two.

They had known each other a long time. His eyes drifted over his friend's face. She was now gazing up at the clouds. For some reason she looked really pretty. Clean and fresh, even though she had paint all over.

There was a blue smudge right over the dip in her upper lip. He curled his finger, tried to think of a way to wipe it off, but he wouldn't be able to reach it without dropping her. He could always wipe it away with his face somehow, with his cheek or his nose, or with his lips.

Huh. What would kissing Teresa be like? She'd be furious with him. He smiled as he considered it; Teresa was always fun when she got mad. It'd be even better than dousing her in cement.

Nah, it'd be like kissing my sister. Besides, Rebbekah would be flaming mad herself. Four years of dating counted for some sort of commitment.

"What are you staring at?" Teresa was looking at him almost cross-eyed since their faces were so close.

"Uh, nothing. You have a blue moustache."

She was reaching up to wipe it away herself when he tripped over the edge of the cement pile. He struggled to keep his balance but couldn't manage it. The freshly mixed cement oozed up over his shoes. She gripped him a little tighter.

"Nuh-uh. You're going down." He dropped Teresa carefully into the goo and held her there with one hand so that her back got good and soaked. After a few moments he reached out a hand to pull her up.

She surprised him by yanking hard. Pulled off balance, Will fell and landed beside her. Before he could scramble up she opened the back of his shirt and plopped a pile of cement down his back, then reached her hand up and rubbed it well into his hair with a gleeful laugh.

He shook his head. "I'm done," he said. "I can't win with you."

"Meg." Teresa ran her fingers through her cement-free hair. "It's time for break. Come on over."

Meg walked over to the van. "Did you get all of it out?"

"Yeah, but shampoo would have helped a lot. Christiana thought it was pretty funny. She brought me a bar of soap and watched me the whole time. She told me about a time when Joaquin was playing in the mud and started to eat some. Their mom was mad."

"How do you understand her? She talks so fast." Meg watched her sister re-braid her waist-length hair. She was usually jealous of it but this was one time she was glad to have hers short. Meg's paint rinse had only taken five minutes.

Teresa wrapped the two thick plaits around her head and pinned them tight. "You should practice more."

"Hey, you're the Spanish major, not me." Teresa didn't understand how stupid Meg felt when she was stumbling over the few words she knew. *I have never been eloquent. I am slow of speech and tongue.* Who had said that? Someone in the Bible.

Moses. That was it. Meg yanked her hair back into a ponytail. Moses had had a brother with a better speaking gift, but God had made Moses go anyway.

"Speaking of mud," Teresa said. "That rainstorm last night really enhances our plan for revenge. I think it's about time for Taco's payback." She beckoned Jamie over from where she was sharing a Coke with Pete.

Jamie spoke quietly once she reached them. "Are you ready?" The other two nodded.

Meg glanced at the hose where Diego was wringing his shirt out and Taco was helping him pick dry paint out of his hair. She raised her voice. "Who wants to race?"

Both the girls responded heartily, as planned. They jogged down the road, about seventy-five feet back from Gertrude, and took their places.

Pete stood in front of the van, ready to call the start. "On your marks… get set… GO!"

Though the mud slipped them up a bit, it only took a few seconds for the girls to make their way down the road.

Paco and Diego looked up with interest to see the three girls flying down the lane towards the van.

Their race didn't take very long. Jamie passed Gertrude's nose, winning the contest. Meg, who was coming in a close second, slipped in the mud just as she reached the van. Diego heard Paco's intake of breath as she fell and knocked her temple on the dull bumper.

The next thing Diego knew she was lying motionless in the mud.

"Taco! Taco!" Will ran toward them. "Come here! Quick!"

Taco hadn't even made it into a standing position before Diego was on his knees in the shallow puddle next to Meg's still form. He vaguely heard snatches of everyone's worried questions.

It had to be Meg, of all people. And they were a long way from medical help.

He bent his head over her face, praying for the feel of a light breath on his cheek. It was there…and it wasn't very light, either.

He pulled his face back a little so that it rested a few inches away from hers. Were her eyelids fluttering? He reached back without taking his eyes from her face and gently took hold of her wrist. Her pulse was strong.

Was that a faint smile twitching at the corners of her lips?

With a jolt of understanding—and a little anger—he expelled a quick breath. *The little fake.* Her eyelids fluttered open, bright pupils reflecting the blue of the sky and two small Diegos looking down with frowning eyebrows. A giggle escaped her lips.

He forgot that his face was still quite close to hers and stayed still, gripping her wrist more tightly now. He wanted desperately to give her a good strong shake. Did she realize how much she had scared him?

Why had she done it? If it was a joke then it wasn't funny. Granted, she was only sixteen, but there were limits to his humor.

Just then she sprang up and Diego was forced to move back. In less than a moment she was in front of Paco, and before the man could react she had rubbed two huge handfuls of mud on his face. Teresa and Jamie had been prepared, too, and plastered his hair and ears. They were all laughing, including Paco.

Diego sat back on his heels and smiled a grin devoid of amusement. So Paco was the reason behind all this. *I still don't think it's very funny.*

Teresa was the first to notice his expression. "Sorry about that, Diego." She didn't seem too apologetic. "Didn't mean to scare you. We didn't even think to tell you… See, we had to get Taco back for something." She explained the story of the day before in short detail.

"And you know, Taco," she turned to him, "we figured that, though this was full of trickery and quite misleading, well, it was the same thing you did to us, and we were hoping to wring a useless prayer out of *you*."

Taco was still grinning as he attempted to wipe the mud from his face. "Okay, okay—you win. I deserve. Is good job—you scared Taco. Now we are level—even, sí?"

All three girls nodded their agreement. Diego hoped they were even— he didn't want to fall for another of their pranks in the future.

"Wow, that couldn't have happened better—way to go, Meg." Jamie held up her hand for a dirty hi-five.

Will clapped Teresa on the back. "You gals even had me scared for a moment there, and I knew what was going on."

"I almost had myself scared for a second." Meg held up a fist and laughed. "I really did almost hit my head, but the thump you heard was this."

"I think you had Diego scared the most." Rick spoke up from his seat by the cement pile.

Meg didn't even glance Diego's way as she replied to her dad. "Ah, it was worth it."

Night had fallen over Monterrey, muffling the city with shadows. Lights shimmered over the hills and receded in the distance to merge with the stars. No haze hung in the mountains tonight, and the view was clear.

Meg leaned on the balcony edge and let the light breeze wash over her face. The air was dryer and cooler than it had been on previous nights, holding steady at a perfect temperature. It was a blessed relief from the heavy humidity they had been forced to work in for the last week.

A week. They had been in Mexico for five days. The mission experience was different from what she had expected. She wasn't quite sure if she liked it or not. At least she hadn't gotten more than a twinge of homesickness, though she missed her brothers, and her Wisconsin hills, and her mother's conversation. But the days were too full to think about it much, and at night she fell asleep immediately, weary from a long day's work. Besides that, she had her dad and Teresa, a little bit of home always available.

It was also because of the people. Diego, Taco, Jeff, Adela, Yolanda, Ruth... And of course Christiana and Joaquin, who had continued to skip across the road every day. Hispanics were a very beautiful people. She loved looking at the different faces, the mixtures of Spanish and native Mexican Indian in each. *Mestizo* was the term, she had learned—it meant "of mixed Spanish and Indian descent." Adela was more Spanish looking—smooth oval face, creamier skin, light brown eyes. She was also very short. Perhaps the Riveras had conquistador blood in their veins. Diego, on the other hand, was more Indian looking. He had the darker skin, the high cheekbones, the strong nose and chin. And, though he wasn't tall, he was definitely above average in height compared to most of the other Mexican men Meg had seen. She didn't know if that was an Indian trait or not.

He had really been scared on Tuesday. Meg still smiled whenever she thought about it. *Ha.* She had had the hardest time keeping a straight face as she lay there, the dirty water seeping through her shirt. When somebody had dropped in the mud beside her she had assumed it was Taco, but the cheek that had rested lightly against her nose had had a little bit of new-whiskered roughness to it. Taco had been clean shaven that morning, but Diego had showed up at breakfast with a slight shadow to his jaw.

The smooth, thick hair that had brushed over her eyelids as she fought to keep them relaxed had clued her in as well. Taco's was short; Diego's was ear-length.

She also doubted that Taco ever smelled like cinnamon.

Sure enough, her eyes had opened to find Diego bending over her. All she had been able to see from that close of a distance were his eyes; their comfortable brown had blackened to night. Poor guy—he'd gotten wet and muddy, too. Her dad had been right when he told her that it had probably not been a very kind thing to do to Diego. But she had meant it when she had said it was worth it.

No, she hadn't expected any of this. Not a Taco, not a Diego. Definitely not a growing love of Mexico. She decided to take advantage of the quiet moment alone, and bowed her head. With her elbows resting on the ledge and hands opened palms-up, she thanked God.

Five minutes later a quiet shuffle on the stairway made Meg drop her hands and turn. She straightened and looked up into the dim stairway, unable to discern who the intruder was.

"I'm sorry." Both Meg and Diego spoke at the same time.

"Sorry? Why are you sorry?" Diego continued down the last two steps. Had he been watching her long? Meg nervously backed against the ledge. Oh, why had she raised her hands? It wouldn't be half so mortifying if she had simply crossed them.

Diego stopped before her. "Don't be embarrassed." He continued down the last flight of steps and disappeared into the sanctuary.

Meg no longer felt like praying. She tucked her hair behind her ears and slowly started down the stairs. Why *was* she so embarassed? It was no big deal. *Just let it go.*

Pete was the first to see her when she entered the sanctuary. "Meg, want to play Shanghai Rummy?" He and Jamie were setting up the card game. Teresa sat between Will and Diego on the edge of the stage, a small carpeted platform raised a foot above the tiled floor. Diego had a guitar cradled loosely in his arms and was strumming lightly as the three talked.

"Nah, I'll just watch." Meg plopped down on an extra folding chair.

Teresa was talking to the guys. Diego nodded every now and then, while Will was being the usual jester. He was trying to balance a spoon on the end of his nose. After about five tries he breathed on it again and placed it on Teresa's. Though she swatted his hand away and continued to talk, the spoon didn't fall off for a good five seconds.

Meg suddenly felt very much the young one. Pete and Jamie were at their touchy-feely stuff again, and Teresa had everyone else at her side. Meg turned to go back outside but Pete's voice stopped her.

"Hey, Meg, you promised you'd give me a Joya tattoo. I've got a uni-ball pen with me. Let me get it, it's in my Bible case."

"Hey, Pete, we gotta play this game first." Teresa stopped her monologue and raised her voice so Pete could hear her from the adjoining kitchen, where he had apparently left his Bible. "Maybe Will or Diego wants one. Meg can practice on them." Diego's guitar stopped. "Diego, get over there. Meg's going to give you a tattoo."

Meg sat down on a folding chair. *Great*. She was going to have to do this for everyone.

Diego approached her looking a bit puzzled. "A tattoo?"

"Not a real one." Teresa spoke for Meg as she took her place at the card table. "She's just going to draw it with a pen, on your arm. All you guys can get one, then we can take a picture of you three at the work site tomorrow, showing us your *grande* muscles."

"Okay." He pulled out a chair and plopped down eye-level in front of Meg.

Chapter Eight

Meg tilted her head. "Where do you want it?"

Teresa leaned over and pulled up Diego's sleeve. "Put it on his upper arm." She traced a circle on the designated spot.

Meg stopped herself from rolling her eyes. Diego could make up his own mind. But then again maybe he liked it, coming from Teresa.

Pete handed her the black pen and she uncapped it. Hopefully the tattoo would end up looking presentable. She had doodled the design on her work jeans earlier in the day, which was what had evoked the tattoo request from Pete. It had looked real on cloth, but working from this position—on skin, no less—would prove more challenging.

She scooted her chair around to better face the side of Diego's arm, then looked around. As she expected, a mostly-empty Joya bottle rested on the table by Pete. He drank the stuff like water, and bought three or four every afternoon from the tiny family-run store across the street.

At her request Pete lent it to her for a visual. She slid it close enough to eye the label. Diego had turned his head sideways to watch her.

"You're going to have to roll your sleeve up." She dropped the cap in her lap and waited for him to comply.

He took his time, rolling the material tightly so that it wouldn't fall and get in her way. She waited for him to say something but he only watched her. Maybe he was waiting for her to speak. *Too bad. I'm not chatty Teresa.*

His arm was ready, so she reached out and began the *J*. Her hands were still cool from being outside in the wind; where the edge of her palm rested on his arm, she felt smooth, warm skin. He kept absolutely still as the pen skimmed lightly over his arm. Meg kept her eyes firmly on the letters as she made the *O, Y,* and *A*. From the corner of her eye it was obvious that he was watching her every facial expression.

It was unnerving. *What is he looking at? What is he seeing?* The design was taking way too long to draw. She wanted to hide, somehow, but the one time she tried to let her hair fall forward, it brushed against his arm and got in the way of her pen.

In the middle of drawing the circle she finally looked up and straight at him. Her pen stilled. Everything stilled. All she noticed was his eyes, the ones she had been avoiding for the last five minutes. They looked clear into hers for a second, as still as everything else. Her breath caught in her throat when his gaze left hers and moved over every feature of her face before returning to her eyes. She resisted the urge to look away—how many of her faults did he see?

What she saw made her falter. It was not what she expected. He had a slight curve to his lips and his eyes were—soft?

No guy had ever looked at her like that before.

What was wrong with him? *Hello.* This wasn't Teresa. This was Meg, who had never been asked out. Meg, the plain one, the little sister.

He wasn't listening to her unspoken arguments. His smile increased just a little.

"I—I gotta go." She stood and the cap fell out of her lap onto the floor. Her gaze stuck to her hands as they both bent to pick it up. She hopped back when she almost knocked her head on his. Though she handed him the pen when he straightened, she couldn't make eye contact.

"I'm tired." A quick glance revealed that he still hadn't taken his eyes off her. What did he want her to see there in his face? She wasn't practiced at reading those kinds of looks. She hardly realized those kinds of looks existed.

Better to leave. Everyone else was so involved in the card game that they wouldn't notice, and Diego—Diego should expect *some* kind of reaction.

Once outside she stopped and wrapped her arms around her waist. *I don't get it.* He hadn't been flirting—the paint fight was flirting, and this was a lot different. It was—it made her feel valuable or something.

Appreciation. That was the word. That's what was in his eyes.

She felt a big smile start on her face. *Wow.* There was probably no substance behind that look, but still, he had noticed her. He had complimented her without saying a word.

Her eyes raised upwards till she was staring straight into the black sky. *Thank you, God! Maybe that wasn't the best thing you'd want to happen, but it sure made me feel good.*

"Al mundo Dios amó a su Hijo Él nos dio, y todo aquel que creyera en Él no perezca mas tenga vida eterna." (For God so loved the world that he gave his one and only Son, that whoever believes in him shall not perish but have eternal life.)

Meg sat in the warm metal folding chair, her back straight, her legs crossed and sticking where the skin touched. She was trying hard to listen to José Rivera—husband of Yolanda and pastor of the Elim mission—as he gave his sermon, but the Spanish was running together. There was no air conditioning in the sanctuary, which made it impossible to determine whether it was humidity or sweat on her skin. A slow trickle of perspiration down her front made her sit up straighter; she pressed her light cotton tank against her skin to absorb it.

Her head dropped forward a little in fatigue before she caught it and jerked back upright. *I'm trying to listen, God.* She really was, but she was so tired and she didn't know Spanish. Jeff had told them that he had learned all of his Spanish by ear, most of it from José's sermons. Jeff used to translate the familiar Bible verses in his head as José spoke, and would write down unfamiliar words to ask Adela about after the service. It had sounded like a great idea to Meg, but today she found herself distracted. The heat was a distraction, the baby crying in the back of the sanctuary was a distraction, the constant struggle to stay awake was a big distraction.

Meg's eyelids ignored her and dropped like lead anytime she gave in half a centimeter. So she sat erect, head high, eyebrows lifted higher than usual to keep her eyes open.

"Now for some music." José spoke the phrase in English and it caught Meg's attention.

The biggest distraction of all stood, guitar in hand. The thought of Diego Ramirez had kept her awake almost all night after the tattoo incident, and now she was paying for it.

As Diego and three other young Mexican men took their places on the stage, Diego's eyes met Meg's across the room. She immediately looked away, reminders of the struggle from the night before coming back.

Maybe he is The One. No, he couldn't be, because now she had said it so it wasn't going to happen. *Of course* he wasn't the one—he didn't even know her very well.

But he was the first guy who had ever noticed her like that. Maybe no one else ever would.

She wasn't going to see him again after this trip was over.

But she could come down and volunteer next summer. And then—

Her mind was playing the same incessant games this morning that it had been last night, when she had rolled over in bed countless times and punched her pillow in frustration. She just couldn't get her thoughts to shut up.

She always did this, with every new good-looking guy she met. This one was no different. *Just get over it.*

But this one *was* different. He was attracted to her.

Meg! She needed to stop. She was reading way too much into that one look.

She simply hadn't expected it from Diego. She wasn't a knock-out and she knew it. Meg had always figured some guy would be attracted to her after he knew her for who she was, because her inside would be pretty enough that it shaded his view of her outside. But Diego had definitely noticed her outside last night.

There. He was *not* The One. It was totally based on sensual sight.

I hate being sixteen.

Diego wasn't looking at her anymore, he was adjusting his stand. *Good.*

She looked around for somewhere to place her gaze other than up front. Teresa sat a few rows ahead and to the left, between Will and their dad. She was sharing a hymnal with Will. He was holding it, but he wasn't looking at the words. He was looking at Teresa—who seemed tense.

Meg suddenly remembered something else from the night before. Around one-thirty in the morning Teresa had rolled over and said something in her sleep. *"Will, she's not right."*

Teresa's words, mumbled into the side of her pillow, had caught Meg's attention. Meg grinned. The words had been spoken quickly and softly, but Meg had shared a room with her sister for fifteen years and was accustomed to discerning her sentences. Teresa was famous for talking in her sleep, and Meg always tried to get as much out of it as she could.

Last night she had rocked Teresa's shoulder lightly back and forth. "What about Will, Reeses?" She had kept her words soft and tried not to laugh.

"Mmph." Teresa had been in a deep sleep, which was usually when Meg could get the funniest things out of her.

Meg had brushed the long strands of hair out of Teresa's face. "What about Will?"

"She's wrong, she's wrong." Teresa had frowned in her sleep.

"Who is?"

"Will, no." The words had been choked.

Meg had started to think it was more of a nightmare than a dream. When two tears had trickled down Teresa's face, Meg figured it was time to wake her up. Teresa's eyes had opened wide and gone immediately to Meg's face. "Where's Will?"

"I'm guessing in his bunk, asleep."

"What? Where's Rebekkah?"

"Probably sound asleep in Wisconsin, where we left her. Are you awake?"

Teresa had closed her eyes for a minute. "Uh, yeah. Sorry, I just had a really weird dream." Her eyes had opened again. "What did I say?"

"Oh, nothing. You just mumbled. Do you want to pray with me so that it doesn't come back?"

"No, no, I'm fine. You can go back to sleep." With that Teresa had rolled over and sighed.

Easy for you to say. Unfortunately Meg had never gone to sleep in the first place.

Meg shook her head. Now she was back in the sanctuary where the whole scene with Diego had taken place, finally ready to sleep, but now was not the time or the place for it.

Diego's voice penetrated her recollections as he started the quartet in on a song. His eyes were closed and his voice was loud and clear as the group sang. The tune was in a steady 3/4 beat and had a definite Mexican flavor to it. Occasionally Meg caught the word *Cristo* and *Dios* but otherwise she let the music wash over her.

Why couldn't she just focus on God? Why did she have to think all of these stupid things? *Please take this away, Jesus—help me to just leave Diego alone.* Her eyelids slid shut as she prayed. Soon her thoughts faded, and the music grew distant...

Silence! Meg opened her eyes with a start. José was back on the stage, and Diego and crew were taking their seats, their guitars back in their cases. She had missed the whole song. Almost involuntarily she watched Diego from the corner of her eyes as he sat and ran his fingers through his hair. She couldn't help it. From the moment she had walked through the doorway into the sanctuary at breakfast, she had had an instinctive homing device on him. It had continued through clean up and as the whole group had helped set up for church. She knew exactly where he was in the room, all the time. It was so annoying. He hadn't seemed to have been watching her, either—his face hadn't been turned in her direction. Their eyes hadn't met until he stood for his song.

Why *should* he be watching her?

"*Vamos a orar.* Let us pray."

Meg bowed her head with everyone else as José wrapped the service up with a final blessing. When he was finished, she raised her head and fought the urge to look at Diego. She made a beeline for the door and walked out into the courtyard. The hot sun glared on her as she walked to a bench in the shade. *I'm going to be one big wet skirt pretty soon.* It was a good thing there was a pattern on her skirt so any wet places didn't show.

Small Mexican children poured out of the sanctuary, set free from their mothers' laps. Meg smiled at the rapid Spanish they yelled at back and forth; they were full of energy despite the heat. She closed her eyes and wiped the beads of sweat off of her forehead with the back of her hand.

She was glad she hadn't worn make-up. *I would have sweated it all off, anyway*. Earlier that morning she had stood in front of the mirror and had deliberated putting some on. For the first time all week, she really wanted to wear it, because Diego was going to be at breakfast—and maybe he would look.

She had decided not to wear it, not for such a stupid reason. Let him see her all bleary-eyed and red-cheeked. She hadn't cared on the work site—why should she now?

Meg fanned her face with her bulletin. *I should have worn it*. She was sure her face was now the color of chiles, like it always got when she overheated. *Oh, well*. Eyes closed, she leaned back against the cool cement wall to enjoy the shade. The laughter and shrieks of the children hung in the air.

"You fell asleep." At Diego's voice Meg's eyelids flew open. He was standing over her with a smug grin. Kerryn—Jeff and Adela's three-year-old—rested on his shoulders, her arms around his head.

"When?" Meg smiled at Kerryn, then quickly rubbed her face again. *Oh, man*. She was probably glistening like a wet fish.

"In church."

She hadn't thought he had noticed. "*Lo siento*. Yes, you caught me. I did hear the first part of your song, though, and it was very beautiful."

"*Cantamos tres canciónes*." Diego laughed.

"Three—what?"

"We sang three songs."

She really *had* dozed off.

Diego winced as Kerryn grabbed a fistful of hair and pulled his head back. He loosened the little girl's hands and held them securely in his own before speaking to Meg. "You look tired."

"I am." *In other words, I look terrible*. She knew how guys worked. If they said a girl looked tired it meant she looked bad, and if they said she looked refreshed it was a compliment.

"Can—" Diego's words were interrupted by Kerryn's hands. They had been playing with his ears, but now they slid across his mouth. She began jabbering something to him in Spanish. He replied quietly, gently took hold of her hands, and swung her down to sit in his arms. "Can we get you something to drink? They are serving orange juice in the kitchen."

"That'd be great. *Gracias.*" Meg had learned that he appreciated any attempt she made at Spanish, even if it sounded stupid to her. So she was beginning to try her hand at small words here and there. But she certainly couldn't understand the exchange that had just gone on between him and Kerryn. She couldn't even understand him when he spoke three simple words about his singing.

Despite Diego's teasing, she couldn't help closing her eyes again, for a minute or two. A faint breeze lifted a few baby hairs from her forehead. If God could just kick up a little breeze. . . and keep Diego away from her until this mind disease was cured. Diego seemed to have singled her out again, with the drink offer and that smile. *That is not good for my emotional stability.*

What had happened to the difference between sixteen and twenty-one?

Chapter Nine

After he had deposited Kerryn with Adela, it had taken Diego over five minutes to get back out to Meg because three different people had stopped him to compliment his singing. When he finally approached Meg's bench with orange juice in hand, he saw that her eyes were closed. Her head had dropped to her shoulder.

"Margareta." She didn't move a muscle at his whisper. "Meg." Still nothing. He sat next to her—perhaps she would sense his presence. She gave a small sigh but stayed still, obviously asleep.

The bench was in a somewhat out-of-the-way spot but it was close to the girls' dorm. He knew Teresa and Jamie were in their room, so he left the orange juice in the shade at Meg's feet and went to knock on the door. Teresa answered.

"Meg is sound asleep on the bench and she looks very uncomfortable. I thought—" he suddenly realized how stupid and obvious he looked. *Their dad wouldn't even go to the hassle of getting her a pillow.* "I thought maybe you could take her her pillow."

Teresa smiled. "Why don't you do it? I'll go get it for you."

Two minutes later he returned with Meg's pillow. He set it down on the bench, then debated whether he should shift her or not. The position she was in looked extremely uncomfortable, so he reached out and cautiously took her by the shoulders. She went easily, curling her legs up onto the bench until she was almost a ball.

It still didn't look very comfortable, but he didn't want to wake her. She might not appreciate what he had done. A glance over his shoulder assured him that no one else had noticed his forward actions. He left her in the shade and headed up to the roof to pray.

𝒳❋

The buzzing of a circling fly pulled Meg to consciousness. She winced at the intense blue of the Mexican sky. It was silent in the courtyard.

Silent! There had been kids here before. She sat up and found her pillow across the bench. *Who…?* She looked up to the sky once again. The sun had sunk beyond the walls of the mission. How long had she been sleeping?

"Ugggh, I need a shower." Her sweat from earlier had dried and now she just felt dirty. Her hair was matted; half of her face felt tingly and warm. She moved to stand and knocked something over near her feet. Orange juice spread on the concrete, tiny rivers of it flowing down into the cracks. *Diego.* He had brought her orange juice, and she had fallen asleep again.

"*Buenos días*, or should I say *buenas tardes*." The proverbial object of her thoughts appeared from around the corner of the building. He *would* show up now, before she had a chance to shower. He got to see her at all of her best moments—fresh out of bed, no makeup, sweaty, drooling.

"Hello." She looked up at him and quickly ran her fingers through her hair. What could she say to scare him off?

"Did you have a good sleep?"

"Yeah."

"I did not think you were the tanning kind." Was he teasing or for real?

"I'm not." She looked up. "I was a bit tired from last night."

"Ah, sí. But I thought you went to bed early last night?" *Was* he teasing? She didn't know him well enough yet to read his expressions, and it was irritating.

60

He stuck his hands in his pockets. "Everyone is hanging out in the sanctuary."

She nodded shortly. "Thanks for letting me know. I'm going to go shower first."

He nodded and continued on his way. Once he had disappeared into the sanctuary, Meg grabbed her pillow and climbed the stairs to her room. Jamie and Teresa had spent some time tidying up the area; Meg grinned when she opened the door to find all of Teresa's clothes thrown across the extra beds.

She managed to find a clean T-shirt in her own neat suitcase, pulled a relatively grime-free skirt from the hangers hooked over the edge of her bed, and headed for the shower room.

Showers in Monterrey were a sort of ordeal. There were two places to shower at the mission—in the girls' dorm, or over at the main building. Teresa always walked over early in the morning to use the facilities above the sanctuary, which were more dependable. Jamie also used those most of the time, but Meg didn't bother. At either location she inevitably either finished a shower sweating more, or else covered with goosebumps.

Though the afternoon air was sweltering, Meg opted to use hot water this time. It was uncomfortable, but at least she would feel clean when she finished. The water and soap quickly rinsed away the sweat, grime, and sleep from her body. Meg stood under the beating drops and let them relax her.

She rubbed the shampoo deep into her hair, then stood still to let it rinse out. *Did Diego bring that pillow out for me?* Nah—he couldn't have gotten it from her bed without going in to the girls dorm, and she knew he'd never do that. It had to have been Teresa.

Meg sighed, then stomped her foot, sending the metal drain cover spinning. "Meg, stop it now. It doesn't matter who got your pillow." She closed her eyes and lifted her face to the water. *God, help me to focus on something else.* She needed help if she was going to be able to stop reading into Diego's every look, or trying to get him to notice her more. "Keep my thoughts from dwelling on him, Jesus. I—"

Her prayer was cut short when the water turned icy.

Meg turned off the shower and reached for her beach towel. After dressing she started to work on cleaning her share of the room. Her thoughts returned to Diego, this time intentionally. She didn't know *that* much about him, although from what she'd seen, he was a strong Christian. Everybody at the mission respected him. He was a gentleman—that had surprised her. She knew very few young men in the United States who would open a door or pull out a chair for her, or for Teresa or any of the other girls. Part of it was that Mexico's culture was different from America, but the gestures still made her feel special.

Yet she knew other men who were committed Christians, and who had the same respect for women, but she didn't get crushes on them. Will, for example. *But he's like my brother.*

Mostly she was thinking about Diego because he was an older guy who was actually noticing her. She had never even thought of Will that way, especially because he was probably going to marry Rebekkah.

Her towel was slipping out of her hair so she unwound it and spread it across the top bunk. "How would I be acting if Diego had a fianceé or a wife standing next to him?" She put her pillow at the head of her bed and smoothed it down. "Would I even think twice about him?"

She was sure she wouldn't be thinking this much about him. And after all, his wife really *was* out there somewhere. She picked up all of her dirty clothes and added them to the laundry pile. If she pretended Diego's wife was sitting with them when they were together, she could treat him the same way she did Will.

Her work finished, she ran a comb through her hair and walked over to find the rest of the group. Teresa, Will, Pete, and Jamie were the only ones in the sanctuary. Meg frowned. She had thought Diego would be there too. Then she grinned. *Guess he's busy talking to his wife, huh, God?* The thought helped.

Teresa looked up. "Hey, there, sleepyhead. Finally decided to join us?"

"I had a good nap." Meg crossed the room and sat down beside her sister. "You should have taken one too, after all those bad dreams you had last night." She turned to Will with a grin. "I think you were giving Reeses some nightmares—ow!" Teresa had subtly but firmly pinched her arm.

"Me?" Will looked at Teresa. "What'd I do now?"

Teresa shook her head. "I don't remember much. I think it was something about college stuff…"

Meg wondered if a bruise was forming on her skin where Teresa's hand was clamped. *Yeah, sure it was college stuff, and sure, you don't remember.* But Meg wasn't about to say anything more.

Will smiled. "College is enough to give anyone a nightmare. Hey, Meg, are you going to give Pete and me our Joya tattoos?"

"Oh…yeah." Meg shook her hand free from her sister. "I'm sorry, I kind of forgot last night."

"I'd say you did." Diego entered the room and rolled up his sleeve as he did so. "Look at what happened when I tried to finish it." Everyone laughed at the crooked circle he had attempted.

Okay, Meg. Now, couldn't she see his wife walking in with him? Meg looked up and blushed. "Sorry." She turned to Pete. "You still have that pen?"

"Sure." He dug it out of his shirt pocket and tossed it to Meg. "Let me know when you're done with Will's, and I'll come on over." He turned back to his conversation with Jamie. Meg grabbed the bottle in front of him and moved over so that she could reach Will's arm.

She started to outline the first letter. It was amazing how much more comfortable she felt when Will was the subject. Even though he was watching her intently, her design went quick and smooth over his skin. She was concentrating deep enough that Will startled her when he spoke in low voice.

"Do you know what's wrong with Teresa?"

Meg's pen stopped moving, and she looked up at him for a minute. He wasn't teasing her, he was serious. "In regards to what?"

"Me. I think she's ignoring me."

"Why?" She continued to work on the circle. This was the same spot in her artwork where she had quit on Diego the night before.

"Stop laughing. I'm serious. I don't know why."

"Your guess is as good as mine." Meg looked at her sister, who was learning a guitar chord from Diego. Meg hadn't noticed anything in Teresa's actions towards Will. Towards Diego, yeah—she had been spending a lot of time with him. *Why?*

Come to think of it, Diego had never responded to any of her sister's schemes. And maybe that was why Teresa had picked him—because he was the one guy not paying attention to her.

No, that wasn't it. Teresa wasn't that petty, and she wasn't much of a flirt. Did it have something to do with Will?

Meg added a few last strokes and capped the pen. "Let it dry for a minute or two."

Pete was waiting for his turn, so Meg turned her attention to him. When she was finished, Pete stood and flexed his arm. "Hey, guys, look at the way this tattoo changes shape!"

"Trying to show off your non-existent muscles, Pete?" Meg got tired of him always acting as if he was the greatest thing since sliced toast.

Diego seated himself next to her. "That was hard on him."

She felt her face flush again. "I was just teasing."

"Maybe the teasing makes him show off more."

"Like he does it to get a laugh?" That made sense.

"No. Maybe he tries to make himself look good because he feels self-conscious."

Meg capped her pen and looked at Diego. "You think it bothers him that much when *I* tease him?" She looked down again.

"It might." Diego shrugged.

Meg was quiet. Did most men feel that way? Maybe men worried about strength the way women worried about being pretty.

"Do you draw much?" Diego leaned back.

"Yeah, quite a bit. I don't think I'd want to pursue it as a full-time job, but I love it as a hobby—something to do for fun."

"You are good at it." She could tell his eyes were on her again. "What *do* you want to do for a job?"

"I'm not sure. I'm not very interested in having a career—you know, a nine-to-five job, working away from the home. I want to stay home and raise my kids. If God gives them to me."

"That's the largest career of all, raising kids—for both men and women. The best, if God calls you to it."

She looked up. "Yeah, I believe that if you're going to be a mom, God wants you to stay home with them. It's a built-in mission field that a lot of women choose to ignore."

"I think you have it right. I think fathers should also try to be at home as much as they can."

"What do you want to do? Jamie said something about pastoring."

Diego nodded. "Possibly. I'd like my first priority to be my vocation as a husband and father, though—if and when I become one."

"Oh, I'm sure you will." *Great—I hope he doesn't think I'm volunteering!*

Diego didn't answer and Meg decided to avoid eye contact for now. Her actions over the next couple of days would determine how easily she kept her thoughts and emotions under control—and talking with him about dreams of family would *not* help.

"I think it's my turn to head to bed early." Diego stood.

"Yeah, I need to go catch up in my journal."

He offered his hand to her, then pulled her to her feet. "Good night."

"Good night." Meg's eyes trailed him to the door, where a faint glimmer of a young woman—*Mexican, I think*—moved to follow him.

When Teresa and Jamie came in to the dorm later Meg was just finishing up copying Colossians 3:1-2 at the end of her journal entry.

Since, then, you have been raised with Christ, set your hearts on things above, where Christ is seated at the right hand of God. Set your minds on things above, not on earthly things.

Chapter Ten

Meg crawled through the hole that was supposed to be the back window of the van and lowered herself to the shoulder of the road. Tough grass grew along the edge and scratched her ankles above the sock line. She blew out a long breath between her lips. An unusually large jolt had woken her just as she had been drifting into sleep with her head on Teresa's lap. Diego had steered Gertrude off of the highway and was now under her engine, his legs the only visible part of him. Meg was glad she couldn't understand the muttered Spanish floating out from under the vehicle, especially when she watched Teresa's eyebrows raise.

I am so tired. Six hours of sleep a night was not enough. Next weekend she'd have to remember that, even if everyone else *was* staying up till midnight singing worship songs. Meg leaned against the side of the van and felt her eyes fall shut. At least she didn't have to do anything for a while now. Better this than the work site.

Now there's a good mission thought. She was here to work. Right.

Diego scooted into sight. He winced, apparently having scraped his back on the gravel, and wiped the sweat from the back of his neck. "Could someone get me a wrench from the toolbox under the seat." Will picked one up. "No, the five-eighths." He disappeared back underneath the vehicle.

Meg closed her eyes again. At least there were some tools along, and a knowledgeable mechanic—though he was taking an awfully long time. What if Diego couldn't fix it? They had to be almost twenty miles from the work site, and farther still from the mission. Nobody would have telephones out here in the country; she didn't even see electric lines.

Walking in this heat was not her idea of an adventure.

Diego hauled himself up from the ground. His face was shining with sweat and streaked with black grease. Meg had never seen that annoyed look on his features before. Without saying anything he walked to the driver's seat, turned the key, and listened to the engine run for a few seconds. He must have liked what he heard because he motioned for all of them to get back in.

The rest of the ride was quiet until Jeff spoke, right after Diego turned off the car. "Guys, we really need to cut down on the paint."

Will looked at Teresa. "Maybe we're running low because you dumped a whole bucket of it on Diego."

"Don't even start." Usually Will's teasing made Teresa laugh, but she didn't seem to appreciate it today. "Like you wouldn't have done the same thing. And I still haven't gotten all the cement out of my hair."

"Hey, take it easy." Will raised his hands in defense. "If your hair bothers you that much, chop it off."

Teresa had been growing out her hair since eighth grade. Will should have known better than to say something about it.

Teresa tried to slam the van door on her way out, but the latch never caught, so she ended up looking silly.

Inside the church the three girls painted under a heavy silence. Jamie had insisted that she be allowed to use the roller, even though she had gotten it for the last two days, and Meg was stuck once again with the tedious paintbrush trim work. She had already found several spots that Teresa had missed and pointed them out to her, much to Teresa's annoyance. The humid air that refused to leave the building wasn't helping anyone's temper, either.

Finally Diego appeared in the doorway. "Time for break." From the edge in his voice, Meg was glad he wasn't painting with them. They dropped their brushes, relieved to quit for a while.

Will and Pete were already sitting down to the right of the lot. "Hey, James." Pete cupped his hands around his mouth as Jamie walked out into the hot sunlight. "Get me a grape Joya."

Jamie's scowl grew deeper. She strode over to the case, grabbed two bottles, and moments later dropped one in her boyfriend's lap. "Do *not* call me James." She didn't wait for the bottle opener to come around, but twisted the cover off her own drink with her bare hands. "And learn to say please. I'm not your servant. Next time you want a Joya, get it yourself."

Pete ignored her as he flipped the top off of the bottle with his teeth. He took one guzzle of the drink, then spit it out on the dusty ground. "This is warm. You know I hate warm pop."

"Well, sorry! It's always my fault, isn't it?" She turned her back on him and walked over to the rest of the group. Pete stood, bottle in hand, and followed her. At the case of pop he stopped and plunked his opened bottle down on the ground beside it.

Meg watched him rummage for a cold one. "Are you going to waste all that Joya?"

"It only costs two pesos."

"Fine." She backed off and watched him choose one. Diego still had not taken a pop, and she was the only other one left deliberating.

The air that swirled around them was stifling. People retreated to their own spots in the yard. Meg smiled. Ordinarily people grouped together in twos or threes to enjoy their break, but today they were all looking for places to be alone, and cool. Her dad was stretched out under the only tree. He hadn't even bothered with a Coke.

Diego was still standing beside her. He looked at her, then reached out and took the apple Joya.

"Um… I was going to take that one," Meg said.

He expelled a frustrated sigh and extended the bottle to her. "*Aquí.*"

"No, no. You take it."

"Really, Meg. *No me importa*; you can have it." He set the bottle down in front of her.

He should know by now that she couldn't understand him when he mixed his English and Spanish. "No, I know you wanted it." She reached over the apple drink, took a bottle of orange and opened it up.

"You hate orange."

Meg looked up at him. "I can drink whatever kind I want."

Diego picked up the apple and mumbled more incoherent Spanish under his breath. He walked over and leaned against the wall, near—but not too close to—Will. Meg was left standing alone beside the van.

She sank down to make the most of the limited shade provided by Gertrude and closed her eyes. They should all just go home and take naps. Forget the church; they weren't getting anything done at this rate anyway. She took a drink of pop, then made a face. It *was* warm.

Why was Diego so upset? He was supposed to enjoy mechanical work. He'd never been anything other than pleasant with her before.

Well, he was human. So was she, and everybody else. *I should have known this was coming.* They had all been with each other around the clock—it was amazing that they had gotten along so well until now.

Patience. This was part of the reality of the mission field. Was she ready to give of herself even when she had only gotten six hours of sleep for the last four nights in a row and everyone she came into contact with was rubbing her the wrong way? This was probably mild compared to situations that arose with year-round mission work.

She couldn't make it the next four weeks on her own, that was for sure. What was that verse Jeff had given them? *I can do all things through Christ who strengthens me.* Or that other one—*Blessed are the flexible, for they shall not be bent out of shape.* Except it wasn't a Bible verse; Jeff had made it up.

Pete and Jamie rounded the corner of the building in an argument. Their relationship had turned into a constant yo-yo. Right now Jamie seemed close to tears as she deposited her empty bottle in the box near Meg. Pete followed her move.

"Hey, James." He tripped over his discarded first pop bottle and then kicked it out of his way. "Why are women like guns?" He answered the question himself. "Because the longer you have them around, the more you want to shoot them."

Meg wondered if Jamie was going to kick Pete.

"You'd better be careful. Soon you aren't going to *have* a woman. Sometimes I don't know why I waste my time. You are the rudest, the most unfeeling person I know."

Meg stood. There were still hours left to this day before they could head back to Elim as she wished.

Will picked up his damp shirt and slung it over his shoulder before rounding the corner of the church to see where everyone was. He had been working hard on the roof, and it was time for another break. Diego was pushing a wheelbarrow back in Will's direction and Pete was shoveling some cement powder, under Taco's watchful eyes. Will laughed. Taco seemed very comfortable being the supervisor. He was leaning on a shovel with Pete's sporty sunglasses covering his eyes. Meg was heading across the road; she must be planning to make use of the bathroom facilities there. Teresa was on her stomach under the small, scrubby tree near the other side of the church.

She sure had been acting strange around him lately. She kept ignoring him, turning away from him, not making eye contact. It was frustrating—they were hardly even relating as friends. Maybe it was a hormonal thing.

Oh, great. He looked down at his front. He should have put his shirt back on. Teresa always commented or teased him about his muscles—or lack thereof—when he was bare-chested. She had been doing it since she was thirteen, and he had learned to keep his shirt on whenever possible.

Teresa rolled over. His approaching footsteps must have alerted her to his intrusion. She was flat on her back and raised her hand as a visor against the sun to make out who he was. "Hey, Phoebus." At least she was smiling.

"Hey, yourself." *Phoebus.* Her code name for shirtless guys who showed off their muscles. It was Latin for *sun god* or something; Will couldn't remember exactly. He took a seat a few feet away from her on the warm grass, then decided her position looked more comfortable and stretched himself out full-length. He quickly sat up again when the itchiness of the grass scratched his back.

It didn't seem to bother Teresa through her shirt. She had a bunch of dandelions resting on her stomach and was lazily popping their tops off. Will looked down at her. Teresa was quiet, the sounds of the summer insects hummed in the background. She had made herself a circlet of dandelions that rested on top of her fat braids. The bright yellow of the flowers looked almost orange compared to the color of her hair.

It must be a nuisance to have hair that long on a day like today. *But she really shouldn't cut it off.* He was about to comment on the thought aloud when a flying yellow missile from her fingertips hit him right between the eyes.

He caught it in his hand, then stopped. *Deja-vu.*

It had been a lazy summer afternoon, more than five years ago. Teresa had been a girl of thirteen, her thin face framed by the same thick, long hair, and he had been a man of fifteen. They'd been sitting on the lawn at his house, and she had had a dandelion crown on. His best friend had been bemoaning the fact that she had never been kissed.

"What's the big deal?" he had asked.

"You don't understand, Will. I just want to know what it feels like." Felt like? A girl had kissed him on the bus in seventh grade. Teresa was in for a disappointment.

"Well, okay." He had scooted over in the grass and lowered his head closer to hers. It was weird, but hey, they were best friends, so it might as well be him. Besides, she wasn't half bad looking.

"Yuck!" Once she had figured out what he was going to do she had jerked back. "Not from you!"

"Why not?"

"Because—because you're Will. People don't kiss their friends."

Ungrateful girl. Was the thought really that bad?

He was going to win this one. "I'm going to kiss you. I promise." She had popped a dandelion in his face.

Not long after that she'd chopped all her pretty hair off. Will rolled the dandelion stem between his fingers. Now he was twenty-one and he knew he wasn't gross. And kissing sure wasn't disappointing anymore.

If he was going to fulfill that promise he might as well give her a little chicken peck now. This was a perfect opportunity.

He knew that he needed to catch her off guard. Since high school she'd gotten a lot more rigid about what she called *throwing away kisses.* Will leaned forward so he could see her eyes. She was watching Diego mix cement to her left. He bent at the waist and aimed for her lips.

Just before his touched hers, she looked up and realized his intention. Her head dropped so that his lips met the tiniest tip of the corner of her mouth but much more of the soft skin on her cheek.

Soft… He closed his eyes for a fraction of a second and took a quick, deep breath. That smell—he had never acknowledged it as Teresa's until now. It smelled good, like when his mom was baking sugar cookies.

He felt her face jerk away and his lips were left with empty air. He looked up to find her leaning on her arms, dandelion crown tipped askew.

"I know…" he said. "'Yuck', right?"

"What are you doing?" She stumbled on the words.

"Kissing you."

"Why?" She started to yank the crown out of her hair. It looked like it was caught.

"Here, let me get that."

Before Will's fingers could brush her hair she was up on her feet. "I'll get it myself."

Will stood as well. "Teresa. Wait." He reached out and pulled on the end of the crown; it slid easily into his hand. Teresa turned towards him. "I had a promise to fulfill… Remember?"

"Yeah. People don't kiss their friends." She didn't get mad easily, but she was really hopping right now. *Definitely hormones.*

"Come on, Teresa, I was just playing. I wouldn't have really kissed you or anything."

"What did you call that?"

"That? That was a miss." He grinned. "I didn't really kiss you. You don't have to be so weird. It wasn't going to be a romantic kiss. A mere one on the ten-point scale."

"That was kiss enough." Her fingers reached up to touch the spot where his *miss* had been. She turned and started walking towards the van, which had just pulled up with Jamie, Taco, and the pop.

He watched her walk away, the tension obvious in the set of her shoulders. He couldn't let it sit like this, even if she was overreacting.

He caught up to her and gently took her wrist. "I'm sorry, Teresa. And I'll be sure and apologize about it to your husband someday." He smiled and finally made eye contact with her. Neither his apology nor his teasing had worked—now she looked like she was about to cry.

"I'm sorry I'm being so weird." She pulled her wrist free and started to walk across the road, plucking little pieces of dandelion out of her hair as she went.

Will pulled his shirt back on with a guilty feeling. *I lost.*

Chapter Eleven

Meg bounced in the back of Gertrude as she careened and squealed through the city of Monterrey, Jeff at her helm. Lights of every color whizzed by outside, distorted by the rounded angle of the van windows. Meg's own reflection was visible every now and then when they passed under an orange street light, her face stretched by the glass so that her eyes looked owl-like   and her chin pointed in a stern V. It was eight o'clock and they were headed into downtown Monterrey to hand out tracts for two hours. Meg was looking forward to it. It was their first time out in the city and she'd get to try out a little Spanish.

"What's the phrase again, Teresa?" Jamie asked from the middle seat. Meg's ears perked up.

"*Para usted—es gratis.*" Jeff had taught the phrase to them so that they could say it when handing the tracts to people. Roughly translated it meant *For you—is free*. "Oh, and girls? Make sure you don't say para usted—es*toy* gratis," Teresa added, half-smiling and half-serious.

Diego understood the comment and lightly hit her on the shoulder.

"What's the difference?" Jamie asked.

"It means 'For you, I am free'."

Pete laughed. "No, you don't want to make that mistake."

"Oh, great." Jamie had a hard time with Spanish. "Now you've messed me up. Which one is right?"

"*Es*. Para usted, es gratis. Not *estoy*. No *toy* on the *es*."

"Okay." The two-syllable word from Jamie was pronounced with resolution. Meg could hear her whispering repeatedly under her breath, "No toy on the ace. No toy on the ace."

Jeff broke into the conversation from the front. "Okay, guys, we're at the parking ramp. Let's pray this van clears two meters—that's six feet for you gringos." The van had stopped in front of the ramp entrance, and right in front of them was a long horizontal pipe that looked far two low for the vehicle to squeeze under. Jeff eased on the gas slowly and Gertrude crept forward.

A sudden hush had come over her occupants, so when the *screeeeech* began it was quite noticeable. The awful noise continued as the pole literally scraped what paint remained off of Gertrude's roof. In a few seconds it was over, but the concrete ceiling loomed solid and low as Jeff eased Gertrude into the nearest parking space. Everyone breathed a sigh of relief when the engine was turned off.

"*Vamos, amigos.*" At Jeff's words the side door was opened and they all began piling out.

A warm breeze played about the group as they walked the few blocks to their destination. On their way they passed a fountain full of statues—Meg assumed it was of the Greek water-god Neptune and his muses. Will remarked that the figures needed some undies, which made everybody laugh.

In front of them loomed a tall, orange-red modern brick building, lit up by strong ground lights. It was flat, rectangular-shaped, and reached several stories high. Pete pointed to it. "Hey Jeff, what's that place?"

"I'm not sure."

"What? You live in Monterrey and you don't know?"

"It's just always been there."

"There aren't even any windows."

"I don't know what it's used for." Jeff shrugged.

Teresa studied the building. "It looks like one of those orange wafer cookies—you know, the kind with really good artificially colored frosting

76

in-between those two dry wafers that taste like sweetened communion from the Catholic Church?"

Meg smiled—only Teresa could come up with a description like that.

"Hey, how do you know what Catholic communion tastes like?" Diego teased. "You're a Protestant."

Jamie linked arms with Teresa. "We'll call it the Monterrey Wafer."

"I like that." Jeff nodded. "'The Monterrey Wafer'. Now when other groups come down I'll call it that."

"Pardon me, *Señor Yeff*, but I think it is called the *Faro de Comercio*, the Light of Commerce." Diego scooted up from his place in the back to play the role of tourist guide. "Many nights a laser shines off the top."

"I still like the Wafer thing. But if you have any more questions, guys, just ask Diego. He probably knows a lot more than me."

Meg lifted her skirt to step through a puddle. Yes, Diego knew a lot. For some reason she was feeling acutely sixteen now whenever he spoke to her. Ever since Sunday he had kept a definite distance. At the worksite all week, he had never delegated any responsibility to her.

He had seemed so different last Saturday—the night of the unfinished tattoo, the night she had recorded in great detail in her journal. Then Monday morning had rolled around and he had hardly glanced at her since in five days' time.

She grimaced as dirty water soaked through her sandals. They crossed a wide street and found themselves at the end of another long avenue, filled with lights and people. Bright, expensive-looking Americanized shops lined both sides of the street.

"Okay, folks, here's our destination. You're going to find tourists like yourselves here, and the more wealthy Mexicans, a few street musicians, and a few homeless people. Your mission is to give them these." Jeff reached into the bag he had been carrying and pulled out a large bunch of tracts, separated into groups by rubber bands. "Basically these have the gospel message printed on them, also the addresses of the Elim churches so people know where to come to. Everyone start out with a pile of them. If you run out, find me and I'll refill you. We're going to split up in groups of twos. Spread out and don't be shy."

Meg turned to look around for a partner. Pete and Diego were taking their stack from Jeff, and Teresa and Will were next in line. "Well, Meg, looks like it's you and me," Jamie said from her place beside Meg. She took a stack with limp hands; Meg noticed that her eyes were on Pete. Couldn't she be separated from him for a half hour?

"Sounds good—except neither of us know much Spanish."

"Oh well."

They began walking and taking in their surroundings. Meg saw a lot of couples walking hand in hand or side to side, leaning on each other. Many of the Mexican women were at least two inches taller than the men, or so it seemed until Meg looked at their feet and saw that they wore shoes with three or four inch heels. Why would they want to be taller than the men?

It must be the American influence, which was evident all along this street. Clothing stores with the latest fashions; shoe stores—where no woman's shoe had a heel less than three inches high; jean stores; a McDonald's. Meg felt almost like she was back at a suburban Wisconsin strip mall—except that a musician sat on a corner strumming his guitar, a few coins in the upside-down sombrero placed in front of him.

A sound to their left caught Jamie and Meg's attention. Two young Mexican men leaned in a doorway and were making *chick-chick* sounds at them—it was obviously the Mexican version of a wolf whistle. Meg made the mistake of looking over and making eye contact. "Hey, pretty *señoritas,*" one called with a grin. He continued to speak something and Meg thought she heard *casa*—something along the lines of "come home with me?"

"Hey." Meg and Jamie turned at the sound of Rick's voice to see him and Jeff right behind them. Rick stepped in front of Meg with a frown on his face. "Me—*padre.*" He poked a finger into his chest, then turned it to Meg.

The young man's eyes grew wide and he threw his hands up dramatically. "*Lo siento, lo siento Señor.*" Rick nodded, then motioned the girls on.

"I don't think we're supposed to look at them." Jamie whispered to Meg so Jeff wouldn't hear.

"I know—but it's hard! I'm not interested, it's just an involuntary reaction to look. I follow the noise. Plus it feels really rude to just ignore them."

"I know. We probably just need practice."

Fifteen minutes later, they had made their way down the whole length of the street and had gotten plenty of practice. Rick had eventually stopped shadowing them when Jeff began speaking with someone on the street. Meg and Jamie had come up with a phrase to warn each other with whenever they heard a whistle: "Horseblinders."

They had handed out about twenty tracts already. Meg had been surprised at people's reactions—instead of depositing them in the closest trash can, or even dropping them on the ground like many people would in America, the recipients actually took the time to open and read them, then put them in their bag or purse.

Meg and Jamie posted themselves at the far end of the street to watch the crowd flow around them. Since they were at the end of the line most people approaching them already had tracts in hand.

Meg accidentally dropped her pile and was standing back up from gathering it together when she noticed a Mexican man coming towards her. He was a few inches shorter than herself, looked to be in his mid- to late-twenties, and seemed intent on talking to her. Before she could hand him a tract with a "*Para usted*," he spoke in broken English. "Where can I go with you in the city?"

"*Perdón?*" Had she heard him right?

"Where—where can I go in the city with you?" He seemed to be struggling with the words.

Was that a pick-up line? Where was her dad when she really needed him? "Nowhere." She hoped the aversion she felt was evident in her voice.

He caught her meaning and seemed to flush. "No, no—I mean, where is your church?"

Meg brought her hand over her mouth, then dropped it. "Oh, sir, I'm so sorry! *¡Lo siento!* Here," she said, and handed him a tract. She flipped it to the backside and showed him the address.

"*Gracias, gracias.*" He smiled and went on his way.

Meg turned to find Jamie snickering and joined in. "Oh, man, I was so rude. But the way it sounded—"

"I know. I would have done the same thing."

An hour and a half later they had handed out all their tracts, so they decided to walk back the length of the street. They kept an eye out for people who had been missed by the others. Mid-way down the street they found Jeff talking to an old, tired-looking woman. The lady bid him farewell just as Meg and Jamie approached him.

He was smiling. "I've been talking to that woman for about fifteen minutes. She's a believer, but she's been struggling with depression. She wanted me to pray with her."

"That's neat." *I wish I knew enough Spanish to converse and relate like that.*

"I think we're going to pack it up in five or ten minutes, since you cleaned me out of tracts. Go on and head down to the end of the street, we'll gather at the last bench."

The two girls followed his instructions and kept going. At the next street corner Meg saw Teresa talking to a man who looked to be in his mid-thirties. Diego was a few feet away from them talking to a woman. Meg and Jamie slowed their walk. Meg's eyes welled up with tears when she saw clearly that the woman was missing a leg and that the muscles in her face were motionless and lax. Her right shoulder was humped at an odd angle, and her hair didn't look like it had been brushed or washed in weeks. Meg had seen people like that back at home, and it always made her heart hurt.

Meg stopped altogether when she saw Diego's face. He was smiling and holding the woman's claw-like hand in his own as they talked. Meg could see that the woman was speaking slow and slurred Spanish; Diego's head was tilted slightly towards her as he made out the words.

The only thing that counts is faith expressing itself through love. She had read that verse this morning. Diego really did have a gift with people. Meg knew she would never be that comfortable around someone so different.

"Come on, Meg," Jamie said. Her tone of voice expressed uneasiness and echoed Meg's last thought. They turned to walk away, but Meg's attention was caught by a loud voice. She looked back. The man with Teresa was arguing. Meg couldn't tell what he was saying, but he looked drunk and frustrated. Meg could tell by the look on her sister's face that she was handling it well.

Meg and Jamie made their way to the end of the street and Jamie took a seat on a nearby bench to wait for the others. Meg noticed a young man selling roses who didn't have a tract yet. *Strange.* Someone should have gotten to him by now.

Might as well try him. She pulled one extra tract from the pocket of her skirt, which she had planned on sticking in her journal as a memento. He smiled widely at her as she approached—*oh, no, not one of those again*—but his smile disappeared when he noticed the little white paper in her hand. He began shaking his head earnestly and kept it up even when she offered it to him.

"No, no—I no want, I no want." He pushed the offered paper away. Meg looked at him with confusion; he hadn't even looked at it. "You see, you see," he said. One hand went into his pocket and brought out a small laminated card. "Look, look." In the bright light of the store windows Meg could see a small print of an opulent painting of a saint.

Pete's voice interrupted from behind her. "Don't try. The rest of us already have, and he just argues about his patron saint. He doesn't want a tract."

"Okay." Meg smiled and nodded politely to the man, then turned back to the bench, where most of the group had gathered.

"You guys think *he's* bad." Teresa shook her head. "You should have been there for the guy I had to talk to. He was so drunk his breath could have killed a cat, and he kept arguing with me in slurred Spanglais about how 'the white girls shouldn't be handing things out about their religion if they can't talk about it with the people.'"

"He's got a point." Will leaned back against the bench.

"Yeah, if he was sober. But his logic was pretty messed up. I finally just said goodbye and escaped with Diego. The guy was muttering to himself when we left."

Jeff took a seat next to Will. "I think in the instance of tracts it's okay if you don't know a lot of Spanish, because it's all on the cards. If we were doing a survey or something it would be a different matter, but I don't have a problem with this. If people are interested, the addresses of the churches are there. In the cases where someone did want to talk, you guys just directed them to Diego or me or Teresa, and we helped." He stood and stretched. "Okay, I think we can head out."

Teresa ended up in the back of the group walking next to Meg. "Meg, next time we go out in public you *have* to put my hair up for me beforehand."

Meg glanced at it—it was hanging loose down her back. "Why? It looks nice."

"Yeah, a little too nice—I had people coming up to me and touching it."

"They've probably never seen anything like it. You're like a Norse goddess."

"Or something. These people definitely don't have any sense of American personal space."

They had walked a block or two when suddenly Teresa giggled.

"What?" Meg asked.

"The people behind us," Teresa whispered.

Meg glanced over her shoulder to see a young Mexican man and an older woman—his mother? They were talking and looking covertly at Meg as they walked a few feet behind the group. "What are they saying?"

"I'll tell you later."

⚘

Diego, walking a few feet away from Meg and Teresa, slowed his pace to more easily catch the conversation between the young man and his mother. "She is pretty," the mother said. "And look, she has no wedding ring."

Was she talking about Meg, or Teresa? He glanced over his shoulder and caught the young man staring at Meg. Diego shoved his fists into his pockets. The guy was at least twenty-five. Couldn't he tell she was too young?

"Yes, she is very pretty. I'm surprised she is not already married."

Diego couldn't help looking over his shoulder again. Meg was oblivious to the man's Spanish praises. Teresa, however, had a large smile on her face. She caught Diego's eye and raised an eyebrow. What did that gesture mean?

He paused until he could fall into step beside her, then spoke in Spanish. "You Americans should wear rings on your wedding finger while you are here." He tried to keep his tone light.

"I seem to be fine—my sister is the one with all the admirers." Her Spanish inflection carried a bit of teasing.

He looked sideways at her. Did she suspect him to be one of them? She had been the one to give him the pillow last Sunday, and had probably watched the whole scene from the girls dorm. Of course she suspected him—girls always picked up on those kinds of things. Especially when their sister was involved.

"Are you guys talking about me?" Meg peeked her head around Teresa. "I heard *hermana*."

Diego spoke to Teresa in Spanish. "She tells me she is not good with languages, but she is picking up vocabulary quickly." He switched to English to reply to Meg. "What if we are?"

He tried to make eye contact but she looked away. "I was just wondering." She wrapped her arms around her middle and fell back.

"Did I offend her?" Diego hoped his words to Teresa were out of Meg's hearing, but said them in soft English just in case they weren't.

"You really want to know?" Teresa looked him in the eyes. At his nod she spoke. "I don't think she would have cared, except that you've been treating her like she's ten years old, all week long. She's probably tired of feeling inferior."

The truth in her words stung. "I did not realize I was doing that," he said, then paused—was he being honest? He hadn't consciously thought about the distance he was imposing, but he knew why he was doing it, and it wasn't fair to Meg. It wasn't her fault that he was disappointed she was sixteen.

Chapter Twelve

"Oh, gross. Look at that. We're going to eat that?"

Jamie's whisper was loud enough for Will to hear. He was reclining with the rest of the group on plastic chairs around two dented metal tables. In celebration of the completion of the church walls, Jeff was taking them out to supper for *grengas*—shavings of roasted beef and pork covered with melted cheese and wrapped in soft flour tortillas.

The object of Jamie's disgust was a rounded slab of raw pork and beef. Blood seeped out of it as two young men sliced thin strips off of it for the grill. Their aprons were stained red, and thin ribbons of blood ran down the tiled paneling under the counter where they stood.

Teresa wrinkled her nose. "Is that sanitary?"

"Don't worry, they cook it thoroughly," Jeff said.

Will leaned back in his chair and narrowed his eyes at the young Mexican meat-slicers. They were grinning and whispering to each other, and looking pointedly at the three girls. He looked to see if the girls were noticing—they didn't seem to be, although maybe they were choosing not to acknowledge it. *Buenas chicas.* They had learned well since arriving two weeks ago that Mexican fellows could be pretty forward. Will had walked along the street with Teresa a few times to go to the corner store for a

Joya, and he had been amazed at the brazenness of the men on the sidewalk. Good thing he was there with her.

Will tapped his fingers on the tin surface of the table. Pete had his arm around Jamie's shoulders and was twisting a curl of her hair around his finger. On the way to the grenga stand Will had been seated in the very back seat with them, and he had been practically forced to keep his head turned to the window so he wouldn't have to watch any more nudgy-kisses. Things had gotten progressively more intimate between those two; from the moment they met at breakfast until the minute they parted at bedtime, they didn't break contact. Hand in hand, hand on leg, head on shoulder…

Now he sat at the end of the table, trying again to avoid watching them. If they were married it would be no big deal—it would even be a good thing, as long as it stayed within the bounds of propriety—but he knew commitment was far from Pete's mind.

"Can we sit here?" Diego stood between Pete and Jamie's places on the left side of the table, a plastic chair hooked over one arm and Kerryn hanging from the other. His question had been directed at Pete. Was Diego trying to separate Pete and Jamie without being confrontational? Will smiled. *I wish I was gifted at that*—but being subtle was not his forte. He had a sneaking suspicion that he would soon have a one-on-one talk with Pete.

"Ah, sure." Pete and Jamie were forced to move apart. Once Diego was situated with Kerryn on his lap, Jamie turned to look across the table. "So, Meg, are you dating anyone?"

Meg began to pick at her napkin. "No, I'm not."

Diego pulled his unopened bottle of Coke away from Kerryn, who had almost dropped it on the tiled floor.

"Anyone in the picture?" Jamie asked.

"Not really." Meg's smile was slight but genuine.

"Ever dated anyone before?"

Will looked at Jamie. What was this, twenty questions about Meg's romantic life? Jamie wasn't going to get much out of her. There was nothing to tell.

Maybe he could help Meg out. "Meg's decided not to date."

Meg's narrowed eyes, directed at him, immediately made him wonder if he'd said the wrong thing. She didn't need to worry—he could defend her. He might not agree with all of her views, but he respected them.

"Ever?" Jamie's look seemed to ask if she'd heard him right.

Will grinned. "Nope, never."

Jamie turned to Meg with her head cocked. "How are you going to find someone to marry if you don't date?"

Meg took a deep breath before answering. "Well, people have been managing for thousands of years without our present system." She smiled but this time it looked a little nervous.

"I don't think it's a matter of finding someone." Teresa leaned forward so that she could see everyone's faces. "It's a matter of God bringing two people together, and He has a lot of different ways of doing it. Look at the couples in the Bible."

Pete had his elbow on the table and was resting his head in his hand. "Yeah, like David and Bathsheba, Samson and Delilah, Jacob and his four wives—oh wait, that's not quite a couple."

"If you think God brought those people together then your theology is pretty messed up." Teresa raised an eyebrow at him, though it was obvious to everyone that he was kidding.

Pete took a swig of pop. "Dating is like test driving a couple of cars before you know which one you want to buy."

"Good point," Will agreed.

Teresa propped both elbows on the table. "Except that it's more like you take it on a trip to Florida and drop it back at the dealers' full of your garbage, with 1,000 miles off the odometer, and tell him you don't really want to buy it after all—and then ask him for another car.'"

"Also a good point," Will agreed again.

"And the car isn't new anymore," Meg said. "It's like—"

Teresa dropped her hands to the table. "Yeah! It's now labeled as *used* to whoever ends up buying it. Everyone knows how quickly a car depreciates in value after you drive it off the lot."

Will looked to Meg to see if Teresa's second interruption in a row bothered her. He had been watching the sisters relate their whole lives and knew that Teresa tended to verbally push Meg aside at times. He had elbowed Teresa about it countless times in the past, and she was getting a lot better, but there were still times—especially when the discussion was something that interested her—that she dominated a little too much.

Meg didn't seem to mind letting Teresa run with this one.

Jamie waved her hand in Pete's direction. "Forget the car analogy, Pete. Dating relationships are more like test marriages."

"That usually end in divorce," Meg finished the thought. Though her tone hadn't been at all offensive, Will saw Jamie flinch at the comment.

"What, are you one of those people who thinks that the divorce rate is a result of dating?" Jamie's tone was clearly skeptical.

"Well, you give your heart away every time you have a relationship with someone, and by the time you get a husband there may be very little left," Meg said.

"I wouldn't say you 'give your heart away.'" Will looked directly at Meg. "It depends on how much you're doing physically." When people who weren't Christians dated, it might set a pattern of brokenness, because they were sleeping with a lot of people. Then, Will agreed, there was nothing saved for marriage. But when it was Christians, they usually weren't going that far.

Teresa directly contradicted his thoughts. "A lot of Christians end up sleeping together, Will. It's not that they plan to, or that they're any more weak than I am, it's the set-up. But physical intimacy aside, the emotional attachments can be very hard to let go of, at least for women."

"But that's just a part of life and love." Jamie shrugged her shoulders.

"*It stinks.*" Teresa almost hit the table in her vehemence. Will's eyebrows lowered—she spoke as if she had experienced it, but as far as he knew, she had never seriously dated anyone. How would she know? She was avoiding eye contact so he couldn't figure it out from her face.

"I don't think God wants us to get that hurt." Meg was also looking at Teresa in slight bewilderment.

"*Diego, ¡tengo* mucho *hambre!*" (I am very hungry!) Kerryn spoke loudly, breaking the conversation. Will watched her turn to look up into Diego's face.

"*Toma,*" he said, without taking his eyes from Meg's face. He flipped the cap off of his Coke and slid the tall green bottle towards Kerryn. "*Ten una bebida.*" (Have a drink.)

Jamie brushed her hair back over her shoulder. "So how would you go about it, if you're not going to date? You don't want an arranged marriage, do you?" Will could tell she was only half-joking.

Meg was trying not to laugh. "Well, Dad's pretty good at dropping names of what he calls eligible bachelors. And we've got a special answering machine for any interested parties; you know, 'if you want to date Teresa, push one, if you want to date Meg, push two, if you want to discuss marriage, push three.'"

Rick spoke up from the other end of the table. "Did you tell them about the detailed touchtone quizzes they have to pass before they can leave a message?"

Will couldn't resist. "When I pushed the one button, all I got was an error message."

Teresa giggled. "That was because the machine has a caller i.d. service, too."

"No, options one and two are just trick questions." Meg winked at her dad. "Didn't you catch the clue word—'date'?"

Jamie shook her head. "No, I'm serious, guys. How're you going to get from being friends to being engaged, Meg?"

Teresa was about to answer, Will could tell, so he jabbed her shin with his foot. She glared at him, then sat back and looked at her sister. Meg was taking her time in forming a reply.

"I'm not quite sure, really," she said at last. "It's different in every situation. I think God is creative and gives every couple their own special story. I do know that you have to take it really slow and pray a whole lot."

Will shrugged. "You can take it slow and pray a whole lot while you're dating, too."

Diego smoothed his hand over Kerryn's tousled hair. "*Sí*. But I would say that you should watch the person you are interested in for a long time first—you will be surprised how much you can learn without talking to them. And what you see is the way they really are, not how they want you to see them—always agreeing with you, changing so that you will like them. You only show your best sides when you are on a date for a few hours. In marriage you see all of the worst and must love anyway."

Meg looked like she was trying not to be pleased at Diego's affirmations of her ideas. "It's a lot more important to *be* the right person than to *find* the right person. I want to work on having good friendships with guys instead of looking for a husband in everyone I meet."

"But you have to be careful how much time you spend one to one." Teresa brushed a buzzing fly away from her ear. "And it's good to have your family involved as much as possible. They can give you good insight into the person's character."

"What if your family doesn't care?" Jamie asked. "Not everyone's home is as perfect as 'the Atwells'."

Ouch. Will hoped Teresa and Meg weren't bothered by that. He watched as Jamie turned her head so she was looking out at the street. Will couldn't quite see, but he thought there might be tears in her eyes.

A loud thump sounded as Kerryn's bottle hit the table. Fizzing brown liquid gurgled out and spread steadily to all corners. Everyone stood quickly; Meg was the first to grab napkins for soaking it up.

"I should not have given a three-year-old Coke, I guess." Diego scooped up Kerryn as he spoke indirectly to everyone else.

Kerryn arched her back. "*¡Más, Diego, más!*" (More, more!)

"*No, no más para tí.*" He stood, Coke dripping off his pants, and carried her to her mother at the other end of the table.

Will gathered the pile of soaked napkins and carried them towards the trashcan. Kerryn was still reaching out for Diego as he walked back to his seat.

Pete set his empty bottle onto the table and lifted his hands. "You guys are taking this way too seriously. Dating is for fun, to get to know someone, to learn how to relate to the opposite sex. No one even thinks about marriage till after college."

Jamie turned to look at him. "Yeah, but don't you think there's a possibility of marriage with every person you date? It might take a couple of years, but you wouldn't date someone if you knew you weren't going to marry her, would you?"

Will cringed. She shouldn't ask questions like that unless she could handle the answer.

"That brings up a good point," Meg said. "No matter what, there are only two ends to dating. Either you break up or you get married." She pulled her tiny ponytail out. "I don't want to share myself, and learn all of his likes and dislikes, or spend hours dreaming about getting married to someone, if he's going to end up marrying another woman."

"But why is that bad?" Jamie asked. "You spend hours with your guy friends, and you know them really well."

"But that's not romantic." Despite the seriousness of the conversation, Meg was aiming her hair band at Will's nose. "I have unconditional friendships with them—I don't have to worry about losing them, like I do when attraction is involved. From what I've seen, when a couple breaks up, their whole friendship disintegrates."

"I think you can still stay friends."

"But you've formed so many memories. Your hearts are getting woven together, whether you realize it or not. Whenever you get hurt—whether it's physical or emotional—you're left with a scar. And after enough breakups, you get callouses."

"But you've never dated anyone," Jamie said. "How do you know? You've never even tried."

"I've watched other people get hurt. I've tried to learn from their experiences so I can protect myself." Meg was looking a little less composed. It had almost turned into an interrogation.

"I think Meg has a point," Will said. "With friends—you're happy when they marry someone else. Maybe we should treat our dating partners more like friends."

Teresa shook her head. "Maybe you can do that, Will, but I can't."

"One of the main problems," Meg said, "is that most people, especially Christians, see marriage—and dating—as a right, but they are gifts." Will could tell it was hard for Meg to get the words out and he was proud that she had the courage to. "I don't go out and buy my own presents at Christmas, my parents give them to me. I can give God a list of things I want in a husband, but ultimately He's the one who chooses the package. He doesn't need me to go around unwrapping presents that belong to other women. I don't think he even wants me peeking under the paper. I'm going to wait till God sends me someone that has 'For Meg' on the tag."

"But how can you compile a wish list without dating to see what you want and don't want?" Jamie's eyebrows drew together.

Teresa broke in for Meg again. "I do it by watching my dad, and guys like Will and his brothers. I pick up quality and character standards from being around them."

Will sat back in his chair and crossed his arms. So she thought he had the characteristics she was looking for, eh? He almost smiled, but a glance at Teresa stopped him. She was giving him that look, the one that said he'd better uncross his arms and sit up straight, because he wasn't *that* special.

"Okay, guys. Here's the first batch." Jeff stood at their end of the table balancing a plate full of steaming food.

Will felt his stomach respond. Enough talking about romance. What he needed after a long day of work was some beef.

"Well, you can make all the rules you want, Meg—just don't box the rest of us in." Jamie patted Pete's hand as she handed him a grenga.

Chapter Thirteen

"Aw, isn't she cute?"

Katie let out a tiny coo as if to affirm Teresa's comment. Teresa and Meg sat on the steps leading to their dorm, Katie on Teresa's lap. Rick, José, Will, Diego, Pete, and Jamie were playing basketball at the nearby hoop. Their grenga feast earlier in the evening had supplied them with new energy. Meg opted to stick with the baby, since she couldn't make a basket unless nothing depended on it. Teresa was staying quiet, though she watched the game intensely. Usually she was as peppy as any cheerleader when a game was going on—and she often was on the court herself, in Will or their dad's face.

Meg watched the dynamics between the players. Pete, up against Jamie, had already pulled quite a few moves that Meg would have considered more than personal fouls. The others were somewhat oblivious to it, being caught in their own good-natured rivalries.

"Jamie sure doesn't seem to mind Pete's holds." Meg stuck out her tongue. "Those two. So much for following the mission's rules. She practically smothers him." Meg couldn't help remembering Jamie's stinging comment from earlier. "*You can make all the rules you want, Meg—just don't box the rest of us in.*"

Teresa looked over. "I know it's hard, but you have to cut her some slack. She's had a rough time of it lately. Her parents just got divorced."

"I didn't know that." Meg winced as she remembered more of the conversation from earlier. Jamie had said that dating was more like a test marriage—*and I responded that it ends in divorce.*

Oh, man. I really put my foot in my mouth there. "No, I didn't know that," Meg said quietly. "That explains a lot."

Another verse she had copied into her journal came to mind. *Be completely humble and gentle; be patient, bearing with one another in love.* Just because it was annoying to constantly be around Pete and Jamie's public displays of affection didn't mean that she had the right to judge them or write them off. And if Jamie's life was being shaken up, of course she'd look for stability in Pete.

Meg watched the couple on the court. "I know Jamie likes the feeling of being in love. I'm sure I'll be just as giddy, when it happens to me. The romantic stuff is fun." Her attention was diverted as Diego made a three-pointer. "But seeing them makes me want to save it even more for the one and only, you know? I just can't relate to throwing it away now."

Teresa nodded. "Yeah, I understand. But Jamie doesn't see it as throwing anything away. Each person is different, Nutmeg. It's like—well, when Jeff was talking about proposing to Adela—how in Mexico they get cubic zirconium engagement rings. You're holding out for a diamond, pure and expensive and flawless."

"Good analogy. Cubic zirconium sparkles, but it's only a copy of the real thing. Like Jamie and Pete's relationship."

"Not necessarily. Cubic zirconium serves the purpose just fine. I wouldn't quite call it a copy. It's just not as expensive. Dating at the wrong time *can* result in a good marriage. Look at Mom and Dad."

"That's true."

Teresa shifted Katie to her shoulder. "Cubic zirconium can be flawed, like a lot of areas in Jamie and Pete's relationship are. But so can diamonds. God is the Master Jeweler, and he's the only one who can fix the flaws."

Meg leaned back to look at the diamonds in the sky. Was she too strict with her purity standards? Was it possible to be too pure? Or maybe she was prideful. Would any man ever get past that?

"You know, the person I don't understand is Will." Teresa shook her head. "I get Pete—he likes having a pretty girl on his arm, and obviously enjoys the kissing. And Jamie is looking for fulfillment, self-confidence, all those areas where Jesus should be but where she's vulnerable because of her dad. But Will—I don't know. I mean, Rebekkah is gorgeous, so there has to be some sexual attraction there, but for four years?"

"Who knows why Will does what he does."

"It's just that I can usually figure him out."

Why was it bugging Teresa so much? She normally could care less about other people's dating habits. "Rebekkah knows. You should ask her."

"From what I know of Rebekkah, she just doesn't seem like Will's type."

Meg laughed. "Yeah, you'd think Will would need someone *really* unique." Meg tapped her foot. "Teresa, can I *please* hold her now?" Her older sister had hogged the baby for a good ten minutes, and Meg was itching to cuddle her.

"I guess." Teresa sighed and gave Katie's smooth cheek one last kiss before she handed her carefully to Meg. The older girl stood and made her way over closer to the game, applauding as their dad made a lay-up.

Meg set Katie gently on her lap so she could look into the baby's round face. Katie was wide awake, though it was nearing eight o'clock, and stared past Meg's right shoulder at some unseen spot. Suddenly she smiled and kicked her feet. *Maybe she's seeing angels.*

"Hey, little frog." Meg cupped the tiny socked feet in her hand. "Where're you trying to swim to—"

Her words stopped as an unexpected spout of whitish liquid came up from Katie's mouth. "Uh-oh…" It ran down the baby's chin and neck. "We'd better find your mama and a burpy diaper quick." Meg stood, holding Katie close enough to support her but far enough to keep the liquid off herself as she started across the court towards the sanctuary. She kept one eye on the ball to make sure it wasn't going to come flying by Katie's head. Diego had just made a rebound and was dribbling back in her direction to the invisible three point line. Meg paused to watch him dribble it between his legs; she knew that he'd seen her when he looked up and winked. She wanted to stay a moment more to watch, but the spit-up was

Diego leaned against the doorjamb. "You have a very nice voice."

Meg startled, and the movement woke Katie, who started to cry. "You weren't supposed to hear me."

He didn't answer but moved into the room, stopping himself from making eye contact. It seemed like he had been looking away from her all night—at dinner when they had all bounced ideas off of each other about romance, and especially when Jamie had asked Meg if she was dating anyone. Meg was too perceptive—once she realized what was on his face, all of his careful efforts to hide his feelings would be wasted. "I did not mean to bother you, but I needed a drink." Well, he *had* wanted a drink, but he had also wanted to know where she had gone to.

She looked up at him and took in his complete appearance before quickly looking back to the baby. Diego followed her glance and looked down—was she uncomfortable with him not having his shirt on? Her hair hid her face so he couldn't tell what was going on inside that head.

He decided to go into the kitchen. It didn't take him long to pour the water and return to Meg. "Would you like a glass?"

"No thanks." Katie was squirming and starting to fuss in Meg's arms. Meg tried to find a better position, but after a few tries, Katie only cried louder. Diego took a seat a few feet away from them.

"Maybe I can get her to sleep?" He reached his hands out.

Meg looked pointedly at his chest then, and he could tell she was noticing that he was sweaty. She didn't look ready to hand Katie over with him in his present condition. "Oh, yes, I forgot." He dropped his hands. "I will go get a clean shirt."

"Don't bother. I'm sure Katie doesn't care."

"Her mama might. I will go wipe off with a kitchen towel."

He went again to the kitchen, then resumed his place beside the two girls. Katie was almost wailing, and Meg looked ready to give her up.

Meg held Katie under the arms and lifted her into his hands. "Maybe she needs some bigger arms around her."

Diego took the baby and popped the pacifier in her mouth. She was soon tucked securely into his arms, and it seemed to do the trick. The pacifier stayed in and she began to swat at his face. He caught one hand with his mouth and held it gently between pursed lips before he let go and kissed the top of her downy head.

Though his eyes were on Katie, his thought were on the young woman sitting next to him. Here was a chance to really talk to her. It had been a long, hard work week, and he had spoken little to her. He had been observing her for two weeks and that had only piqued his interest in finding out what she kept hidden behind her quiet eyes and closed lips.

The sleeping baby didn't stir when Meg reached out and touched her cheek. "You really know how to make people feel comfortable."

"You're not comfortable with me." He made sure that his tone was even and not accusing, and watched for her reaction.

"I guess not." She shrugged and continued to look at Katie.

"I am sorry if I have done anything to make you feel that way." He stopped himself from covering her hand, which was playing with Katie's fingers. Why *was* she uncomfortable? He could guess a few things. Perhaps because of the way he had been treating her, or because he was older and she felt she couldn't be herself. Maybe she had subconsciously picked up on his evaluations.

"That was really kind of you last night," Meg said, "when you held the hand of that woman—the one missing a leg. It always makes me want to cry when I see people like that."

She had seen that? He looked her in the eyes and noticed they were moist. He took a deep breath. *Should I tell her?* He wanted to learn more about her, but he didn't know if he wanted to open up quite so deeply about himself. *But that's the only way I'll be able to get her to be open with me.* She would trust him more if he trusted her with his past.

"She reminded me of my mother."

Meg was silent, waiting for him to continue.

He swallowed, then exhaled. "My father frequently abused her. One night it was so bad that she became unconscious. I was ten years old. She woke up with the mind of a child again—much like the woman I talked to last night." He swallowed hard. "My father left then, and never returned. Me, my brother, and my mother were left with no money. My brother was fifteen. To get money, he sold drugs. He is very like my father—he yelled at my mother but beat me instead." He felt his arms tighten around the sleeping baby. He had shared his story before, with Jeff and the Riveras and a few others, but it never got easier.

"When I was fourteen my mother died. I would not stay with Felipe. I spent more and more nights here at Elim for protection. When I was seventeen I became a Christian and moved in permanently. I had a job for a year doing car work, but then I quit to be able to help full-time at the mission." He smiled at the memory of the turn-around of that season. "By this time, Jeff was a brother to me, and I was happy. I learned guitar from José, and I learned English from the American groups who came down during the summers."

"José plays the guitar?"

"*Sí*. He is excellent."

A soft knock sounded at the doorway. Meg and Diego turned to find Adela standing there. "*Katie está dormida?*" (Katie is asleep?) she asked.

"*Sí. Ella está soñando, yo creo.*" (Yes, I think she's dreaming.)

Adela walked over and Diego stood to place the child against her mother's shoulder. Katie took in a slight breath, then let it out as she settled familiarly into her mother's body.

"Here." Meg passed the pacifier to Diego. "This fell on the ground, so it's probably dirty."

"*Gracias.*" Adela took it from him. "Well, time for bed for me. *Hasta luego, amigos.*"

As soon as Adela was out the door, Diego returned to his seat beside Meg. There was so much more to tell, but perhaps it was getting late.

"I'm sorry for what I said earlier." Meg drew her knees up to rest her chin on them.

"What did you say?" He couldn't think of anything she needed to apologize for.

"About you abusing defenseless females. That wasn't very sensitive of me."

"Ah, don't worry. I didn't even think of my father or brother when you said it. You didn't know."

Meg nodded and turned a little to watch him. The glow of the ceiling light cast long shadows across her eyes and chin and highlighted her nose and mouth. *That mouth.*

He decided to look elsewhere. A thin eyelash rested on her cheek.

"Hold still." He reached up to brush it away with his thumb as her eyes shut, but he missed, then drew closer to be able to see better. She was only a few inches away from him, close enough for him to trace her cheek with his fingertips if he wanted, time enough to imprint the memory of the smell of her hair.

"Got it." He pulled his hand away and shoved both hands into his pockets. He leaned against the wall and kept his face far away from hers. The exchange had been so fast that he didn't think she had noticed anything out of the ordinary, but it was still lucky for him that her eyes had been closed. He might have ruined the evening if she had seen what he was feeling.

"Hey, Papa. How was the game?" Meg was speaking past Diego. He turned to see Rick in the doorway of the kitchen.

"Good." He took a long drink from his own glass of water. "Diego, you bowed out on us."

Diego hadn't even noticed his entrance. How long had he been there? Had he seen the brushing of his daughter's eyelash?

"Sorry, sir. I got distracted."

"I see." Was that a slightly raised eyebrow? "I thought I told you to call me Rick."

"Sorry, Rick."

He smiled and went back into the kitchen. Diego heard the glass clink in the sink.

Diego reached up to rub the back of his neck. "I should go to bed."

Meg moved to stand, but he was quicker and was able to offer her a hand up.

"*Hasta luego*." She spoke to him over her shoulder on the way out.

"*Hasta luego*."

Chapter Fourteen

"*¡Señorita—señorita!*" "*¿Como se llama?*" "*¡Usted es muy bonita!*"

Meg laughed at the jabberings of the Mexican children tugging at her skirt. The mission group had just attended a Tuesday night service at Taco's church in another part of the city. Many children had come with their parents, and were now eager to touch and talk with *las señoritas bonitas.*

Meg was surrounded by six or seven of them. The questions they were asking her were all simple, but the words were coming so fast that they sounded like a single stream of gibberish.

"*Más despacio, por favor* (more slowly, please)," she asked as she knelt down beside them with a smile. One little boy came up behind her and draped his arms around her neck. She turned around to face him. "*Ven aquí, niño.*" (Come here, kiddo.) She reached out her arms and gathered him into her lap.

"*No soy niño.*" (I am not a baby.) He spoke slowly, as she had requested. "*¡Tengo cuatro años!*" He held up his four fingers proudly. Meg laughed, then tickled his belly lightly. At least this little man spoke the language at the same level she did.

"*No, tu no eres bebé.*" But he *was* tiny for a four-year-old. "*¿Como te llamas?*"

"Diego." He squirmed in her arms.

"*Sí?*" Meg looked around. "*El nombre de mi amigo es Diego.*" (My friend's name is Diego.) She lifted her free hand and motioned towards the doorway where Diego was watching the goings-on with a peculiar smile. The smile grew wider as he pushed himself off the wall.

Little Diego reached up a small hand and fingered her hair. "*Por qué es blanco?*"

"*Dios* —" she paused to search for the verb. Had she learned *to make* yet? "*hacer esta manera...*" What had she just said?

The boy seemed to understand her explanation for her light hair—that God had made it that way. Or else he really didn't care. He nodded and squirmed again, wanting to be let down. Meg lowered him to the cement pavement, then looked up to find Diego standing over her.

"*Su nombre es Diego.*" She pointed to the little boy skipping away.

Diego broke into a big grin. "*Es lindo.*"

She frowned. "*Que es lindo?*"

"Cute, adorable, sweet."

She stood and dusted off her long skirt. "*Como se dice 'Diego' en inglés?*" (How do you say 'Diego' in English?)

"Yames."

She giggled at his mispronunciation.

"Sorry," he said. "We were speaking Spanish, so I was not thinking with English sounds."

"I'm going to start calling you Yames," Meg said.

"Okay." The corners of his eyes crinkled. "Mar— Meg, did you realize that those were the first words you spoke in English for the past five minutes?"

Her shoulders dropped and she tilted her head slightly to the left. "You're right." She had hardly realized that she had been using Spanish words.

"And maybe I am wrong, but it looked like your conversation with little Diego was in Spanish, too. He understood you." He raised his hand halfway as if he were going to pat her shoulder, but abruptly dropped it. "My Spanish lessons are paying off already."

She smiled. "Maybe." For the last few days, every time they spoke to each other, he had been giving her the Spanish version of her English words and insisted that she repeat them. He'd been saying little things in Spanish, too, and refusing to translate for her. But there had never been a conversation between them that wasn't part English.

She turned to see that a group of young girls had formed a circle with Teresa in the deserted street and had started a hand-clapping game. The words sounded almost like a chant, and grew faster as the slapping quickened. The group burst into a chorus of giggles and cheers as one girl finally ended up "out," then a new round began.

Meg observed the game from the side of the street. It looked familiar, and after watching a couple of rounds to get the rhythm, she decided to try her hand in it. When they finished the next round, she stepped into the circle. "Can I play?" She looked at Teresa.

The girl who had just gotten out nodded enthusiastically. "*Sí, sí.*" She pointed to Meg's left hand and said something that Meg didn't catch. Meg frowned and shrugged at her, holding up her hands.

The girl next to her took a hand and pointed to the ring on one finger. "This—ow!"

Of course. Rings would really sting when the slapping got fast. "Just a minute," Meg said. She rolled the gold band off the middle finger of her left hand and made her way over to Diego. "*No tengo pocketas,*" she explained as she tugged at her pocketless skirt.

"*Seguro.*" (Sure.) Diego grinned and took the ring she held between her fingers without touching her hand. "By the way, *pocketas son 'bosillos' en español.*" He tucked it into his pocket.

She turned to walk back to the circle, then paused to glance back over her shoulder. No, he wasn't looking at her. He didn't even notice that she'd turned around to look back at him.

He had just been helpful today, that was all.

Ten minutes later she and Teresa were two of the three finalists left in the game. Meg was just about to place her hands in position when the sound of a car engine sounded from up the street. A bunch of shrieks came from all the girls present, and Teresa yelled "Auto!" It had happened three times since the game started, and each time someone alerted the group to the approaching vehicle. There was no danger involved—the cars only went about ten miles an hour—but the girls enjoyed the excitement of it and hammed it up.

When the Bug had passed and the group was back in place, Meg tried to regain her concentration. She could only understand about three words of what they were chanting, but she knew that when they got to *¡Tres!* she needed to pull her hand away.

The girls around them chanted as the slapping grew faster. A few seconds later the fateful *¡Tres!* sounded, and the one young girl remaining got slapped by Teresa. Her friends teased her and pulled her out of the circle while Meg moved closer to stand opposite her sister. The girls clustered in and began the chant. Meg tried to concentrate on the game but found it distracting to be in the finals with her sister. She always lost to Teresa's competitiveness.

This time, when the *¡Tres!* came, Meg was too slow. Teresa slapped the tip of Meg's fingers as she tried to pull them away in time.

"Ah ha ha ha!" The group around them shouted and pointed fingers at Meg. "*¡Fuera! ¡Fuera!*" (You're out!)

What were they saying? Meg put up her hands. "I'm not very good at this."

"Come on, Nutmeg, at least you made it to the finals." Teresa smiled at her, but Meg turned to leave. Enough of watching Teresa in her element.

Meg drew herself away from the circle and headed towards Diego to retrieve her ring. He was sitting against the clean adobe wall waiting for her, rolling the ring in his fingers and examining it while she approached. He held up the small circlet so that it reflected the light shining from inside the small church. It looked very small and out of place in-between his fingers. "*Tienes dedos pequeños.*"

He spoke too fast for her to catch any of the meaning. "Stop speaking in Spanish. I'm not that far yet." She didn't know why, but suddenly she needed an outlet for her frustrations.

"What is wrong?" He looked up and peered into her face.

"I just feel so stupid." She rolled her eyes so that she stared at the ceiling. *Don't cry, Meg.*

"Sit down." He patted the cement in front of him.

She shook her head and remained standing.

"Okay, then I will stand." By standing he brought the distance between them to about six inches. She stepped back. She didn't want him to know just what was going on inside her, including her awareness of his closeness. She decided to sit down.

"Okay, my friend." He followed suit. "You do not have to tell me, but I am trying to make you feel comfortable, sí?"

She nodded. He had opened up to her the night before—the least she could do was share a little right now.

"I always feel so second-rate compared to Teresa." She kept her face turned away from him. Teresa and her girls had started another game. She could feel his gaze on her but she couldn't return it.

"How are you second-rate?" He obviously didn't agree with her statement, from the smile in his voice.

"She's gifted at everything. She's pretty. She's smart. My Spanish will never be as good as hers. She is equipped in every way to be here—her personality, her charm, her language gift, her comfortability. I just get tired of always being in her shadow."

Diego tapped the tip of her nose to make her look at him. "That is not true. You may feel like it at times, but it is just that—a feeling. Stop being sorry for yourself."

She would have felt even worse at his reprimand, but he said it with nothing but kindness.

He dropped his hand. "You are tired. Do not worry about so much." He leaned forward. "*Toma.*" He slid her ring off of his pinky and held it out to her. "*Tienes dedos pequeños.*" He said the words quietly, slowly. "I was telling you that you have small fingers."

She put her hand up in the air, fingers spread. He seemed to hesitate, then flipped the ring so that it was held securely between his thumb and forefinger, and slid it onto her ring finger. The brush of his fingertips and the circle of metal were warm in comparison to the night air, and he had it almost past her knuckle before she realized it was the wrong finger. "No— it goes on my middle finger." She kept her hand still as he slid it back off and onto the other. "Thank you."

She stood and walked a little ways down the hill to seat herself on the low curb. Paco's church was higher up in the foothills than Elim was;

power lines were visible along the top of the ridge, far enough away that they looked like toothpicks. The last light-blue patches of evening sky were fading behind the hills' silhouettes.

She rested her elbows on her knees. A light breeze waved her skirt against her legs. She felt the tears start to flow, for no reason. She buried her head in her arms. It felt so good to have a good cry. *I know why I'm so emotional—it's that time of the month.*

But Diego *had* been right—she did feel too sorry for herself, and she compared herself to Teresa way too often. It wasn't fair to Teresa, or herself.

Meg sniffed and wiped the tears from her cheeks and eyes. The others appeared to be getting ready to go. She crawled into the van before they came, curled up in a back corner, and hoped they wouldn't notice her red face. Her dad was the next inside, and he sat down next to her. Meg switched positions so that she was tucked underneath his arm, resting her cheek on his chest. He didn't ask any questions but smoothed her hair away from her face and held her all the way home.

Chapter Fifteen

Will had to get Teresa out of his head.

He didn't know when it had started, but it was there. Maybe it had been pressing his cheek to hers at the work site a week before. Maybe it had been watching her in her element the night before at Taco's church. Maybe it was the fact that she seemed to be completely ignorant of him, and he missed her company.

He had awakened this Monday morning to the sound of a rooster crow and pictures of Teresa floating in front of his eyes.

When I wake, I will see your likeness. That was the first verse that he saw when he flipped open his Bible for a morning Psalm. The rest of the verses blurred as he imagined Teresa's smiling face.

Determined to erase it, he had tiptoed down the stairs to the second floor for a bracing cold shower. He had almost knocked Teresa over on his way to the men's room as she exited the women's. Her hair was wet and hanging down her back, literally steaming in the cool morning air, and it smelled like flowers. She had on a pair of perfectly modest pajamas, too, but the combined picture with the faint memory of his thoughts the night before was enough to make him trip the last step into the bathroom.

"Watch out, the water's hot today." She had warned him over her shoulder as the door closed behind him.

Five minutes later he had ended up in front of the mirror, combing his hair back, telling himself to deal with it. This was nothing he couldn't handle. It was just physical attraction, and it had happened before with other girls.

But never with this frustrating intensity, and never with Teresa, of all people. She would probably be totally disgusted at the thought. The last thing he wanted was for her to see it, and he was doing his best to hide it, but it was extremely difficult because she could read him the way she read Spanish advertisements: quickly and with complete comprehension. Besides that, he had more of a chance at winning the Mexican lottery than he did winning her affection.

So all day he had tried not to watch Teresa. He had tried not to watch her at the work site, when he was installing the windows and she was painting the walls in the interior, with only a panel of glass between them. And he tried not to watch her when he saw her napping on the grass after lunch. When she laughed as she beat him in the final round of Lightning before dinner. Even when she slurped up her soup across the table from him.

At least she was out of sight right now, and he could give his eyes a break. It was so bizarre, having known her for a lifetime and suddenly seeing a completely different woman. How long would it be until the old came back? Part of him hoped it was soon, but most of him never wanted to go back.

Maybe talking about it with Rick would help. Then again, he wasn't just a second dad to Will—he was also Teresa's dad, which might influence the advice Rick gave too much.

"Hey, Will. Where's Teresa?" Meg skipped over the last step, which he was sitting on.

"Uh, I think she's over by Gertrude, but I'm not sure." *Yeah, right,* he wasn't sure. He had watched her walk there after dinner and he had been on the steps ever since.

Meg tilted her head back as she walked across the courtyard. The entire horizon lit up as a stroke of lightning branched its way across the sky. By its eerie light she could see several layers of clouds piled high on top of each other. She hadn't heard any thunder yet, but the flashes seemed closer than they had even five minutes ago. She hoped the storm would hit sometime tonight. It would clear and cool the air, and she'd be able to sleep better.

Meg made her way to where her sister had spread an old blanket over the sand and prickly grass next to the van. Teresa was completely stretched out, and she patted the open space next to her when she saw Meg approaching.

Meg lay down next to Teresa on her back and propped her head up with her hands so that she could watch the lightning display. The flares were higher overhead now, and more brilliant. In the far distance thunder was beginning to rumble softly.

"What's everyone else doing?" Teresa's voice was just above a whisper.

"I don't know. Will was just sitting on the stairs doing nothing. I think the others were in the sanctuary." Meg looked back up into the sky. "Look at that one!" She drew in a quick breath as a bolt traveled the exact same path several times in a row. "That looks like a strobe light or something."

"S'pose we'd better go in?"

"Yeah, pretty soon." Meg looked over into her sister's upturned face, illuminated by the street lights, and was surprised to see Teresa's eyes tightly closed. A tear was waiting to fall in the corner of each eye.

Meg reached out and touched her sister's shoulder. "Reeses? What's wrong?"

Teresa opened her eyes and gazed at her sister without saying anything. Then the tears started to flow.

Meg sat up and moved so that she could both support and embrace her. The older girl clung to Meg, but still didn't say anything. Meg smoothed her sister's hair from her face and let her cry silently for a couple of minutes, still unsure of the reason for the unexpected tears.

The breeze that had been brushing through their hair and around their faces suddenly gusted into a wind. The two girls looked up to find the storm rapidly approaching. The little palm trees were swaying in the wind, their branches whipping into tangles. By unspoken consent the two girls stood up and started for the main building. Even if the others hadn't left the sanctuary yet, they could find a secluded spot.

But the sanctuary was deserted and dark. Meg felt her way across the room while Teresa followed close behind with the blanket. They curled up in the far corner, where they had the best view of the storm.

"What's the matter?" Meg asked again. The words seemed to echo in the empty room. "Sorry," she said in a lower voice. She dug into her pocket, pulled out a crumpled but unused tissue, and handed it to her sister.

"Thanks." Teresa wiped her eyes. After a few sniffs she crumpled up the tissue again. "It's Will."

"Will?" Meg waited for more.

"Meg, I just can't get him off my mind. He's been so nice to me on this trip. If I need anything, he gets it for me. He can tell when I'm down, almost as good as you can. He always tries to cheer me up. He's just always there. And I've been such a bear to him."

"He's always been like that with you, hasn't he? And yeah, you have been a bit of a grump. He asked me what was wrong with you a week ago, but I didn't know."

"Nothing that I want him to know about."

"I'm not sure where you're going with this."

Teresa brushed her hair away from her face. "Meg, I've struggled with my emotions concerning Will since I was fifteen."

"You mean you—liked, or was attracted to him, or—"

"*Am* attracted to him. Extremely."

Yikes. Meg thought back on the trip. Why hadn't she picked up on it? Why hadn't Teresa told her about it? They were best friends. *For five years?* "You're kidding."

"I know, it's crazy." Teresa laughed but it caught on a hiccup. "I started liking him when I was a sophomore in high school, but I never said anything. I had his full attention, even though none of it was romantic. Then two months later Rebekkah showed up, and I lost him."

"Oh, Reeses…" Meg hugged her sister. "I can't believe I never even noticed."

Teresa shrugged. "After a couple of months it got better. I never had a chance…he knew me too well, kind of like a worn out shoe—comfortable but never noticed, taken for granted." She sounded like she was about to break into tears again. "Once he and Rebekkah started going out seriously, I realized that he'd chosen his one and only, and I was kind of able to bury all those feelings. Kind of. I talked with Mom about it a lot, and she helped me. Mostly I tried not to spend too much time with Will. I always made myself think of him as hers. But I still didn't quite get rid of it. Love is a permanent disease."

"Love?"

"I don't know what else to call it. I think I'd die for him. And I don't know why in the world it's him. I mean, I do, but I don't. He's such an oaf. And he's got a beautiful girlfriend."

"You're beautiful." Meg was sure Will had noticed that at least.

"Not to him."

The weather outside was getting wild. The whole sky would light up while the lightning streaked and forked its way through the clouds, making the room and courtyard outside as bright as day. Then everything would go dark, but only for a few seconds.

Meg pulled the blanket over her legs, glad to be inside. "Do you think Will knows?"

Teresa shook her head vehemently. "He has no idea that I feel this way, and I don't want him know; it'd make things really hard if he did. But it's eating at me, and I'm wrecking the friendship anyway—I can hardly stand to be around him. I feel like my thoughts are a big untrained Labrador retriever that I'm taking for a walk in the woods—they keep straining and pulling at the leash, totally tiring me out. So far I've been able to keep hold of the leash, but I'm getting sick of it. The world says 'Run with the dog! He's just being normal.' A part of me wants to tell him, so bad."

Meg shifted so that Teresa could rest her head sideways on her lap.

Teresa rested her hand on Meg's knee. "And I'm constantly around him, always seeing all the things I'm looking for in a future husband. We know each other so well. And without Rebekkah here in Mexico…"

"You're having a hard time seeing him as belonging to somebody else?"

Teresa nodded.

"So that's what you were talking about in your sleep," Meg said.

"What exactly did I say?" Teresa's tone was flat, as if she didn't really want to know but had to pacify her curiosity.

"You kept saying 'She's wrong, she's wrong. Don't, Will, she's not right.'"

Teresa had to laugh at Meg's imitation of her restless sleep-talking. "I was having dreams of Will and Rebekkah's wedding day that night. I was one of the bridesmaids. It was awful."

"Yuck." Meg's words were drowned by a loud crash of thunder that shook the ground and reverberated throughout the air. Teresa waited till it had echoed off to speak again.

"Besides not wanting to initiate anything, it's really hard that he doesn't know my struggle, because then he doesn't realize how hard he makes it for me when he keeps on hanging around me. And sitting by me, and talking to me—" Teresa paused. "He kissed me the other day."

"What?" Meg's voice crescendoed as she sat up straight and stared at Teresa. "So he *does* realize you're beautiful."

Teresa shook her head. "I don't think it has anything to do with that. I was just laying there, relaxing at break. He came over and sat down by me. I wasn't watching him or anything, and then I turned and looked at him, and his lips were about two inches from mine."

Meg raised her eyebrows. "And he kissed you—on the lips?"

"No...not really." Teresa closed her eyes at the memory. "I turned away really fast, so all he got was my cheek. But then he was just bent over me, with his face next to mine, and he didn't move or say anything. I couldn't really see him, but after a couple of seconds I jerked away. I couldn't take it. I felt like—you know that song, 'If you can't be with the one you love, love the one you're with?'"

"I can't believe he was that insensitive to you. What a jerk."

Teresa put a finger to her lips and pointed up. The boys' dorm was above them. "I can believe it. He promised me, a long time ago when I was probably twelve or thirteen, that he would kiss me someday. He said something about it the other day when he tried. I don't think it's something he does routinely. I hope not. I don't think it meant anything to him." She blew out a long breath. "I just wish he would have said something first, given me a little warning or asked me."

"Well, I'm sure he thought that if he asked he wouldn't get one." Meg peered down at Teresa's face. "*Would* he have gotten one?"

Teresa rolled her eyes. "No. But that doesn't mean I wouldn't have enjoyed it."

"I would have slapped him. Did you yell at him?"

"I couldn't. I wanted to cry, so I just walked off. I think he thought I was mad at him, but I wasn't. I mean, I was frustrated, but mostly I just had to act really angry so he wouldn't see how much he'd hurt me."

Meg bit her lip. "I could shake him."

"But he didn't mean it that way."

"Yeah, right. Stop defending him. You're in love with him. I have the clear head here."

"But he's so innocent of it all; he's like a little boy."

"My foot. He's twenty-two years old. You should say something to him."

"Like what? 'I don't want you to marry Rebekkah; marry me instead?'" The two girls grinned at each other. "I don't want him to even to think about it. I'll live."

"In misery."

"Oh, be quiet. I think I just have to get away from him."

"How? He's our next door neighbor."

"I talked to Jeff again about coming back to Mexico."

"Again?"

"The first week we were here I explained how I'd finished college and was looking for a longer-term mission project in Mexico. He told me yesterday about a new mission that they are starting in Hermosillo. They really need help there. He said it would be a great opportunity."

"Cool." Meg reached out to give Teresa another hug, which was returned tightly. "Well, I'm always here if you need someone to talk to. Do you want to pray quick before we head to bed?"

"Sure."

The prayer was kept short because both sisters could barely contain their yawns. Teresa flipped the blanket over her shoulder. "Tomorrow's another long work day."

Diego watched in amusement as people shuffled one by one into the kitchen for breakfast. Jeff had given them the day off, in celebration of reaching the halfway mark on the church. They'd even been allowed to sleep in—*it must be almost ten-thirty already.* Will had said something about them not waiting lunch for him. Diego didn't know how anyone could sleep that late.

Meg came in next, and joined Teresa, Jamie, and Pete at the table. Diego was enjoying a rare morning off, and had already eaten. Later he was going to take them all to the market.

"So, is there a VCR around here?" Jamie yawned as she poured syrup over her waffles. "I think we should have a movie night tonight. We haven't seen any since we came here."

"I think there is one in the boys' dorm room upstairs." Diego rested his arms on the tabletop. "I can bring it down tonight."

"What movie do you want to watch?" Teresa stifled another yawn.

Jamie smiled. "I've got a couple in my suitcase—including my very favorite. I saw it five times in the theaters."

Diego picked up his fork. Was that the movie everyone had been talking about for weeks, back around Christmastime?

Clare Cook & Bethany Patchin

"Sometimes I think you like that sissy guy better than you do me." Pete sounded like he was only half-joking.

Jamie elbowed him in the ribs. "Come on, Pete. You were with me every time I saw it."

"Hey, that part with the frozen dead people is cool."

"Yuck." Teresa shook her head. "I didn't see it, and I don't want to."

"You didn't see it?" Jamie stopped eating. "Teresa, you *have* to see it. The romance is so good. And the dead people are really fake, anyway."

"Aren't a couple of the romance scenes pretty explicit?" Meg pushed a piece of waffle around her plate with her fork.

Jamie shrugged. "You don't really see much of anything. They're not very long, and they're hardly explicit compared to most movies."

Diego swallowed the rest of his orange juice. Hardly explicit? He didn't want to watch any movie that even bordered on it, especially with the girls sitting right there watching along with him. How uncomfortable. And if it was at all visually provocative he wouldn't even want to be watching it alone. *I will set before my eyes no evil thing.*

"They ruin a good love story with those scenes. Hollywood portrays love as hormones." Meg scuffed the thin carpeting with her foot for a minute and accidentally knocked Diego in the shin. At her quiet apology he shook his head to wave it off.

"We can fast-forward them if you really want me to." Jamie leaned forward to be able to see Meg two seats down.

Meg shook her head. "Thanks, but I'd rather not."

Diego scooted forward on the bench. "Would you watch people doing that in real life? If it was not through a movie lens—would you be embarrassed to come across a couple doing what the characters do?"

Jamie coughed on a strawberry. "Well, no—I mean, yes, I'd be embarrassed, and no, I wouldn't watch it in real life. But that's the whole point—it's just pretend."

"But it's *not*." Meg shook her head. "The actors actually had to take their clothes off. They're not faking that. I think that's pretty gross."

"Hey, they're just having fun." Pete wiggled his eyebrows. "Honestly, Meg, they really don't show very much."

116

"I just think it's really dangerous. From a girl's perspective. I know that if I watched it, I would probably get caught up in the love story, and I'd be a lot more permissive about what the characters do. I really try to be careful about what principles I'm allowing myself to soak in when I'm watching a movie. Because I can be so tempted to compromise."

"But you've got to be able to separate reality from fantasy, Meg," Jamie said. "You make it sound like you have no say in what you take in."

"I think it could be subconscious, if I watched enough movies."

"But this is just one. It's not going to cause you to lose control someday when some guy finally gets past your purity hang-ups and kisses you."

Diego saw Meg flinch. Teresa apparently saw it, too, because she quickly changed the subject. "Don't they swear quite a bit?"

"Well, there *were* all those people dying," Jamie said. "Don't you think that's what they actually said?"

"Maybe." Teresa tilted her head in consideration.

"That's not the point." Meg spoke quietly as she pushed her plate away. Her hand was shaking a little. She glanced over at Diego for a second before looking back at the table top.

He cleared his throat quietly. It was enough to bring Meg's eyes back to his for a second—she really was taking note of everything about him right now. He allowed his eyes to smile at her; hopefully she would understand the message.

She understood something, because the corner of her mouth turned up and she quickly looked away.

"There's no more swearing than you hear in school." Jamie gave an exasperated sigh. "I didn't even notice it. Meg, I just don't understand—you haven't seen the movie. How can you say if it's good or not?"

Meg rubbed the back of her neck with one hand. "I've talked to several people who've seen it." Her tone was mild. "And I read a couple of detailed reviews."

"Oh, come on." Jamie rolled her eyes. "Most of it is based on history. Just think of it as a documentary."

"I still think I'll pass this time." Meg stood to take her dishes to the kitchen.

"Fine. You're so much better than the rest of us."

"I didn't mean to sound that way." Meg stopped and turned to look at Jamie.

Diego spoke up. "I need to go get some parts for Gertrude. Jamie, would you like to come with me?" Maybe he could get her to simmer down a little. Plus it would be good to get her away from Pete for a half-hour.

"No thanks." Jamie was stacking Pete's dishes on top of hers.

Maybe he could whisk Meg away for awhile, then. He walked to the kitchen and peeked around the doorway. "Meg, I need to run a few errands. Want to come?"

She stopped rinsing her cup. "Sure." She sounded relieved.

He deposited his dishes, then followed her out of the building. She squinted as the bright light washed over her.

"Do you need anything?" Diego asked.

"I don't know, do I?"

"I'm just going to get a few parts for the van. We won't be going anywhere special."

"Okay." She allowed him to open up the passenger door for her, then hopped up into the seat. He stopped himself from putting a hand on her back to help her up.

He turned the key and listened as Gertrude wheezed to life. He looked over his right shoulder and stretched his arm across and behind Meg's headrest for leverage. A few strands of her hair tickled his arm.

It was getting progressively harder not to touch her.

"Are you okay?" he asked.

"Yeah."

"Jamie hurt you." He edged the vehicle carefully out of the gates.

"Maybe she's right." Meg turned in her seat. "Do you think I have purity hang-ups?"

He kept his eyes on the road. "I don't think you can ever be too pure, Meg. It is good that you are sealed. You make it much easier for guys to be around you because you do not flirt, and because you dress modestly." He didn't want to think about how difficult it would be to be around her if she didn't.

"Thanks." Meg looked out the window. "I feel so conspicuous sometimes. I don't fit in, my fashion is completely out of date—although it's better here, being at the mission, where everyone dresses that way."

Diego almost laughed. "Believe me, not everyone dresses modestly."

"Even when the groups come down? What about the rules?"

"I think it is usually innocent, especially with the younger girls. They don't understand how easily something becomes immodest in a young man's eyes." He was surprised at how well she seemed to understand it, at her age. Rick and his wife had done a good job with their daughters.

Meg was quite the package, and it wasn't just her outside. He had met many girls who never had a positive word to say about young men, and he would never have opened up to them. Then there were the young women visitors who followed him everywhere, and manipulated ways to sit by him, and talked to him whenever they had the chance, and took many pictures of him. Meg never did any of that. He always had to go to her.

She had her temple resting against the window and her eyes were closed for a moment. Obviously she felt comfortable being in silence with him.

She shifted, and he suddenly realized he'd forgotten to take his arm off of the back of the bench seat. She apparently didn't, because she moved again so that her head dropped onto the top of the seat, bringing her cheek straight into his cupped hand.

He relaxed his fingers around her face for a millisecond before her eyes flew open. Diego and Meg reacted simultaneously; she straightened in her seat and he drew his arm back to the steering wheel.

Was she blushing? Maybe the pink on her cheeks wasn't embarrassment. He looked at her eyes and they met his for a long moment. He forced himself to keep the wonder off of his own face. Had the simple skin-to-skin contact affected her that much?

A loud horn drew his eyes back to the road, and he saw that he had almost drifted over the center line. The store was just up ahead.

Diego turned in to the parking lot. "Want to come in with me?"

Meg looked at the building for a couple of seconds. "I think I'll just wait."

Diego nodded. "Make sure you lock the doors."

Meg watched him disappear into the old brick shop. Was this where he'd learned mechanics? She reached up to rub her cheek. How could she not have realized that his hand had been by her face? It wouldn't have been so bad if she could have immediately brushed it off, like she would have if it had happened with Pete. But she'd gotten flustered, and he had noticed and given her that look, without saying anything. He probably thought she was a flirt.

The constant consciousness of his nearness was starting to be annoying. Now that he was treating her like an equal, she just wanted to be friends with him, but she tensed up whenever he was around. Everything came into sharp focus where he was—she would notice the details of what he was wearing, or doing, or eating. She heard every word he said to anyone in the room. And her mental list of his likes and dislikes was growing daily. She hadn't realized that until she'd caught herself watching at dinner last night and predicting which dishes he would fill his plate with.

She'd thought she had it bad that Sunday after tattooing him, but that was just reacting to flattery. This had nothing to do with what he felt for her—most of the time it seemed as if he wasn't even aware of her. He seemed to be distracted and almost disregarding her.

Diego reappeared into the sunshine and she directed her attention to her lap, where she began to fiddle with her ring. No need to watch him approach the car.

The driver seat springs squeaked and the door slammed behind him. A candy bar came into her peripheral view, held in his thick brown fingers. "Hungry?"

Had he noticed that she had only been able to eat half of her waffle during the movie discussion?

"Why wait?" She quipped the slogan as she grabbed the Snickers bar from him.

He pulled the candy back. "It is ironic you should ask that, because this very morning I read a Bible verse that I have been pondering all day— *'They that wait upon the Lord will renew their strength...'*"

Chocolate does it faster. "I was just quoting the commercials. 'Why wait?' is the Snickers slogan."

He tapped the bar against his chin in contemplation. "But it is still a good question. Why should we wait? There is an analogy to be drawn here."

"Leave those to Teresa." Meg reached out for the candy bar.

"No, no." He tapped his chest with his thumb. "Listen to the wisdom of your elder. Chocolate," he waved the bar just out of her reach, "is best if you save it for dessert. In the same way, romance is best if you save it for after a main course of friendship." *What is he getting at?* Was he talking about them?

"So why are you giving it to me for breakfast?" *Whoops.* Hopefully he wouldn't think that she was insinuating that he was giving her romance. Or that she wanted it.

"Maybe I won't. Maybe I will eat it all myself."

Her stomach growled.

Diego made a face. "Alright, alright."

She took the bar from his hand and ripped open the wrapper. He fumbled in his pocket for the keys.

Diego peeled out into the street and they chugged down the road. "So was it worth the wait?"

"Completely."

Rick was the last one into the van and found that the only seat left was next to the door. Will was in the passenger seat, supposedly to help Diego navigate through the traffic to the market. They were laughing about something. *Probably comparing notes on my daughters.*

Rick shook his head. No, thankfully they were each keeping their thoughts to themselves.

Next to him, Teresa lifted his arm and placed it around her shoulders. "Wake me up when we get there."

Rick looked over at Meg, who was on the other side of Teresa. "Are you ready for a nap too?" Meg shrugged but laid her head on Teresa's shoulder, her cheek against his hand. It reminded him of when they were ten and eight and would curl up next to him on the couch during football games.

Diego suddenly swerved and hit the brakes. The girls slid against Rick and pushed him against the armrest. Had they reached the market? Diego pushed the gas pedal to the floor and they screeched around a van. Apparently not.

Diego drove like an Indy 500 finalist, but that was okay. Jen had accused Rick himself of that many times, particularly when the kids were babies. Their family had survived, and Meg and Teresa were used to it by now.

Where was that market, anyway? Perhaps Will's navigational skills had gotten them off-track.

Rick looked at the daughter dozing against his shoulder. Will hadn't yet done anything that would reveal his interest to Teresa, but that was good— the young man needed to make a decision about his girlfriend at home before, or if, he chose to pursue Teresa. Then again, maybe Will had no intentions.

Diego drove the van up over the curb and onto the crowded plaza, where he maneuvered into a parking spot. The two girls jerked up and rubbed their eyes.

Chapter Seventeen

Meg blinked a few times to clear up the haze of sleep.

Will turned around in his seat and raised his arms like a Superbowl champion. "Are you ready to shop?" Everyone ignored him as they scooted to the door.

A variety of sounds and sights surrounded Meg the instant she was on the sidewalk. This was a different side of the city than the street by the Monterrey wafer had been. People bargained in rapid Spanish for everything from blankets to meat to spices. The air was dusty and carried a variety of smells. Stands full of pottery and silver jewelry were scattered throughout the square, all of their owners busily seeking customers from among the passersby.

"Go ahead and split up into groups." Diego waved at the bustle behind him. "There are a few side streets with nice shops. Let's meet back here in an hour and a half."

Everyone agreed and began to wander off in small groups.

"Let's go look at the jewelry." Jamie tugged on Pete's hand, which had stayed entwined with hers even as they exited the van.

"I want to go look at those dead pigs." Pete disentangled his fingers from hers and started towards an open stand with red slabs of hanging meat.

Teresa grimaced. "I think I'll opt for the jewelry. I bet they have some cool rings."

"I'm with you gals." Meg linked arms with them and they started weaving their way through the displays.

Over her shoulder Meg watched the three young guys head towards the butcher stall. Her dad seemed content to take a seat on a nearby bench to people-watch.

Jamie immediately went to the necklaces, while Teresa went to a locked glass case. On top of the case were some less expensive rings in a black velvet display. At least, Meg thought they were less expensive—they weren't as intricate or as shiny as the ones in the case. But she wasn't good with peso conversions.

Teresa had her hands on the glass and was scanning the rings without expression. Meg stepped up across from her and peered into the case.

"Ooh, look at that one." Teresa suddenly pressed her index finger to the top.

"Which one?"

"Third bunch across, fourth row down. Wouldn't that be a pretty engagement ring?"

Meg leaned over farther to see better. It stood out from the others—a thin band of braided gold and silver with a tiny diamond-shaped amethyst embedded in the center. A perfect Teresa ring.

Meg's focus was drawn to the top of the case, where a new reflection appeared. She looked up to find Will right behind Teresa, his right palm on the case and his chin almost resting on Teresa's shoulder.

"Which one are you talking about?"

Meg forced herself to look away so that she wouldn't glare at him. It was none of his business. It was annoying when he butted into conversation like that. Not to mention that Teresa was probably excruciatingly aware of him and what she had just said. Had he caught the last part of her words?

Will reached out and nudged Teresa's finger off the glass. "I can't see." He took a long look then stepped back. "They all look the same to me. I'd get a big one myself—more for your money."

"Duh. The bigger the stone is, the more they charge." Meg hoped her expression told him to get lost.

"I'm going to go look at the blankets." Teresa pushed a braid back over her shoulder and turned to join Jamie a few yards away.

"Want to go check out those bloody pigs with me?" Will offered an arm to Meg. She grudgingly slid her hand through to loosely rest in the crook of his arm. *Insensitive boor.*

As they approached the meat stand she noticed a few dead chickens strung up next to the hanging pork. Meg forced herself to look at Diego and Pete, who were chomping on freshly-grilled chicken legs.

Meg shuddered. "Do you guys realize that only a little while ago there were flies crawling all over those?"

"Mm hmm. And flies defecate every three seconds." Pete waved his drumstick.

"I do not worry. Heat kills bacteria." Diego wiped his mouth with the back of his hand. "Here, try it."

"No thanks. I'm full from the Snickers bar."

"What?" Will turned to her. "Where'd you get one of those? They only sell Mexican candy at the *Abarrotes*, and I can't read the wrappers to know what I'm buying."

Meg smiled. "I've got friends in high places." A stand to the right suddenly caught her eye. "I'll leave you guys to your roasted flesh—I'm going to go look at the dresses."

At the dress stand she slowed down to enjoy the variety of gowns on the rack. The floral designs were embroidered in bright colors and lined the sleeves, waist, and hem of each. The tops were full with wide necklines, and the skirts flared to mid-calve. *That would really puff out if I twirled.*

Meg narrowed her favorites down to four colors—lavender, red, yellow, and blue—and finally chose the blue after five minutes of going back and forth. Teresa would have snapped up the purple one in a second, but Meg had a harder time with these kinds of choices. Better to deliberate and make sure it was the right one.

She placed it gently over her arm and stepped over to the counter, where a young girl sat with a cash box. *Oh no.* This girl probably didn't know any English. How was Meg supposed to ask how much it cost? Suddenly she couldn't remember anything beyond *Me llamo Meg.*

"Fifteen dollars." The girl smiled at her. She must have seen Meg's panic.

"I only have pesos." Meg pulled out a wad of colorful bills. She hoped the girl wouldn't rip her off, because she had no idea how much worth the different designs on the bills indicated.

The girl took the money, then handed most of it back. She didn't look like the cheating type—and even if she was, it was still a great bargain for hand embroidery. Meg didn't need the extra money like this girl probably did.

"Did you do this?" Meg traced a line of curling roses with her finger. The girl brought out a paper bag.

"No, my mother." She took the garment and folded it expertly, then inched it into the bag.

"She does beautiful work."

The girl smiled and nodded, then handed Meg a few coins.

"No, keep them. No *bosillos*, see?" Meg lifted the sides of her skirt.

"*Sí.*"

Meg went to find her dad. She knew he would like the dress. Ten feet from the jewelry stand she noticed that Will was arguing with the vendor. The side of the case was open and one group of rings was on the top.

Will was motioning to the fourth row. Meg stopped and tried to see what ring he wanted. The vendor pulled one out and Will took it from him to hold it up to the light before he slid it onto his ring finger. From her viewpoint, Meg thought it looked like the Teresa ring.

Was he buying it for *Teresa*? Or maybe for Rebekkah?

He wouldn't buy anyone a ring unless he was serious. He might be casual in some areas, but when it came to commitment she knew he wasn't the kind to act thoughtlessly.

The vendor reached under the case and pulled out a black velvet box. He began to speak rapidly, apparently saying something about the cost by ticking off numbers on his fingers. Will looked completely lost, and was shaking his head. He reached into his pocket and pulled out a wad of bills.

"Here," she heard him say. "This is all I have. Take it."

Meg took a step backwards. Spendthrift Will, the king of Salvation Army bargains, offering all he had? This was one significant ring.

If it was for Rebekkah, then he was beyond insensitive—to pick the only ring that Teresa liked?

The salesperson seemed satisfied with what Will had given him, and placed the ring in the box. Meg turned to walk away before Will could see her. She had to find her dad. Maybe he knew what was going on.

He was still on the bench, but now he looked like he was about ready to fall asleep. Meg plopped down next to him and cradled her bag in her lap.

"What did you get?" Her dad tugged at the bag.

"A dress." She pulled it out carefully.

"I like it."

"Thanks." Meg folded it in a different way so the wrinkles wouldn't get too deep. "Dad, I just saw Will buying an expensive ring."

Rick tilted his head. "Funny—I don't picture Will as the jewelry type."

"*Dad*. Seriously. It was Teresa's favorite one in the case. Either he was buying it for her or for Rebekkah."

"You don't know that. Maybe it was for Rachel."

"I don't think he'd use up all of his spending money for his mom."

"But you think he'd use it all on Teresa or Rebekkah?"

Meg brushed a fly off of her knee. "I don't know, but I saw him hand over a whole fistful of bills to the vendor, and he didn't get any change back."

"What were you doing, spying?"

"No." Meg paused to think of an excuse. "I was just walking by, and it caught my attention."

"I don't know why Will's buying it, but we can't make assumptions. We'll find out eventually. Just don't say anything to Teresa about it."

"Oh, I wasn't going to. She told me about how she likes him and I don't want to get her hopes up." Meg leaned back on the bench and scanned the area. Will and Teresa were now standing in front of a pottery stand. Teresa seemed to have recovered from Will having practically kissed her neck back at the ring vendor, because she was laughing with him about something. *That's good.*

Jamie and Pete were strolling around 'window' shopping, once again glued at the fingers. They had lime chills in their other hands. Meg squinted, then made a face when she saw the chili powder topping on Pete's. *Yuk.* Whenever the lime-chill vendor came around the mission on Sunday afternoons, she always ate hers plain. The thought of a sweet lime icy with chili flavoring was enough to make her shudder.

Diego was talking with a pretty young woman selling spices. The smile she kept flashing at him revealed teeth lined up in a row like Peppermint Chiclets. She was probably about twenty years old and had long black hair and big eyes. *The opposite of me in every way*—other than the fact that they both seemed to notice how attractive Diego was. Meg sighed. There was that Mexican wife popping up again. *Thanks a lot, God.*

But that was what she needed. She didn't want to notice how wonderful Diego was, because then she started thinking about being married to him, and one thing led to another, and then in her mind she was thirty years old, the mother of his six children. They were living in a poor Mexican slum doing mission work, with no electricity or running water, and he was gone all day evangelizing, and she had no friends because she still couldn't speak Spanish, and so she was left with her poor children who were so deprived that they didn't know what a computer was and had only met their grandparents twice.

Diego might be the most intriguing man she had ever met, but he wasn't worth that.

"So do you think you'd ever be able to barter in Spanish?" her dad asked.

"Are you kidding? I can't even barter in English." She always gave in because she felt like she might be quoting an offensively low price.

"You have to have more faith in yourself. I think you'd be able to catch on to Spanish very quickly if you were more immersed in it. Hasn't Diego been giving you lessons?"

"Yeah."

"You seem to enjoy his company." Her dad stretched an arm behind her shoulders.

She let her head fall back so that she was looking up into the cloudless sky. Maybe telling him would help to get it back into perspective.

"I think I enjoy it a little too much."

He rested his hand on her shoulder. "Don't beat yourself up about enjoying someone's company, even if he's a guy. Your future husband wouldn't be mad at you for that."

Meg rolled her head to look at him. "Duh. I know that. That's not what I'm worried about."

"What—are you attracted to him? Because that's pretty normal, too."

Meg sighed. He was always so basic, so cut and dry. It was good to have a married man's perspective to balance her silly girlish thoughts, but he didn't quite understand. "It's more than that. I get so—I mean, I start to think along marriage lines—" she laughed and looked back up at the clouds so he wouldn't see her embarrassment, "but then I just get overwhelmed. I don't want to marry someone like him."

"Why not?"

She watched a pigeon swoop. Why not? How could she phrase it without sounding narrow-minded? "He's from a totally different culture."

"I thought you didn't like American culture."

"Well, he loves to read. I love to work with my hands."

"He's a mechanic, isn't he? I bet he understands you."

"We speak different languages. We would have terrible communication problems."

"Your mom and I speak plain English and I still can't understand her half the time."

"Are you saying I should marry him?" Meg sat up and looked at him.

He put up his hands. "No, no. I'm just talking about friendship. Don't miss out on a good relationship because you're so worried about your attraction to him."

"But how do I form a friendship without letting him know what I'm feeling? That's so hard." She sat back again.

"Run silent, run deep."

"Huh?"

"Grandpa was on a submarine in World War Two, and that was their motto. They cruised as deep as they could, and everyone on board maintained complete silence, so that no one on the surface could detect them with radar. That's what you have to do. Don't broadcast your feelings to all your girlfriends, keep quiet about them when Diego has the radar up, and keep them deep, between you and God."

When Diego had the radar up? What did he mean by that? Diego never even looked for signals from her.

That was probably just the dad thing kicking in—he assumed young men would notice her just because she was his daughter and he considered her beautiful.

Meg rested her head back on his arm. "Run silent, run deep. That's a good one. I'll remember."

Chapter Eighteen

"Oh, a mall!" Jamie added a skip to her walk. "I haven't been shopping in ages. I finally have a chance to spend the money my mom gave me, and everything's probably cheaper here."

"Not really." Diego turned in his seat. "The mall is made for wealthy citizens and American tourists like all of you." He smiled. The money that a typical mission helper would spend in one evening was enough for Yolanda to buy a week's worth of food at the local supermarket. But the Mexico experience could only expand one's horizons so far in one trip. The Americans just didn't see things from a perspective of need.

"But we went to the market," Pete said to Jamie. "That was shopping."

Jamie snickered. "Like I was going to buy anything there. All those cheap pots and blankets, and they were asking three times as much as they were worth."

Diego stuck his hands in his pockets. "But if they were selling them across the border in Texas, they'd cost at least twice what they do here." A lot of the blankets and clothing he'd seen were well-made and worth more than their makers would ever charge, considering the hours of time that had been put into them. "And you would pay it, because of the way it is packaged and sold in a special store."

"That's true." Will slung his arm around Teresa's shoulders. "But I found some pretty good deals at the market. Spent all of my money, but I made some guy really happy. That's worth something, isn't it? Especially on a mission trip." Though she laughed with the rest of the group, Teresa still shrugged his arm off.

Meg was wearing the leather sandals she had purchased at the market, Diego noticed. She thought the fact that the soles were made from old tires was cool, and he hadn't seen her without them for the last two days.

They turned the corner to see the main doors of the building before them. Pete, first in the group, opened the door and let it swing behind him, not bothering to hold it for Jamie. Jeff caught it and pulled it open to hold it for her, but she made her way quickly inside without looking for his gesture. Diego heard Meg and Teresa both thank him as they went through.

High glass ceilings and bustling, well-dressed crowds greeted them. To the right was a currency-exchange store, and directly in front of them was a sparkling new black Volkswagen Bug on display in the middle of the plaza-like room. Lining the four sides of the area were stores selling everything from clothes to jewelry to CDs. It reminded Diego of being back in Chicago. This was part of the city life he did not enjoy.

"Is there a McDonald's around here?" Meg asked.

Diego clicked his tongue against his teeth in admonition. "Shame on you—you skip Yolanda's meatloaf and then fill up with unhealthy French fries."

Will dropped back. "I ate three helpings of the meatloaf, and I'm totally ready for a Supersize Value Meal."

The group stopped in front of one store where Jamie and Pete waited. Jamie pointed to a pair of jeans in the window. "Aren't those great jeans?"

Teresa looked them over. "Well, they look like jeans to me. I can't usually tell much difference. Besides, they're probably seventy bucks, if Gap costs the same in Mexico as it does at home."

"It does." Diego leaned against the window. He owned a pair of Gap pants, but they were hand-me-downs. One of the group members had left them two years ago and they had become Diego's favorites. But he saved them for special occasions.

Jamie sighed. "I'm just sick of wearing skirts."

"I think you look nice in them," Diego said.

Meg leaned against the glass front. "We wear pants at the work site." He watched her tuck her hair behind her ears. She never complained about skirts, or when men tried to open doors for her. Though she was only sixteen, she seemed very much a woman. Moreso than Jamie, though Jamie was three years older.

Jamie switched her purse to her other shoulder. "But it's not the same. Those are just my old khakis."

"I've actually liked the skirts," Teresa said. "They're a lot cooler than sticky jean shorts in this heat. And they make me feel like a girl."

Diego trailed them to a shoe store, where all of the shoes had a chunky high heel. So silly, all of the Mexican women trying to be tall like Americans. Why couldn't they be happy the way God made them?

"Those are awesome!" Jamie pointed to a pair of brown shoes towards the front of the display. "Let's go in."

Pete turned to Will. "Hey, Will, why do women have smaller feet?"

"I don't know, why, Pete?"

"So they can stand closer to the kitchen counter!" Pete finished his joke off with a hearty laugh. Diego snickered, more at the others than at Pete's joke. Will, Teresa, and Meg were all laughing at Pete's complete personal enjoyment of his own humor, but Pete wasn't paying attention.

Pete had made "women jokes" before in Diego's hearing, but Diego had noticed that Meg and Teresa always refused to be riled. Jamie didn't like Pete's humor very much, but her boyfriend didn't seem to care.

"Pete, that is so chauvinistic." Jamie had one hand on her hip. "You are so sexist."

"He's just joking, Jame," Meg said. "Come on, Will, I'm in need of sustenance."

The hungry blondes went looking for the food court, while Teresa, Jamie, and Pete headed in the opposite direction towards one of the department stores.

Jeff fell into step with Diego. "I've noticed that you have been spending more time with this group than you usually do with others." His quiet Spanish held a teasing note.

Diego glanced sideways at him. "They're more my age. Usually we get high-schoolers."

"Are you sure it isn't the one high-schooler in this group who's interesting you? You haven't missed an outing yet."

"There is nothing for me to do at the mission right now." Diego hadn't said anything to Jeff about Meg, but his friend obviously knew him well enough to read his restraint when he was around her. Jeff probably had also noticed that Diego hadn't denied any of his accusations yet.

"Be careful, Diego. I trust you completely, but it's easy to lose your level-headedness. She's only going to be here two more weeks."

Two weeks was a long time when they were around each other fifteen hours a day. But Jeff knew that. Diego patted Jeff on the back. "It only took you two with Adelaida, and Meg has already been here for three."

"I just can't say anything, can I?" Jeff rubbed the back of his neck. "Adela and I aren't the best example of obeying the mission's rules about Mexican-American relationships."

"But you did obey the rules." While the groups were in Monterrey, Elim preferred that they keep their focus on the reason for being there—serving God. Afterwards it was completely up to the individuals. Which meant Diego could correspond with Meg, and visit her frequently while he finished his last year of college. They could continue their Spanish lessons and she could practice in person with him, since she did not learn well by books. Then, in a year or two, she could quit college and they could be married and come back to Mexico, like Jeff and Adela. They would start a church and she would be his helper, and they would have many beautiful children.

He was jumping ahead of things, yes. But it was nice to dream.

Teresa dropped her purse onto the tabletop in-between Will's and Meg's meal trays. "Ughh."

"Want a French fry, O huffy one?" Will dangled one between his fingers like a long cigarette.

Teresa took a seat next to Meg. "Yeah." She plucked the golden sliver from his grasp and tucked it into the side of her mouth so she could speak. "I just ran into Pete and Jamie kissing behind the sales rack."

"So?" Teresa watched Will as he took a big bite of a quarter-pounder. He ate hamburgers the same way her twelve-year-old brother did, without any manners whatsoever. A piece of lettuce hung from his lips, stuck on a glob of mayonnaise.

Teresa pushed a napkin towards him. "So, it was disgusting, kind of like you at the moment."

"Thanks." He ignored the napkin and opted instead for his tongue.

"It was enough to make me want to toss Yolanda's meatloaf."

"Ah, simmer. It's no big deal."

Sure, maybe for you. Teresa wanted to roll her eyes but she knew it would evoke a lecture on the joys of kissing from Will.

"But the mission has rules." Meg crumpled up her hamburger paper. "It's a little disrespectful to be breaking them."

"Oh yeah. I forgot about The Rules." Will leaned back in his chair. "But it's not a Mexican-American relationship, and it's not like we're at the mission or anything. Give them a break. They're dating. They're in l—, well, they like each other a lot."

Teresa rested her elbows on the table. "It would be different if they *were* in love." Her voice was pointed. "Or even if they had liked each other for five years or something like that. But it's been all of, what, two months?"

"Hola." Diego's voice came from above her. He rested his hands on her shoulders. "What are we all tense about?"

Teresa glanced at her sister's face. Did Meg think anything of Diego's casual touch? She had definitely noticed—her glance had followed his action before she reached for her pop. But it didn't seem to bother her, Teresa was glad to see. Teresa knew it was the gesture of a brother, and she was quite used to his affectionate attitude towards everyone—except Meg. They hadn't been much into the second week before Teresa had taken note in her journal that Diego seemed to be singling Meg out in subtle ways. One was by never laying a finger on her. Meg seemed to clam up every time he was around, but Teresa had caught her watching him in unguarded moments, too many times to count. There was a current

ning between them that was almost tangible to anyone who knew
them well.

But Teresa had done a good job of keeping her mouth shut. Meg should appreciate all of the things she wasn't saying—because it sure wasn't easy.

"We're talking about kissing." Will wiped his mouth with the back of his hand.

"I see." Diego sure sounded interested in the conversation. *Typical guy.* "So, who wants to kiss?"

The three Americans snickered, Teresa the loudest. *My sister does.*

"Nothing personal, Diego, but I'd rather go for the lovely woman across from me." Will waggled an eyebrow at Teresa.

If only he was serious. "You go for it and I'll run." She glared back at him.

Will looked back up at Diego. "Is Jeff really strict about the mission rules?"

Diego stole one of Meg's fries. "Which rules?"

"About relationships."

Meg folded her napkin in half. "Teresa was getting frustrated with Pete and Jamie's lack of tact."

Diego took the only seat remaining, opposite Meg. "Well, I broke the rules myself once, a long time ago."

"What? You?" Teresa couldn't believe that a man with such character had disobeyed.

Diego nodded. "I was seventeen, and I was dating Raquel."

"Who's Raquel?" Will looked confused. He always was horrible with remembering names.

"José's second daughter," Diego said. "She's married to Enrique now."

"So, you kissed her?" *Good old Will, never one to be subtle.*

"Yes. But I would not do so anymore."

Will laughed. "I'd hope not, if she's married."

Teresa covered her eyes with her hand. Why did he have to turn everything into a joke?

Diego smiled. "Well, any woman you date will eventually get married. It's something to take into consideration. I was kissing Enrique's future wife. Now, I wish I hadn't. And I hope my wife is not on a date right now kissing someone else."

Teresa nodded her head. Pete's and Jamie's spouses wouldn't be happy if they knew what was going on in the Gap right now. "What if you *had* married Raquel, though? It's okay to kiss the person you know you're going to marry." Teresa rested her cheek in her palm so that she could watch Diego's expressions.

"I thought I *was* going to marry her."

Will shrugged. "Well, you have to kiss a few frogs before you get a prince. Or princess, in our case."

Meg began to paint a design on her napkin with the rest of her ketchup. "Frog-like is not a word I'd use to describe Raquel, from the pictures I've seen in the Rivera's living room."

"Why do you think God made kissing?" Diego seemed to be directing his question towards Will.

"Well—I don't know. A way to express emotions."

"Do you think He places any boundaries around who you should do it with?"

"Women within five years of my age that aren't relatives or married?"

"Well, that's a start." Teresa couldn't keep the sarcasm out of her words.

Diego laughed. "Yes, you are on the right track. But I have come to the conclusion that I think He designed kissing to strengthen the bond between two people who are publicly committed to spending the rest of their lives together."

Teresa set down her pop. "I think when you kiss someone it should be because you are bestowing devotion, not taking gratification." She hoped it wasn't completely obvious that her comment was directed at Will.

"Happy birthday to you, happy birthday to you, happy birthday dear Meg, happy birthday to you!"

The song, sung in varied original keys around the group, ended in a loud off-colored harmony from Pete. Meg nodded her thanks and rolled her eyes as she grinned. *Such a group of friends I have.* She looked around the circle quickly before taking in a big breath. The glow of the seventeen candles gracing her cake reflected in the eyes of her friends. Her own eyelids slid shut as she held her breath. *God, I wish—oh, I don't know what I wish for. I'm open to suggestions.*

No, wait, He might actually be listening to her, and she didn't want another supernatural dream. She had already had far too many dreams about Diego—not that those dreams had been supernatural—especially after finding out his thoughts about romance and kissing at McDonald's.

She opened her eyes and quickly blew around the circle of candles, running low on the last few. At the sight of the one remaining candle Pete yelled out, in keeping with the tradition, "Hey, Meg, one boyfriend!"

She used the very last sputtering bit of air in her to breathe it out. "Sorry, Pete."

"You carry out your convictions to the last candle, don't you, Meg?"

"Ha ha."

"Let me grab the knife,"Teresa said. As she spoke, both Diego and Meg reached down to start removing the candles. Their fingers brushed on the way to two different ones; Meg jumped back with an "Ow!"

Diego looked up.

"The wax was still hot." Meg peeled a thin layer of candle off the tip of her finger.

Teresa started handing out the plates. "Okay, guys, this is one of Yolanda's specialties. Sorry, no ice cream, but we've got milk to drink over here."

The late afternoon sun was beginning its climb into bed behind the western mountains. The orange glow bathed the surroundings in warm highlights and dusty shadows. Meg seated herself on a step with her birthday treat and looked out over the city as she took the first bite.

It was Friday evening and they had come to El Obispado, known in English as Bishop's Palace—a grandiose pre-revolutionary building resting on the top of a hill that looked out over a large part of Monterrey. From where Meg sat, she could see a cemetery to the lower left, and farther away there were a few skyscrapers. She twisted around to once again take a look up at the dome-topped cream-colored building towering behind her. At the top of the stairs was a set of huge wooden doors with square inlays. It was a beautiful structure, definitely Spanish looking in its architecture.

Meg looked over and saw that Teresa had begun clean-up by herself. *Aw, let her. It's your birthday, and she's been grumpy all day.*

No. Meg stood to help. When she reached the clearing, Will and Diego were putting the leftovers back in the van. The two girls let them, then sat back against the broad trunk of a nearby tree.

"One boyfriend, Meg. Is he by any chance Mexican, with a first name that starts with a 'D'?"Teresa's tone was half-teasing but fully aggravating.

"Lay off, Teresa." They had started the day off with a picky fight in the bathroom about sharing their toiletries. Teresa had been upset about what she called Meg's messy habits, just because Meg hadn't kept up on her laundry and had taken a pair of her sister's clean underwear without asking. Meg had had just about enough of Teresa's nagging and stinginess on this trip and decided to tell her so. Teresa had just blown it off, which aggravated Meg more. *Teresa never takes anything seriously*.

Teasing was one thing, but pushing the limits, when Diego was standing just a few yards away, wasn't funny.

"Save it for later." Meg didn't want to ruin her birthday. Maybe tonight they could actually talk about it, but when Will and Diego stretched themselves out on the grass, Meg hoped the glance she shot at Teresa was enough to keep all mention of boyfriends quiet.

As he reclined, Will's eyes and thoughts, as usual these days, turned to Teresa. He took in every feature of her face as she leaned against the tree. He loved to watch her. She didn't seem to be in a particularly good mood, but he still enjoyed being with her. She was funny when she was grumpy; besides, he had been dealing with her moods for twenty years.

Where had Pete and Jamie disappeared to? Probably behind a bush somewhere. Though they had been ready to kill each other only two days before, they were now back to their normal intimacy. *They really are too chummy*. It made him uncomfortable.

His eyes once again strayed to Teresa's form. If only he knew that he had a chance with her. He'd caught her looking at him a few times in the last week, but never with any sort of tender expression. And every time he caught her like that, she'd turn her glance into a glare. How was he supposed to woo her when she didn't want to be wooed? She knew too much about him—he was her jester, not her knight.

He dug his finger into the change pocket of his jeans, where he kept the ring he had purchased at the marketplace. It was a symbol of hope, and knowing that he had spent as much money on it as he had gave him a bit of courage. There was no way he couldn't go through with it now. Some day—and he hoped it was soon—he was going to place it on Teresa's finger, and she was going to be happy about it.

"Man, I'm glad to be past sixteen." Meg seemed to be addressing Teresa. "Sixteen just seems so—I don't know. It's just young."

Teresa rolled her eyes. "Seventeen's not that much older. You're still not an adult." She gave Meg a patronizing smile.

Will felt his eyebrows raise. Ooh, she was feisty today. *Poor Meg.*

Meg's eyes narrowed. "I just feel more like one of the rest of you now."

Teresa glanced at Meg, looked pointedly at Diego, and then back at her sister. "Yeah, well, twenty-two's still a long ways from where you are."

What did that mean?—oh. Teresa was talking about Diego and Meg. Was there something going on between them that Will hadn't picked up on?

Diego was obviously waiting for Meg's reply. Teresa's comment must have been correct, because he had that look of anxiety about him. *I hear you, buddy.* That made two of them unsure about their chosen Atwell women.

From the look on Meg's face, Teresa had just spilled one of Meg's secrets. Teresa wasn't usually that insensitive. Will turned to her. "Hey, simmer, Reese." Teresa looked at him, then bit her lip.

Meg looked like she had tears in her eyes. She set down her piece of cake and swallowed hard. "Well, at least I haven't secretly been in love with my next door neighbor for five years." She was looking straight at Teresa.

Teresa had been in love with someone for five years? How had that escaped him? There *had* been that one Josh guy when she was fourteen, but that hadn't lasted longer than a month.

Wait a second. Meg had said neighbor.

Does she mean me?

Meg's eyes were wide, apparently in shock at what she had just said. Teresa had gone white, and had turned to stare at the building.

It had to be true.

Why was Teresa looking away from him if she loved him? Being in love with him was an awesome thing. And if she'd just turn and look at him, she'd see how much he returned her feelings. *Come on, Reeses.*

Love. For five years? *And I thought it's been hard to wait the last two weeks for her.*

Holy Texas Longhorn. Meg hadn't said Teresa *liked* him, or that she had a crush on him—Teresa *loved* him.

Teresa stood shakily and reached out to rest her hand on the picnic table. "I—" She swallowed down the rest of her words and started walking fast towards the other side of the building. What was wrong with her?

"I'll be back in a few minutes." Meg took off in the other direction.

Will glanced at Diego, who looked mad.

What was wrong with everyone? This was a great revelation! Meg hadn't just made Will's day, she'd made his life. He had to go find Teresa and explain everything to her.

Teresa loved him. It made him feel incredibly honored and unworthy at the same time. He'd always thought Teresa had high standards when it came to guys. She had only ever dated once. Will would have guessed he was the last person deserving of her affections.

Yet now he was finally given reason to believe that he held them.

He stood and started walking in the direction Teresa had headed. *Delight yourself in the Lord and he will give you the desires of your heart*. He couldn't remember having had such an answer to prayer in a long time.

Where was that woman? His woman. He liked the sound of that.

As he came around the corner of the building, he saw her curled up in a cranny against the wall, her head buried in her arms. She was crying. He approached her slowly, not quite sure if she would run from him, but itching to say something. He crouched down next to her and slid an arm around her shaking shoulders.

"Love, why are you crying?"

She looked up and wiped her nose with the sleeve of her tee. "Just go away."

"Please talk to me." *Please say it*. He wanted to hear it from her own lips—*I love you*.

"I am so stupid…I'm sorry, Will, I can't—"

He bent closer and touched his forehead lightly to hers in an effort to make eye contact. She was almost cross-eyed when she returned the glance, and he laughed softly. He brought his hand up to trace the tip of her nose. "Don't cry."

He wasn't doing very well with words.

He brought his lips centimeters away from hers. Time to bring her ideal of a first kiss into being. He hovered for a second when he realized that, in all her dreams, he had most likely been the prince giving that kiss to her. The thought was enough to cause him to close the final distance.

Teresa's sob caught on a hiccup, then stopped completely. He drew away for just a moment, long enough for her to steal a breath, then brought his arms around her and his lips back to hers, where they belonged.

She needed to feel what he was feeling. He wanted to show her that he loved her, to revel in their mutual devotion. This was nothing like kissing Rebekkah. This represented a depth in both of them that he hadn't realized was possible.

She seemed to be feeling it. At least she wasn't sitting there like an ice block, which was a nightmare he had had countless times in the past few weeks.

She didn't really know how to kiss, but he was glad. He brought his hand up to smooth a few hairs away from her cheek, and that seemed to break the spell. She jerked her face away from his and used his shoulders to push herself to a standing position.

The force of her shove knocked him back off of his heels. "Teresa!"

He watched her run as he tried to regain his balance. What was wrong with her? He knew she had enjoyed it. Couldn't she tell that he loved her by the way he had kissed her? That hadn't been a kiss for himself, it had been a *giving* kiss.

Teresa didn't stop, but he managed to catch up to her halfway along the next side of the building.

He reached out and placed his hands firmly on her shoulders to turn her around. Why did the silly girl keep crying? Her face was covered in new streaks. "What is wrong with you?"

"What is wrong with *me*?" Her shoulders were rigid. "Well, let's see. I was just completely mortified in front of everyone, and then you pushed another kiss on me, just because I was vulnerable—"

"Hey, wait a minute." She made it sound like he had taken advantage of her. "I didn't push that kiss on you. I gave it to you because you wanted it."

She opened her mouth in disbelief. "So you go around granting a piece of Will to whatever female happens to want one? Well, let's get one thing straight—I don't want anything, William Engle."

She was lying. "Excuse me, but you were kissing me just as much as I was kissing you."

"I was just using you for physical gratification. I knew you had good kissing skills."

Where had that come from? Was that true? She looked serious, and it hurt more than he wanted to acknowledge. Did she think that he had no feelings for her, that he would kiss her if there wasn't something behind it? Was her estimation of him really that low?

If she wanted gratification, she would get it. "Okay, I'll demonstrate some more." Before she could react he drew her against him and kissed her again, stronger this time. It only took a second for her to grab the material of his collar and push hard. She broke the kiss, but Will kept his hands on her shoulders. He wasn't about to let her run again.

Teresa brought her hand up swiftly and slapped him hard across his cheek.

"Ouch!" He brought his hand up to cover his face and grabbed at her wrist with the other.

"Let me go, Will." She was crying again, and trying to tug her hand away from his grip. "Please." Her voice was rising. "Go. Leave me alone. Now."

Will understood exactly why and his anger immediately cooled. "Love, I'm sorry." He slid his hand gently up to her elbow.

"Eat it."

Her braid almost hit him in the nose as she whirled to head for the van. For the third time in fifteen minutes he was watching her retreating back. Only this time she was walking, not running, and her body language clearly conveyed the message that if he pursued her again he would get more than just a slap in the face.

I'm sorry, God. He dropped to the ground and stared up at the sky. He had made a huge mistake. That had not been the right thing to do—any of it. He rubbed his burning cheek. He had gotten his due reward.

…And He will give you the desires of your heart. Not quite. But then again, Will hadn't been delighting himself in God lately—or at least not listening to His leading.

Maybe it was time to start. A week of prayer might be helpful. He would give Teresa space to think, and he would sort through all of his confusion with God's help.

Next Friday he would see where things stood.

Diego found Meg on the other side of the Palace, on a bench tucked away in a stone lookout corner. She sat straight, her body rigid.

"Meg."

She turned to him, then turned back to the view. "Go away, Diego."

He came around and took a seat beside her. He started to speak, then remembered that she couldn't understand Spanish. He forced himself to count to ten.

"Meg, I cannot believe you would say something like that to your sister. *¿Por qué?*"

"She embarrassed me. She's been a jerk all day. And I don't need you to tell me what to do for the fifth time. I'm sick of your advice."

He replied in heated, rapid Spanish. "You think I like doing this? I wouldn't say anything if I didn't have to. How does embarrassing her in front of Will help anything? She has been trying to protect Will and herself, and you just ruined it."

She rolled her eyes. "Diego, *no entiendo* (I don't understand)."

He let out a frustrated sigh and moved up on the stone wall, his back to the magnificent view. The muscles in his arms were tense.

"No, *I* cannot understand *you*," he said quietly, in English. "You disappoint me, Meg." He looked straight at her but she was fiddling with her shoestrings. He reached out and cupped her shoulder.

"I, I—." She lifted her head till her eyes met his, and he saw her composure begin to falter. "I wasn't thinking." Her voice cracked as tears welled up. "I'm sorry, Diego. Please don't be mad at me. I didn't mean—"

She had covered her face with her hands, and with the breaking of her will he slid off the wall and pulled her gently into a brotherly hug. She was crying in earnest now.

"I feel awful. I did the minute the words were out of my mouth. Teresa will never forgive me," she choked out into his shoulder. "I really didn't mean to."

"But you *did* mean to." He smoothed her hair back. "You thought before you spoke, did you not?"

"Yeah." She lifted her head after a few minutes, avoiding his eyes. "It won't change things, but I'm going to apologize to Teresa." She took a long breath. "I'm sorry I cried all over your shirt." She distractedly reached up and tried to wipe away the damp spot on his chest where her tears had collected.

He caught her hand and stilled it close to his heart. "Do not be embarrassed. We are friends, no?" She finally made eye contact with him, and he smiled. "'*Un amigo ama siempre*,' even when the other says something very foolish and turns into a leaky faucet all over him." She half-laughed and half-hiccupped at his words. He released her hand, then reached up to smooth away the tears on her face with both palms. At the feel of her smooth, hot cheeks he caught himself. This was more familiar then a gesture from a friend. He pulled away. No need to complicate the situation.

Meg scooted back to the far side of the bench, and looked away, up to the building. "So is this place used for anything more than a museum?"

"Well," he paused to cough, "yes. It is—how do Americans say it?—a 'parking place,' Jeff calls it? Friday night, you come up here late, you will see many cars parked all along the street. Many couples—" He felt the heat steal to his face. This was not a subject he wanted to be explaining to her.

"I see."

Meg looked out at the city and he visually traced her profile. Did it matter to her that he was from another country? That he had been raised in a different culture, that their children would have coffee skin? When he had watched her pick up that little boy at Taco's church, he could not help imagining that it was their child in her arms, with the dark hair and light skin. Diego had watched her smile at him, tickle his belly, balance him on her hip. He hadn't been able to get the picture out of his head since.

The little boy's name had turned out to be Diego. Had that been a sign? He knew he was stretching it a little, but he couldn't help wondering.

"So, you think seventeen is old?" Diego had picked up on her excitement earlier in the afternoon. He grinned. "You're an old maid now."

Meg turned to face him. He wanted to look into those eyes every day for the rest of his life. He was glad she didn't know him well enough to read his thoughts yet. He stood to stop himself from saying all of the things she wasn't ready to hear. "I'm going to go see how Teresa is doing."

Meg watched him walk away. *'Un amigo ama siempre,'* he had said—"a friend loves at all times." And how much closer was Teresa than a friend? Meg hoped Teresa would forgive her. A tight feeling gripped Meg's chest at the thought. *She'll forgive me, but that doesn't change the fact that I blew it.*

With her arms wrapped around herself she leaned back against the still sun-warmed stone wall. Diego's embrace had been so tight she hadn't noticed the descending night air. She wouldn't forget the sound of his angry Spanish anytime soon.

But she had needed to hear it. The reprimand, though it had made her feel completely foolish, had been appropriate. He had corrected her when she was wrong. It had hurt intensely, but his words had actually been proof of how much he cared for her. Her arms tightened. *He cares for me.* Not romantically, but at least as a solid friend. She had heard it in his words, she had felt it in his arms, and she had seen it in the expression on his face.

Many of his expressions played through her mind now, as she thought back on the last four weeks. She saw Diego's smiles—genuine, teasing, sarcastic, silly. And the way his eyes crinkled when he played with children. She thought of him playing guitar and singing loudly, with no inhibitions, to God. She knew he prayed deeply and laughed ridiculously loudly at times. His voice could get loud, too, when he debated with her.

He was so annoyingly steady and sure. Always listening, allowing silence. *I am so gone on him it isn't even funny.*

It was futile. She would never measure up to him. Did being in love always make you feel this stupid?

What *did* he think of her? She kicked a piece of gravel away from the bench. *I don't even want to know.* He was probably disgusted by her utter lack of emotional control. He was so chummy with everyone else, always giving shoulder rubs and pats to the back. But he never laid a finger on her. *I must be really gross.*

Chapter Twenty

A great green bus appeared at the top of the street and rapidly approached the tiny mission group, who waited at the corner. Meg was positive it was going to pass them by, but at the last minute it squealed to a halt. The grinding sound of the brakes was enough to make Meg's ears hurt.

It was an old school bus, with Mexican beer stickers on the windshield and a vibrant red stripe painted down the side. Dark eyes peered out of the dirty windows as the group of gringos quickly hopped through the sliding door and up into the seat area. It was packed almost to a maximum already, and adding seven more people put it over the limit.

Will, Pete, and her dad quickly made their way to the aisle and grabbed hold of the metal bars overhead to steady themselves. Two seats were open in the very back row, which Diego offered to Teresa and Jamie. Meg stayed close to the door, clamping her hands onto her own metal bar. Diego shared the small aisle with her, but she decided to look out the window instead.

The smell of sweaty bodies and hot metal surrounded her. *No Mercedes Benz here.* But in a way this was more enjoyable.

That probably had a lot to do with the man standing next to her who—

unfortunately for her emotional state—smelled like cinnamon, as always.

She was jerked back as the bus took off once again. The gears ground hard as they accelerated to over fifty in fewer seconds than she thought possible. The bus's shocks had obviously worn out long ago, because the floor shook and repeatedly rose and fell beneath her feet as they hit bump after bump.

The high screech of the brakes began. Though they were still going over thirty miles an hour, the door two feet away from her suddenly started to open. At the sight of the pavement whizzing by, and at the realization that she could easily swing right out the door at any given moment, she involuntarily stepped backwards—right into Diego.

Before she knew it, his arm was across her middle and he held her securely against him. She felt her knees give as if the wheels had crossed a pothole, and her stomach seemed as ready to bottom out as the unstable floor.

"Crazy drivers," he said, with his cheek practically pressed against hers. His words tickled her ear and she couldn't stop the sensation from continuing all the way down to her toes. Could he feel her reaction? *Oh, I sure hope not.*

He didn't release her immediately, as she half-hoped and half-dreaded he would. He waited until the door had opened completely and the wheels were stationary. As he pulled his arm away she could feel the tips of his fingers brush her waist. She expected to feel the warmth of him behind her disappear as he moved away, but he stayed close.

A glance risked over her shoulder showed that there wasn't really anywhere for him to move to. He seemed to smile faintly in apology.

She tried to steady herself against the pole as the bus took off again. It was tempting to lean back a centimeter, to rest against his chest just slightly, but he would notice. She had tried to be extremely careful since last night at Bishop's Palace—if she felt this strong she probably radiated it when she was around him, and she didn't want him to read into *any* of her actions.

Meg glanced back at Teresa and Jamie, who were holding on tightly to the sides of their seats. Because they were in the far back they bounced higher than anyone else. Teresa caught Meg's eye for a second and grinned.

150

Meg warmed at her sister's smile. Last night following the birthday party, Meg had sat on the bunk with Teresa and asked her sister's forgiveness. Teresa had granted it—she was never one to hold a grudge. But she had not added the words, "It's okay" to her "I forgive you." Both girls had fallen asleep within moments of each other without exchanging many more words.

Meg had noticed at breakfast that Will was decidedly ignoring Teresa. Now he stood staring out the bus window without smiling. Teresa had forgiven Meg, but there was still a gaping wound between Teresa and Will as a result of Meg's words.

And then there were Pete and Jamie, on the usual roller coaster. Once again they were barely speaking to each other. Meg didn't know what had happened this time.

Diego's voice interrupted her musings. "So, do you like this part of the Monterrey experience?"

Meg tensed up so that he wouldn't know she was acutely aware that her hair was probably in his mouth. "Uh, it's an experience, all right."

The second time around she recognized the different shift in momentum that signified an impending stop, but she still wasn't strong enough to brace herself. The door flew open and she once again involuntarily backed away at the sight.

"Relax, I have you." He now had his hand wrapped around her upper arm. Though the air in the bus was heavy and humid, the warmth of his grasp didn't bother her in the least. Why was she reacting like this? Only a day before she had cried in his arms and the physical contact hadn't done a thing to her insides. She had never experienced this—this intense *stomach flopping* with him before, and they had been around each other for a jam-packed month.

Then again, he hadn't really touched her until now. What if he would have sooner? She was suddenly glad that he had refrained, no matter what his reasons.

But it wasn't like his touch was any more intentional now.

Was her dad watching? She peered around the other shoulder into the crowded aisle. He had gotten jostled up towards the front somehow and didn't seem to be paying any attention to her.

Diego dropped his hand and nudged her forward. "Better hurry, this is our stop."

The bus driver won't pull away from the curb without checking for stragglers, will he? Meg didn't want to answer the thought, so she ungracefully jumped across the single step and onto the cement sidewalk.

The others made it off in what seemed like record time. Meg looked up to find a park spread out before her. She plopped down on a bench and blew some stray bangs out of her face. The nearby fountain looked all too inviting. She pulled her Bible from her purse and opened it to John. There was a passage about water that she felt like reading right now...

A wind brushed past and lifted the old Elim church bulletin she had been using as a bookmark out of her Bible. The neon blue paper floated across the path, and she watched as a square hand grabbed it—Diego just happened to be walking by.

Her eyes met his and she suddenly realized with extreme horror what was written on the page.

He walked towards her, and just before he made it over—she was almost safe!—he glanced down at it. He stopped two feet away from her and she closed her eyes. *Why, God? Couldn't you at least spare me this final mortification?* This was the cherry on the cake, the icing on the sundae.

When she had sat in church last week waiting for the Spanish sermon to be over, she had watched Diego tune his guitar and had scrawled *Meg Ramirez* across the top margin in about eight different styles.

She was afraid to look at him, but couldn't seem to stop herself. She had to see his reaction.

He was grinning from ear to ear. *He's laughing at me.* She wanted to keel over the bench, cover her face with her Bible, and die.

He handed her the evidence slowly, one eyebrow raised. The grin slowly dropped from his expression and he looked at her intently. "Can I talk with you tonight?"

She swallowed, took it with shaking hands, and tucked it back into her Bible. She was going to rip it and flush it down the toilet when they got back to the mission. Not that it mattered—the damage was already done. She knew why he wanted to talk to her. He was now certain that she had a crush on him and it was time to admonish her as a sister in Christ. She could just hear his words. *Meg, I am flattered, but it would be best if you not think of me that way. Jeff does not want us to encourage these kinds of things.*

Maybe she could excuse herself from supper by saying that she didn't feel well. Because she didn't. She *really* didn't.

Chapter Twenty One

Six more days.

Meg looked around the dorm room that she, Teresa, and Jamie had come to think of as theirs. Each day seemed to go by more quickly than the one before, when all she wanted to do was slow them down.

The dinner bell reminded Meg that this day, too, was already almost over. If only she didn't have to face Diego again before it ended.

No such luck. He was near the door when Meg came into the dining room. Great—he had that smile on his face again, that one he'd been giving her every time he caught her eye since the incident at the park this morning. Like he was trying to remind her of her stupid mistake.

"You look tense." He walked with her toward the tables. "Are you okay?"

"I think I'm just hungry." Meg kept her eyes on the table.

He pulled out a chair for her. "Would you like to go up to the balcony tonight?" His hands still rested on her chair back. "You can see the sun set behind the mountains. It is one of my favorite times of day."

Meg turned her head so she could glance up at him. *No, I would* not *like to.* He was just trying to make her feel more at ease by mentioning the sunset. "Okay."

His eyes were shadowed. "Come up whenever you want after supper." They met hers for one second before he turned and headed for his seat.

Meg tried to eat supper, but when Diego finally rose and left the room, she still hadn't eaten more than a forkful of her spaghetti. A minute later she slid her chair back. *Might as well get this over with.* Maybe if she explained to Diego that she already understood what he wanted to say, it wouldn't be so embarrassing. *The poor guy.* How many times had he had to have this talk? He probably had it memorized by now. And how had she managed to become one of the recipients of it?

Red and gold were blended into the haze of the western sky behind Saddle Mountain when Meg stepped onto the stairs and began to trudge her way up them. The sun had just disappeared, its after-shades perfectly silhouetting the mountain's unique shape.

Diego sat at the far end of the platform, his arms wrapped around one knee, his Bible resting beside him. He must have heard her shuffling footsteps because his eyes were waiting for her. She tried to meet his gaze but could not.

Diego shifted his position. "You got here just in time. The sun goes very quickly." Meg nodded. The darkness was already increasing, thank goodness. Soon she wouldn't be able to see his eyes. Across the valley she could see lights flickering on in various houses.

"Here." Diego scooted around till his back was in the corner of the railing and the wall, and inclined his head to the spot next to him. "You can see pretty well from this point and you will be more comfortable sitting."

Meg sat down with her back to the wall, keeping a good foot between them. The rough surface of the adobe pressed against her sticky tee-shirt and sent a slight shiver down her back. She took a deep breath. "Look. I know what you're going to say. I'm sorry I've been acting like a lovesick sixteen year old, but I promise I'm over it."

Diego's eyes seemed to widen. His hand went to the back of his neck and he massaged it for a few seconds. The silence seemed to be amplified. There was no smile, no reassurance, no dismissal. *Can't he just let me go?*

Finally he spoke. "I was hoping you weren't going to get over it."

What? "Did you say *weren't* or *were*?"

"Ah, were *not*." He rubbed his hand over his face.

"I thought…" She paused. She could feel Diego looking over at her but she continued to focus on her hands in her lap. "I was *sure* you were going to tell me to get over it."

Diego's reply was all in Spanish. He stopped, then spoke again in English. "Margareta, will you look at me?"

She had never heard him call her that before. She had never really liked her full name, but hearing it on his lips in soft Spanish with the extra *a* suddenly made her feel a little weak. It was enough to draw her gaze to his for just a second, but she didn't have the courage to hold it there. The tension was the same as it had been the night of the tattoo, but now—did he feel that same curling feeling in his stomach? Was he saying—what *was* he getting at?

Instead of reaching out with words, he lifted a hand and touched her chin. The action was enough for her to maintain eye contact.

"I do not want you to get over it." Diego locked his hands together again. "I have spent much time with you these past four weeks. I should maybe not have done it." Meg thought she saw a brief smile, but she was too intent on the words to be sure.

"I am sorry if I was wrong about this." His eyes searched her face. "But every day I look forward to seeing you and talking with you and getting to know you more. And the more I do these things, the more I want to keep doing them and doing them." His accent was getting harder to understand.

What was she supposed to say to that? Was she supposed to answer him? She'd be happy just listening to him for now. Before Meg could think anything more, he rattled off two or three long sentences in his native language, then sighed. "I am sorry. I am having a very hard time saying it in English." He reached out and took her hands in his, cupping them almost reverently. "I—I am growing to love you. I do not know if you have the same kind of feelings inside, but I had to ask." His voice cracked. "I need to know if I have your permission."

She swallowed down a bunch of words and clenched her hands tightly within his. "For what exactly?"

Diego turned to look out over the mountain without saying anything. Meg followed his gaze, holding her breath for his answer. The shapes of the upper half of the mountain now blended into their surroundings, with clusters of star-like lights covering the lower inhabited areas. The houses extended up towards them, giving light to some places and causing the shadowed places to look even darker.

He kept his eyes on the horizon as he spoke. "Next week you will be flying home, but I think God has a way for us to continue to get closer." This time when he took her hand, his own was shaking slightly. "I am asking you to pray about keeping up a correspondence with me after you go home. I will visit you on school breaks. And if God wills, I will eventually ask you to be my wife."

Wife? That meant marriage.

He was offering himself as a potential—*probable*—husband.

Was this was really happening to her? She could barely process it all, between the solemnity of his words and the distraction of his hands.

She sat looking at their intertwined hands in silence. He seemed to be serious. He wouldn't be smoothing his thumb across her wrist if he wasn't. Her mind repeatedly rewound and fast-forwarded his words as they slowly embedded themselves in her memory. It was taking awhile, because receiving this new kind of touch from him was absorbing most of her concentration.

"Please say something."

She took a deep breath. "I—I don't know what to say."

"Well, what is the first thing that comes to mind?"

"That I'm just barely seventeen."

He tilted his head a little and his shoulders dropped. "Meg, if you do not want this, say no. I do not need an excuse about age." He was on the verge of looking dejected.

"No—no! It's—it's not an excuse. I just—I mean, I must seem like a little girl to you."

"No."

Meg stilled as she read the undertones in his one word. He turned her hand over so that the palm was facing up, and lightly smoothed her fingers before gently pressing his other hand over it.

She allowed her fingers to curl between his. "Why me?"

"I do not think that is something I want to tell you unless there is a promise between us. That is best saved for another time."

She nodded. "I probably don't have to ask you if you've prayed about this."

He laughed. "No, you don't."

"And you think that God has said it's okay?" If God had implied that, didn't that mean the determined ending *was* marriage?

"I think," Diego seemed to choose his words carefully, "I think God has said it is okay to ask you to pray with me about this. We should take it in tiny parts. Do you want to do this, Meg?"

"I—I think I very much *want* to do this." She pulled her fingers loose. "I just don't know if I can trust my feelings."

"I thought you were over your feelings." He nudged her side with his elbow.

At least he can joke about it. She wriggled away from him, not revealing that he had caught a very ticklish spot. That kind of knowledge was also better saved for another time.

He continued. "I do not want you to trust your feelings. I am asking you to make sure that it is God, and not me, who is pulling your heart to mine."

"Right now all I can tell is that you are tugging."

"I am?" He smiled. "I mean—that is not good." He coughed.

"*Yes*, you are. I should think that was quite apparent three weeks ago—"

"Three weeks ago?" He seemed even more pleased.

"It's just hard right now to figure out what is God and what is you and what is my own feeling." Meg sighed. Diego had done everything right, had acted beyond the private standards she had set; how could this *not* be what God wanted? But she still had to pray, to make sure.

She startled a little as she felt his fingers brush her cheek, tucking some loose strands of hair behind her ear. Such a small touch suddenly held deep meaning. It was so new, so foreign, yet almost familiar. All thoughts of prayer fled.

She wanted to look at him, but was almost afraid to let herself. His glances would carry so much more, now that she knew what was behind them. If she wanted to stay objective she should probably keep a good emotional distance.

It was virtually impossible to keep emotional distance when he was sitting a breath away. She made herself look at him. *Not smart.* No other man had looked at her like this before. It was heady. When his gaze dropped to her lips she almost choked.

"I've never kissed anyone before," she suddenly blurted out.

He smiled a little, a pleased smile. "That is good."

"I'm not going to kiss anyone until my wedding day," she added quickly. He did not smile at that, but cocked his head slightly and looked at her.

Man, why *did I make that vow?* She suddenly wanted to whack herself in the face with her Bible. *Stupid girl. You could have just received a first kiss better than anything you ever dreamed of.*

No, that wasn't true—Diego wouldn't have kissed her this soon. And besides, the first kiss she had always envisioned involved her in a white dress with two shining rings on her finger and a new last name. And that was still the best dream of all.

Diego smiled slightly as he finally asked the question she knew was coming. "*Por qué?*"

Meg took a deep breath. "Because if you love somebody, you will protect them."

He nodded. "*Sí.* I have determined this myself—I had planned to wait to kiss a woman until we were engaged."

Meg fingered the flowery material of her skirt. "But she would not be your wife yet. You don't belong to each other until you make a covenant before God." She paused, then swallowed, feeling her face heat as she tried to get the words in her brain onto her tongue. "Even if you do only kiss after you're engaged, I think that it would be very hard to keep your passions in control when you already feel that you belong to each other." *This is so embarrassing.*

He coughed a little. "But, um, there are different kinds of kisses—you can have *un besito,* or *un beso profundo.*"

Meg's brows furrowed. "*Besito?*"

"A light—shallow kiss. *Beso profundo* is a deep kiss."

"But I think it can go from shallow to deep very quickly when you love someone." She was glad that the almost-dark sky hid the color of her face from him.

"Yes, that's true."

Meg felt her heart sink a little as she realized that he spoke from experience. She had always secretly hope that the man she married would have as little experience as she did—but that was pretty idealistic.

She tucked some hair behind one ear. "It's not something I'm going to be able to flex on later, either, 'cause I made a vow about it."

He reached up and tucked some behind her other. "Well, then, you'll just have to be engaged for a very short time—because you have beautiful lips, Margareta." He pushed himself to his feet and offered the usual hand up. "Let us go our separate ways and pray."

He's ending this so soon? She fought back the urge to be tremendously disappointed. She wanted to sit there and talk with him till the sun returned in the eastern sky. *But my dad wouldn't like that very much.*

He pulled her to her feet in a playful manner, then clapped a hand on her shoulder and led her down the stairs. At the bottom of the flight he stopped. Light from a lamp above them cast a glow over his hair and shoulders. He slid his hand halfway down her arm to cup her elbow. "Meg Ramirez has a nice ring to it." He winked, then turned to head back up the stairs.

"*Buenas noches.*" He paused on the stairwell and looked down at her.

"Good night."

You have beautiful lips, Margareta.

Meg made her way to the girls' dorm and flopped onto her bed. It was still early, only about eight-thirty, and she had the room all to herself. Will and Pete had been playing Frisbee under the floodlights in the courtyard, and Jamie and Teresa had been sitting on the steps of the girls' dorm, far away from the boys. Teresa had given her a long inquisitive look as Meg passed. Right now Meg hoped her sister would just leave her alone.

The whole evening felt unreal. It was stranger than being in a dream. All day she'd been preparing for Diego's lecture, and now—what? Things were different. Diego had practically just proposed to her.

Wow.

Well, he hadn't actually gone so far as to formally ask her. But she hadn't even expected a guy to be interested in her for another two years, especially someone like Diego.

Meg pulled her hair back and held it off her neck with one hand. During all of their talks, while they worked together, even when Diego looked at her, he had never alluded to such a deep interest. But he'd obviously been thinking about it for a while, and praying for both of them. He had waited until God had told him it was okay. None of the guys she'd known had ever done that before they asked a girl out.

Diego had made it so easy on her. They would be committed to each other, with none of the uncertainties of casual dating—yet it wasn't quite like engagement.

God had already given Diego the go-ahead to approach her. Diego's only question had been what she thought about it.

What was she supposed to tell him? She dropped back onto her pillow, then sat up again. She needed to record tonight's events. Maybe getting it out on paper would help her sort out the questions that swamped her.

As she opened her journal she remembered Diego looking at her lips. She let the book go for a second and fell back onto her pillow again. She could not wipe the smile off of her face. *God—I have a feeling I'm going to be 'waking up' this next week even without any kissing. Please keep me from falling too fast*—as if it hadn't already happened. *Help me to obey you.*

A little twinge of doubt suddenly hit. Maybe she had been too strict by making the kissing vow. Maybe it would have been better to only wait for engagement, like Diego had decided. Had it been wrong for her to have made such a sweeping pronouncement without discussing it with the man she would eventually marry?

She flipped open the journal again and found the entry where she had recorded her vow. It opened with a quote from the book *Passion & Purity* by her favorite author, Elisabeth Elliot—a passage explaining how women hold the key to passion in a relationship. Then below it Meg had written out a Bible verse from First Corinthians chapter eight, which Meg had paraphrased.

Certainly kissing will not bring me into the presence of God; if I do not partake of it, I am none the worse; and if I do, I am none the better. But I must be careful that this liberty of mine as a woman does not become a pitfall for the man I love, who is weak. If desire is the downfall of him, my love, then I will not tempt him anymore, for I will not be the cause of his downfall.

Following the quote, she had pasted in a sheet of paper with her vow written on it.

I, Margaret Juliana Atwell, make this vow on this Sunday night at the age of fifteen that I will kiss no man until the day of my marriage, in accordance and response to what I have read in the Scriptures and what God has been revealing to my heart. And with His strength behind me, supporting and encouraging me in my decision, I know I will be able to keep this promise that I have made to my husband, myself, and most importantly my Lord Jesus Christ, whom I love above all others.

Below it she had copied three separate verses about vows: Numbers 30:2, Psalm 15:1 & 4, and Psalm 65:1b. Reading over them again as she lay on her bunk helped reinforce her decision. *I'm glad I did it.*

She filled several pages of her journal during the next hour, till her hand was cramped. She had to laugh as she looked over the scribbled words, often barely legible. Many times she had paused in the middle of writing to daydream of Diego, his voice, the feel of his fingers, his words—going over and over each part of their conversation like rosary beads until every moment was imprinted on her mind. Her distraction apparently showed on her pages, too—around the margins of her journal pages she must have written his name almost fifteen times.

Oh, well. Diego wouldn't care. And besides, all the praying and struggling not to think of him was finally released; it was okay to dwell on him now.

Or is it? Meg absently rolled her promise ring up and down her finger, then took it off and looked at it. There wasn't any real commitment yet. She would just have to watch it this last week. And she needed to pray. She'd sent a few disjointed prayers towards God tonight, but she hadn't really *talked* to him. She closed her eyes.

Fifteen minutes later she finished, with no real sense of direction. Diego just wouldn't leave her thoughts. *I have to pray*—she couldn't go into this kind of thing without praying about it first. That was just the way it was. But it was hard to concentrate, difficult to imagine that God would not want this to be happening. It felt incredibly right.

Please, God. She rolled over on her back and traced the pattern on the plywood base of the bunk above her. *Help me.* She couldn't lose all of her emotional self-control, not now. She needed to be able to think clearly, to focus.

The door creaked open; Teresa and Jamie came in to get ready for bed. Jamie headed over to the other building to take her shower, but Teresa stretched out on the bed next to Meg's. She was quiet. After a minute had passed, Meg turned and propped her head up on her hand.

Teresa looked at her. "Yeah?"

"Diego asked me to come out to the balcony tonight for a talk." It felt good to talk to someone out loud. "I thought he was going to give me a sermon about how I've been acting like I have a crush on him and how I shouldn't see him as any different than Pete or Will. But then he floored me—" Meg dropped her hand and leaned over the edge of the bed. "He said he wants my permission to write me after we leave!"

"Seriously? I mean, he's talking about something serious?"

Meg grinned. "If you call marriage serious."

She had never seen Teresa's eyes that big before. Teresa sat up. "What?"

"Well… he basically said that we'd write for a couple years, and see where it goes, but the general thought is that we'd be looking towards marriage, as soon as I'm old enough."

"Whoa!" Teresa's laugh sounded disbelieving. "I can't imagine—what did you say?"

"I—I don't know." That was what Meg had to say, of course. It would be too sudden to flat-out announce that she agreed with Diego. She was just seventeen, not twenty-one, and she hadn't been the one praying about it. If she said she was ready, then she'd be admitting that she wanted to marry him.

What would it be like to finally know whom she was going to marry? No more wondering or questions, just plans and daydreams about one particular man. Meg pulled back onto the bed and flopped backwards with a happy sigh.

Teresa looked at her, probably noticing that weird smile Meg knew she'd been wearing constantly for the last hour. "Well, what *are* you thinking?"

As if she needed to ask. Teresa could read her so well. "Well, you've seen me doodling on my bulletins in church for the last two weeks." Meg took a deep breath. "But it's scary. I mean—it's huge."

"No kidding it is." Teresa shook her head. "I had guessed that Diego might be interested, but I didn't think—it didn't seem like he was *that* serious. That's a big leap, and you've only known each other, what, four weeks? But you *have* spent tons of time together." Teresa leaned her head back onto her pillow. "Have you talked to Dad?"

"No, I haven't seen him yet." What would he say? Meg wasn't sure how she felt about talking to him about it. "Can you not talk about it with Mom and Dad? I'd like to tell them myself."

Teresa nodded. "My lips are sealed until you tell me otherwise. But I'd really encourage you to talk to them. Daddy has been so great for me with the Will stuff."

Meg nodded. "I will, it's just that it hasn't even sunk in yet—I just wasn't expecting it, you know? I know it's all just emotions, but I'm on a huge high."

"No, really?" Teresa rolled to face her. "I couldn't tell."

Meg got off of her bed and picked up her pajamas. "Oh, wah wah. You're just jealous because I've got the man with the chocolate eyes."

"So? Mine has nice eyes, too."

"Yeah, but you *don't* have hi—" Meg stopped with her boxers halfway up her legs. "Oh, Teresa, I'm sorry. I didn't mean—"

"I know." Teresa hoisted herself off the bunk and wrapped her arms around Meg. "Don't worry. I'm really, really happy for you. Don't feel like you have to temper any of your excitement just because things aren't working out so well for me."

Meg returned the tight embrace. "Thanks. I love you."

"Love you, too." She sighed. "You know, lately I don't even want to be around Will." Teresa pulled her pajamas off of their daily spot hanging on the bunk boards. "He's giving me the silent treatment now. I don't know if he thinks it's all my problem that I reacted like that yesterday, but he hasn't apologized for or even mentioned the kisses. I wish I'd slapped him again."

She sounded so vicious that Meg had to bite back a laugh. Will had better be very careful about what he said and did around her sister. "He's probably as confused as you are."

"I'm not confused. I love him, but he's acting like a jerk. He needs to get some things straight about relationships with women. And he needs to start taking some responsibility for his actions."

"So tell him."

"No, I don't think that'd work very well." The sheets crackled as Teresa pulled them up and tucked them under her chin. "He has to take the initiative because he knows he should, not because I'm telling him to. Otherwise I'll just come off as a bossy pest—one of those nasty contentious women in Proverbs."

"You do have those tendencies."

"Aw, shut up."

"Don't say shut up!" Meg spoke in the same voice their younger brothers did when catching each other saying the phrase their mother detested.

"I miss Amos and Joel and Daniel and Nathan." Teresa shifted to a different position.

"I know." Although frequent e-mails had been exchanged back and forth, the girls had only gotten the chance to talk to their little brothers a few times on the phone. "I miss Mom the most, though. If you and Daddy weren't here I'd be miserable."

"Oh, you would not. You have Diego."

Meg shook her head, even though Teresa probably couldn't see it. "That's not the same. It's not like he's family yet. I need you guys a lot."

"Mm-hmmm." Teresa spoke slowly through a yawn.

"Sorry. I'll let you go to sleep."

Her sister's breath caught on a drowsy sigh. "Okay."

It was a long time until Meg's mind slowed down enough for her to even think about feeling sleepy, and when she finally drifted off her last conscious thought was of the day to come and the man she would be seeing at breakfast.

"Rise and shine, dearest!"

Meg rolled over as Teresa shook her shoulders. "Mmph."

"Come on, dudette. You slept through the bell and breakfast—I tried waking you up but you were dead to the world."

Meg opened her eyes to see Teresa retreating to the bathroom. She was dressed in a fresh skirt and tee, and was braiding her hair.

Why do I have such an expectant feeling? Meg had a happy flavor in her soul, but she couldn't remember. . . oh yes. Memories of the evening before returned with a rush, and though some of the events seemed jumbled with the dreams she had had all night, she knew that everything was for real.

Meg took a deep breath as she thought about the day ahead. How would she ever be able to concentrate on the church service? Diego's presence, his glances, his words were going to be so full now. It would be a wonderful workweek, though.

She dressed quickly in her favorite blue skirt and a light yellow shirt, then headed for the tiny bathroom to comb her hair out and brush her teeth. At the sight of her small make-up bag she paused. She hadn't been using it during the week while they were working—it was too much trouble. Besides, no one had cared.

But someone cared now. She reached for the pouch, then paused. How silly. Diego didn't care about makeup. He wasn't interested in her because of her complexion or the redness of her lips. At least, she hoped not.

She put the bag back on the ledge and opted only for some raspberry lip balm. Of course he wouldn't notice that she had shiny lips. And he wouldn't kiss her, so he wouldn't taste the raspberry.

Meg capped the round container and stared at the berry icon on the lid. She would have to be sure to wear good-tasting lip-gloss on her wedding day. An image popped into Meg's head, one of Diego in a tuxedo, standing close to her as she looked at him through a misty veil. He lifted his fingers to catch the edge of the material and slowly brought it up over her face...

But for some reason she couldn't imagine anything after that point. Maybe it was because his admiration hadn't fully sunk into her comprehension yet—she couldn't believe he would actually want to kiss her. That was going to take some time.

Two arms suddenly wrapped themselves around Meg's waist and she felt herself being weakly lifted an inch off the ground. "Hey, little Meggy, time for church!"Teresa continued to squeeze the air out of Meg's stomach as she spoke in a silly voice.

Oh, great. Every once and awhile Teresa got in a goofy mood and began to physically wrestle with Meg like a kitten playing with a ball.

Meg turned and squeezed her in return, which resulted in an *oof* from Teresa. She mimicked her sister's baby tone. "Okay, little Reesy." A pinch in the waist resulted in a squeal from Teresa before Meg turned to put her lip-gloss back.

Meg practically skipped down the stairs of the girls' dorm and across the cement to the sanctuary. The sun was out, the cars were zooming, the roosters were crowing, Diego wanted to marry her. What a great day. What a great life.

She paused in the doorway and immediately looked for him. There he was, at the front, tuning his guitar. He looked up as if he could sense her presence and gave her a happy smile. No one had ever smiled at her like that before. She returned it for just a second, then ducked her head and turned to look for her dad, to get a morning hug.

The church service went quickly. Meg especially enjoyed the worship time. She even found that she was able to take her mind off of Diego and onto the songs she was singing—when she closed her eyes. Except there was one song—*I Want to Know You*—and she couldn't stop herself from peeking at Diego as the group sang. It was a little frustrating—the words fit human love all too well. *"I want to know you, I want to see your face, I want to touch you, I want to hear your voice."* She squeezed her eyes shut all the more tightly and tried to focus on God.

Meg reached down and slid her hand into her dad's. He gave hers a little squeeze. His hands were like Diego's in their warmth and dryness, but were shaped long and thin like a musician's, whereas Diego's were square and thick. She sighed. It was so nice to have both Diego and her dad with her.

Diego returned to his seat at the end of the song, and Enrique, Raquel's husband, stood to close the service with a prayer. He then went and sat by his wife and their eight-month-old son, who was sitting on her lap. The baby reached for his dad as soon as he sat down beside them.

Meg sighed. Raquel had the beautiful face with high cheekbones, the expressive eyes, the smooth dark skin. She was so much more like Diego. He should want someone like Raquel, who would be more suited to his life than Meg.

But why should Meg be jealous? Raquel was married to Enrique now, and she was a mother. Deep down Meg knew she was bothered because Raquel had dated Diego four years ago and had gotten to kiss him. *I might never get to experience that*. It wasn't fair.

I need to stop. She didn't even really want Diego to kiss her right now. The time was not at its fullest.

The post-church rustlings of people moving from their chairs had begun. Church was over, so Meg stood and stretched. Diego had set his guitar down and was weaving his way to them. He said good morning first to her father, then turned to her. "Hello."

"*Buenos días*." Meg glanced up at her dad's face to find him watching her. The newness of this was all a bit embarrassing. He had never observed her relating to an admirer before. She didn't quite know how to act.

"Mind if I steal her for a moment?" Diego looked at her dad.

"Only for a moment."

For some reason Meg felt tears prick the corners of her eyes at the look her dad gave her. He looked—old, or resigned. She wanted to keep her hand in his, to stay and talk with him. For a very fleeting moment she almost wanted to forget about Diego, though she didn't know why.

Diego nodded towards the door, and she followed him out into the sunshine.

His eyes were settled on her face. *I should have worn the makeup*—but the look he was giving her made it apparent that he wouldn't have been able to tell the difference.

He had his hands tucked into his pockets. "I wanted to let you know that I am going to be gone for the next few days. I am going to travel around to the sister churches and do some repair work. I have been putting it off but I think now would be a good time." He seemed to be watching closely for her reaction.

She tried to swallow it down. How many days? When was he leaving? "This is our last week—" She looked away so he wouldn't see the wetness in the corners of her eyes. *I am way too emotional today.*

He tipped her chin up so that she would look him in the eye. "I know. But my reasoning is, if God has plans for us, we will have the rest of our lives to spend time together. But if He doesn't, then it would be best if we do not spend so much intensive time together now. You need to have a clear chance to focus without me mudding things, and you need time to pray."

She nodded. His reasons were valid, but they still stunk.

"When will you be back?" Time was going to drag.

"I am planning on tomorrow night, so I will probably see you Tuesday morning."

"When are you leaving?"

He glanced at his watch. "In about an hour."

"Okay."

"Promise me you will use the time to pray and think?"

"I promise."

He surprised her by wrapping his arms around her, lightly, for just a second. Then he reached up and tapped her on the tip of her nose. "*Hasta el martes.*" (Until Tuesday.)

She nodded again, then headed back into the sanctuary. She would use the time to pray and think, and to be with her dad.

Chapter Twenty Three

Their last Monday crept by very slowly, especially in the afternoon. After four full weeks of labor, the little cement-block church was nearing the final stages. So while Will, Pete, and Jeff were busy moving dirt piles and cleaning up the site, the three girls were put to work painting the outside of the building.

"I'm getting a real headache." Jamie was crouched underneath a window. She was in charge of doing the trim work, a job for which she had asked.

Meg pressed her mouth tightly closed to keep from replying. It was the fourth time in the last half-an-hour that Jamie had complained of her headache, the heat, or about somebody else's work.

Teresa stretched her body and rubbed her shoulders. "I'm starting to feel it too. This sun gets to you after a while, but we'll be done pretty soon."

"Yeah, I know, it's just been a really long day."

Meg blew a few stray hairs out of her face. "We're all tired, Jamie. You don't have to remind us about it." Meg knew the minute the words were out of her mouth that she shouldn't have said them. *Is it that time of the month? I'm not usually this irritable.*

Teresa glared at her and Jamie was silent for a few seconds before saying in a quiet voice, "I'm going to wash up." She wiped the excess dark green paint from her brush and turned to walk towards the bucket of water in which the paintbrushes were stored.

"So." Teresa spoke as soon as Jamie was out of hearing range. "What's the matter with you?"

"What?" Meg lifted her hair off of the back of her neck. "She's been complaining all afternoon. I'm just as sick of it as she is, I'm sure, and so are you, but we're not complaining. I'm getting tired of listening to it."

"Your attitude isn't a whole lot better, you know." Teresa stopped painting to wipe the sheen of sweat from her cheeks and forehead and sat back on the ground. "Jamie's had a hard couple of days. She's been getting really homesick—you of all people should know what that's like. And then last night she and Pete had some sort of falling out. Give her a little room."

"Sorry." Meg held up a hand. "I won't do it again."

Teresa didn't look convinced, but she seemed to accept the signal for peace. She dipped her roller back into the paint pan. "Are you grouchy because Diego's gone?"

"No!" Meg wrinkled her nose at the assumption. "Of course not. That would be stupid."

"Methinks the lady doth protest too much." Teresa smoothed her roller back and forth along the wall.

Meg sighed. "Maybe so, I don't know. Lately I've been such an emotional ball I don't know what's controlling my moods. It bugged me a little when Diego said he was going, but he's only going to be gone until tomorrow morning. And he left on purpose, to give me time to think and pray."

Teresa painted in silence for a few strokes. "Have you been?"

"Been what?" Meg looked over at her.

"Thinking and praying."

Meg dipped her own brush in the bucket. "Well, yeah. Of course. I haven't had a whole lot of free time because of the workday, but—"

"Nutmeg." Teresa reached out a hand and squeezed her shoulder. "You don't have to justify things. I was just asking. But I don't want to gloss over all of it, either. You have to be listening to God on this one—intently listening. It's the first step to what could be a huge life decision. But you have to be open to a *No*, too."

Meg turned back to the wall and accidentally hit the edge of the trim with her brush. "I—I know that."

"You know, I didn't want to say anything on Saturday night to bring you off your cloud, but I was thinking about when Josh was pursuing me—"

"You mean when you were *dating* him?" Teresa never liked to apply the D word to that relationship because it implied mutual feelings, and she insisted she had never liked him.

"Yeah, whatever. But honestly, I don't want you to make the same mistake I did. Josh was the first guy who ever really paid attention to me—he was the first person who ever complimented me, who treated me like I was pretty. I went along with it because I thought he would be my only chance."

"Seriously?" How could Teresa, of all people, have thought she'd only have one chance?

"Yeah, seriously. I tried to force myself to like him, but it didn't take me long to figure out that I just wasn't attracted to him—he wasn't someone I'd want to marry. If you're manufacturing feelings, it's not going to work."

Meg dropped her hand and turned to look her sister straight in the eyes. "Do you really think I'd ever manufacture feelings for Diego?"

Teresa smiled. "No. What I'm getting at is that you should be careful. The combination of your attraction to him and the fact that you're being wooed for the first time might cloud your objectivity. Females are extremely susceptible to flattery. Just make sure he knows the real you, and that you know the real him, and that both of you know that God is planning it."

"I know that."

"Good. Just make sure you *conoces*, not just *sabes*."

Meg had learned those verbs early on—*saber* was to know facts or information, *conocer* was to know someone or something on a more personal, intimate basis. What she did know was that she was a bit frightened to know deeply what God wanted. She knew she didn't want to hear a *No*.

Jamie came back with two cups of cold water in Styrofoam cups and handed the first to Meg.

"Thanks." Meg reached out to take it. She took one swallow, then lowered the cup. "Jamie." Jamie turned back to her. "I'm sorry about what I said." The cup felt heavy in Meg's hand, a reminder of Jamie's quick generosity. "It was rude." Meg glanced at the clear water, then looked back at her friend. "Will you forgive me?"

"Yes." The awkwardness was still there, but at least the deeper tension had been relieved. "It's all right. I understand you're just as grouchy as me." She gave one of her slow-blooming smiles, handed Teresa her water, and re-did her long ponytail. "I just can't wait to go home. I think I'll be a lot happier once we get back. Only five more days till I get to see my mom."

Five days. *Don't remind me.* Saturday morning at 3 a.m. Meg would climb with the rest onto the bus to go back to McAllen, Texas, and then on to home.

If home was still in Wisconsin.

Tuesday morning during break Teresa sat staring out the window of the church at the gray clouds drooping over the sky. Four more days and they would be on their way home. But it wouldn't be long before she would be returning to Mexico. Jeff had told her last week that the mission wanted her in Hermosillo; now it was only a matter of timing before she would be traveling there to help for at least six months.

She had an idea that she would enjoy that trip much more than she had enjoyed this one. Sure, she would miss having her dad and Meg with her, but she was kind of looking forward to the challenge of being on her own, away from home. Even when she'd gone to college, she had never been farther than an hour's drive from home, and she always returned to her family on the weekends.

Best of all, she wouldn't have to deal with Will. That would relieve a lot of stress. She couldn't even tell what he was thinking these past few days. All of a sudden, since that afternoon at Bishop's Palace, he had been avoiding her. Every time she came into the room, he would leave a couple of minutes later. She had said hi to him once, and he'd just barely acknowledged her presence. Though he had no reason for it, he seemed mad at her.

What is wrong with him, anyway? She had half-hoped, half-dreaded that he would follow her after Meg had revealed her secret, but she sure hadn't expected that kiss. He had said it was for her. Was he telling the truth?

It depended what he meant by it. Much as she hated to admit it, he'd been right about her kissing him as much as he'd kissed her. That kiss had been great, everything she ever wanted in a first kiss. She couldn't help but return it, not when she had waited and dreamed so long. But she couldn't tell him that. And it had all been at the wrong time. He hadn't said he loved her, or anything even close to that.

Well, of course not. He did have a girlfriend, after all.

Teresa bit her lip. He wasn't being fair to anyone—to Rebekkah, or her, or to himself. *He was just using me*—despite his protests.

She still hadn't figured out what he had meant when he said that the kiss had been a giving kiss. That he was giving it to her? Well, that had been obvious! It had sounded like he meant he'd done it for her sake. But he'd only made it worse for her.

How long would it take for them to be friends again?

Telling Meg about it had helped her relieve some of her anger. She had debated telling her dad about those kisses, then decided it would be best if he didn't know for a little while.

Maybe Will had more growing up to do than she'd realized. Or maybe she had just loved him for so long that she hadn't realized exactly who he was. She closed her eyes for a second, but turned at the sound of footsteps across the threshold.

Jeff dropped an armload of rags and old sheets next to the buckets in the center of the room. "Here you go. Since it's only spitting out there, the other guys and I are going to get the rest of these rock pieces hauled away." He gestured with a tilt of his head to the piles of debris outside the door. "If it starts to rain hard, we'll be back. Are you comfortable here? Do you have enough to do?"

Teresa surveyed the walls with full head rotation and answered in teasing Spanish. "I think so."

Jeff nodded and exited. Teresa waited a few seconds, then began directing Meg and Jamie, who had followed Jeff into the room with their cookies and Joya. "Meg, why don't you do the roller work this time? Jamie, you start on this wall, and Meg can come along behind you." She picked up the roller with the longest stick. "I'll tackle the ceiling, since I'm the tallest."

Pete stuck his head in the door. "Hey, Teresa, can you come help us for a while? Jeff says to tell you he was wrong, he thinks there's a storm moving in, and we want to get this pile of junk moved before it hits."

Teresa had already put her roller down. "I'll probably be back in a few minutes," she said to Meg and Jamie over her shoulder on the way out.

⚘

The wind had turned cold during the last couple of hours while she'd been indoors. Teresa shivered and wished she'd thought to bring her jacket this morning. Jeff threw a last shovel of dirt and rocks into the back of the old truck they'd borrowed and laid the shovel on top. Then he and Pete climbed in the cab and Jeff started the engine.

"They're taking it to the dump." Will's voice just behind her made Teresa jump. She turned to look up at him, but he wasn't making eye contact. "Can you come help me carry some stuff across the road to Christiana and Joaquin's house?" He seemed to be looking at her goose-bump covered arms. "Are you cold?"

Teresa rubbed them. "Not too bad. I'll warm up soon with the work."

"I could warm you up." He waggled his eyebrows up and down suggestively.

Teresa jerked her head up. "William—"

"I was kidding...I mean..." Will's face was turning red. "Not that I don't—well, I just meant it as a joke." He shrugged and looked away.

You have incredibly poor taste in jokes. Teresa followed him across the road in silence. She really didn't want to live with that for the rest of her life. How could she have thought herself in love with someone so...so immature? Honestly, other than being a Christian, what did he have to speak for himself? Not to mention the fact that he wasn't available. She'd been

178

deluding herself. Rebekkah could have him; in fact, she was welcome to him.

"About that kiss the other day." Will kicked at a large white pebble in the gravel. "I wanted to tell you again that I was sorry about that. I've felt horrible for doing that to you without asking or anything. I know you can't forget about it, but I'd like your forgiveness. Because we are friends."

Teresa tilted her head enough so that she could see his face, but without having to look him in the eyes. She could feel his gaze on her. What was she supposed to say? He knew everything about her feelings now. She could feel her own face turning red. "I forgive you."

Will was too hard to read. She wanted to go back and paint, to get away from him and his goofy smile, and his little comments that he might be making because they were friends, but might be making because he finally liked her.

Nope. Teresa shook her head. *So much for level-headedness.*

"Come on." Will handed her a shovel. "And you're lying about being cold." He took off his jacket. "Wear this." He tossed it to her and picked up his shovel.

Meg moved to the middle of the room, as did Jamie. They painted in silence for a good five minutes. Meg found herself once again dreaming about what it would be like when she saw Diego again. *You're terrible.* He had only been gone—well, not even two days. How was she going to handle being away from him for months?

Meg glanced over to discover ribbons of tears tracing down Jamie's cheeks. She forgot about Diego. "Are you okay?"

The gentle rhythm of Jamie's painting stroke faltered for just a second. "Yeah." Meg had a hard time hearing the answer.

She hoped she didn't sound like she was prying. "Are you homesick?" Meg knew how terrible that was.

This time Jamie stopped completely. "Yeah. I just want to go home." She took a deep breath and wiped her face with one hand.

"Here." Meg dug into her pocket and pulled out an unused Kleenex. "You got paint on your face." She put down her brush and stepped closer to Jamie so that she could wipe away the mixture of tears and paint.

"Thanks." Jamie snuffed back the rest of her tears and pushed some damp strands of hair from her eyes, taking care this time to use a clean finger. "This week has just been terribly long. I mean, it's only been a day and a half—I feel like a baby—but I just miss everything back home so much. I still feel like a total stranger, even after five weeks here."

Though Meg would never bring it up out loud, she guessed part of the reason Jamie felt that way was because Pete had been her world. Jamie hadn't ever taken the time to make friends outside of the American group, other than with Diego. *I should have guessed.* Of course Jamie would be the one to want to go home so badly, especially if she was having problems with Pete.

Meg took a deep breath. "Doesn't it help to have Pete here?"

Jamie glanced at her as if to gauge if she was being serious or sarcastic, then looked back at her work. "Pete broke up with me last night," she said quietly.

"Oh, Jamie. I'm really sorry." Meg put her arms around her friend and Jamie leaned into her. "I didn't have any idea." She could feel Jamie's tears start to seep through her shirt.

"I didn't think you'd care." The words were spoken without malice. "I know you don't agree with dating, and you're always so busy with something or someone else. I didn't plan on telling you—you've never seemed to want to be around me or talk to me."

A sudden gust of wind and rain struck the church with a blast, battering the windows and roof with water pellets. Meg looked over Jamie's curly hair and watched as waves of rain swept past them.

I'm sorry, God. She had been so preoccupied with her disgust at Pete and Jamie's physical closeness—with noticing and mentally commenting on Jamie's lack of maturity—that she had put up walls between herself and a sister. Worse, Jamie had felt every bit of it.

"Will you forgive me?" Meg leaned back but kept her arms around Jamie. "I have been really rude to you. I've—" she caught on the words but forced herself to get them out, "judged you, and avoided you. I'm so sorry you had to deal with that for four weeks."

"I forgive you." Jamie pulled out of her arms. "Don't worry about it. *Everything's* been rough these last four weeks."

Meg felt a stomach ache start. *I've been so insensitive.* "I really am sorry about Pete. He's probably been your anchor through all of your family stuff."

Jamie nodded. "But that's not necessarily good—I think I've been transferring all of the things I've been missing from my relationship with my dad to Pete, and he can't handle it. Really, I should be getting filled up with God, but He's seemed so far away for a long time. But honestly, I thought Pete cared more deeply—until lately, when he got really non-committal and casual about our relationship. It was like he was more interested in going out and having fun or working with the guys than he was in spending time with me."

"Do you think that's why he broke up with you? Because he wasn't getting enough time with the guys?" Meg hoped she wasn't speaking too honestly.

"Well, I asked him about it. And he got defensive, as if he didn't even see what I was talking about. Yesterday was really quiet. We didn't hardly say three sentences to each other. Then, last night, Pete comes to me and says we have to talk. He said he'd been thinking about our relationship, and he didn't see it going anywhere, and that he didn't think we suited each other very well, anyway." Jamie had once again started crying, and this time it was punctuated by hiccups. Meg placed a hand on her shoulder.

"I just don't get it." Jamie covered her face with her hands and rubbed her eyes slowly. "We've been going out for two months, everything is going fine, and then one day he says, 'I don't think we should keep dating,' and the whole thing's over with. Bam. Just like that. And it doesn't seem to bother him at all. Doesn't he care?" She looked directly at Meg.

Here was an opportunity to show Jamie the reality of the dangers of casual romance—but Jamie was living the results. She didn't need it pointed out. "I don't know what he's thinking, Jame."

Jamie tucked a curl behind her ear. "Maybe he didn't care that much about the relationship, but I did. And he let me go on like that—I gave him so much— and he never told me that this was only something 'for fun' for him… He even talked about getting married, 'hypothetically,' he always said."

"He did?" Meg fought back different feelings of judgment and anger. "What a—I mean, that's totally defrauding."

Jamie sniffed. "I can't just turn off my feelings for him and pretend that we're only friends." *So she did truly care for him.*

Jamie took a deep breath and let it out slowly. "I'm sorry to dump all this on you. You probably didn't want to hear about it, I know."

"No, really—I don't mind."

Gertrude's grinding engine drew up to the church and a minute later Teresa and the guys appeared, their clothing damp and clingy. As soon as they entered the room Jeff grabbed a bunch of paintbrushes and handed them out. "Well, looks like we'll all be painting today."

Chapter Twenty Four

Diego swung the side door of the van open as far as it would go. He offered his hand to Teresa, and she held it lightly as she made the giant step two feet up onto Gertrude's floor. Jamie did the same, except that her hold was much tighter. Diego made sure that she was completely inside before he turned once more to look for Meg's shining hair out in the courtyard.

She wasn't in sight.

Teresa spoke up from inside the vehicle. "Meg said she'd be out in a minute. She had to run down to the kitchen for something."

Diego nodded, not minding the wait. What were a few more seconds? Sure enough, Meg soon appeared around the corner of the building. She obviously knew she was holding the rest of them up, and Diego watched as she hurriedly crossed the courtyard to join them, her dark blue kerchief flapping around her face. He smiled at the sight of her, couldn't seem to keep it from his face. But she didn't see it since her head was bent. Just as she reached the van, the wind tugged off her scarf and send it sailing to the ground at his feet.

He bent down to pick it up for her, but Meg was quicker. With a single motion she grasped the piece of cloth and, evidently not seeing Diego's offered hand, entered the van unaided with a single giant step.

"Sorry," he heard her apologize to everyone. She took a seat in the far back and stretched her legs out to cover the rest of the space beside her. She had barely given him a cursory glance.

He fought down feelings of apprehension. This was not like her. Well, yes it was, on the grumpy days when she retreated and kept that one particular look of hers on her features. But she should be happy—at least, he hoped she felt the same way he did to be seeing her again.

He settled down in the corner of the second seat, diagonally opposite Meg's corner. Jamie and Teresa were next to him but seemed to be ready to go back to sleep on each other's shoulders.

Meg flipped her head forward so that she could retie her hair back in the scarf. Diego watched as she fiddled with the knot.

"So, Meg, have you finished all of your painting yet?" He brought his arm across the back of the seat.

Meg tipped her head up just far enough so that she could see his face, then lowered it again without letting her eyes catch his gaze. He thought he heard her murmur an "Mm-hmm," but he wasn't sure, especially when her hair hid her expression. "What?" Diego tapped his fingers against the plastic upholstery. "*No te comprendo.*"

Meg pulled hard at the knot she had just finished and put her head up slowly, smoothing back the material. "I said no. We have to finish the rest of the outside today since it rained all of yesterday and Tuesday." The words were very distinct and deliberate.

Diego stared at her for a minute. What game was she playing with him? Out of the corner of his eye he saw Teresa reach back behind the seat and pinch Meg's thigh. Meg jumped but kept her expression smooth. She flushed a little and turned to watch the sprawling outskirts of the city disappear behind them. Was it so he wouldn't see her reaction?

Diego caught Teresa's eyes long enough to see them roll and also the shrug she gave him in return.

The day that had started off looking so exciting was starting to lose its allure. If Meg pulled this attitude all day, he would spend several very long hours trying to figure out what was going on.

What had he done to bring on this aloofness? She had been so warm and peaceful on Sunday, and now it seemed like she and he were in some sort of fight. That was silly—they weren't boyfriend and girlfriend. He had hoped they wouldn't *have* any petty squabbles, at least not until they were married and fighting over some silly house thing.

Yet it didn't really feel like a spat. She was acting more like she had during the first week of their trip, when she hadn't known him—only now she seemed even more distanced.

Distanced—was that intentional? Had she been praying and getting a different answer than the one he hoped?

He felt his stomach drop, and it wasn't the kind of flip he usually felt when thinking about Meg. What if she was purposely removing herself from him, trying to prepare him for unwelcome news? What if she had spent the past three days thinking about her choices and had come to a decision?

God, you wouldn't tell her to say no. Diego turned to face the front of the van and let his shoulders slump. He could hear his heart beating quickly. God wouldn't send two opposing answers to the same question, would he?

Hadn't he taken the last three days away from Meg so that she would be able to think clearly about this and see what God wanted? What if one day was as long as he should have risked being gone—what if three was too long, and she had done too much thinking, and decided she really wasn't interested in him, after all? She was so good at hiding her feelings…

Diego stole another quick look at the young woman he loved. Her mind seemed completely absorbed in her observations and not at all concerned with him.

Perhaps she had never really considered his questions seriously in the first place. Sure, she had been excited by the possibilities, but almost any other seventeen-year-old girl would have reacted the same way.

Diego pushed that suggestion away. He understood Meg well enough to know that her feelings about this, about him, ran deep inside her. He had seen her hope and eagerness, and even her innocent longing. This was something she had promised to commit to thought and prayer. She would not have given him that promise or misled him if she knew immediately that she couldn't pursue anything.

But did she have that knowledge now? Was her maturity and commitment to Jesus—which so drew him to her—now pulling her away from him?

It would be a long forty-five minutes until they reached the work site. Maybe once they arrived and everyone started to work he would have a chance to talk to her alone. Hopefully she would be straightforward with whatever she had to tell him. It would be easier to take if she didn't get emotional.

Lord God, if she says no, there isn't going to be an easy way. He didn't want to hear it.

"Be still, and know that I am God." He had just re-read that Psalm this morning. *Be still.* What a tough command in the midst of worry.

⁂

Diego was the first to climb out of the van when they reached their destination. He blinked as the sun's rays blinded him momentarily. It was a good reminder that the day was young.

He turned to help the girls alight. Again the last of the three, Meg jumped to the ground without assistance, and would have kept going had he not laid a firm hand on her shoulder and turned her around to face him.

"Is it not rude to reject someone's offer of help?" In an effort to keep the strain out of his voice, the words came out a little sharper than he'd intended.

Meg looked at him with surprise, the first genuine emotion he'd seen all morning. "I'm—I'm sorry," she answered.

Diego softened his grip so that his fingers only rested on her shirt. "Can we talk, Meg?"

Meg looked around the area, keeping her gaze away from his. "Let's do it later."

He lowered his arm and the wall went back up as soon as the physical contact was broken. He was tempted to take her arm again but he knew that would be unfair. Instead he handed two paint buckets to her, then picked up two more and fell into step beside her.

"Something is bothering you. What am I doing wrong that you are angry at me?" He didn't want to ask the real question that was echoing through his head.

Meg cleared her throat. "Nothing, Diego. *Estoy muy cansada.*" (I am very tired.) She smothered a forced yawn.

*Be still…*Diego bit back a retort. "Come over and work by me. Then we will be able to talk."That was what he had been looking forward to for the last three days.

Meg set the paint buckets down in the shadow of the church, next to the front door. "Diego, if we go off and work together and talk we will seem like a couple. We can talk later, can't we? Besides," she placed her hands loosely on her hips, "I promised Teresa I'd work with her this morning."Without waiting for any reply she picked out her brush from the pile and started towards her sister.

Diego stood and watched her make her way across the brittle, well-worn grass. Her words rang like a repeating echo in his mind.The message was clear: she didn't want to be linked with him.

"*Es mi respuesta, Dios?*" (Is this my answer, God?) he whispered. Her words, her glances, her body language—all of it pointed to the same thing. She was trying to convey to him that she would not pursue the relationship.

Jeff approached with two long rollers perched on his shoulder. "Come help me do the back side."

Diego nodded, crouched down, and poured out a tray of paint. He picked it up carefully and followed Jeff around the building where no one else was working.

Within several minutes Diego was telling Jeff everything that had gone on. Except for a periodical nod or grunt to assure Diego he was still listening, Jeff was quiet, processing Diego's rapid Spanish until it faltered and stopped.

Jeff talked as he worked. "Honestly, I don't know what it is. The best thing to do is to talk about it and get it out. That's what I've learned with Adela." He paused so that he could face Diego. "I doubt she's planning on saying no to you."

"When do you think I'll get a chance to talk to her? It's going to be a long day with this sitting on me."

"You'll live. But I empathize—it wasn't so long ago I had my own women problems."

"You are referring to last night, *Señor?*"

Jeff pretended to bop him on the head with his fist. "Get back to your painting."

When they had almost half of the wall done, Jeff went around to see how everyone else was doing. He came back with a set of keys in his hand.

"All right, Diego." He tossed them to him. "Here's a chance to talk to Meg. Paco's agreed to stay here and continue working while you go find us something to eat and drink. You take Meg with you, don't worry if it takes you a little longer than usual."

Diego fingered the keys. "I don't know if she'll want to come with me."

"Go start Gertrude, and I'll go get Meg." Jeff turned and disappeared back around the side of the building.

Diego started the van and turned it around. A minute later Meg walked around the corner of the church and headed towards him. As soon as she had gotten in beside him and closed the door, he took off down the bumpy road.

The silence hung heavy. Meg seemed content to watch the village's mangy chickens squawk as they flapped to the side of the road, and Diego had to keep his eyes on the road so that he wouldn't hit them.

What should he say? He had no idea how to start. His during-painting prayers for direction seemed unanswered.

A few minutes later they had passed the last of the houses and the road became semi-deserted. Diego glanced over at his companion and forced himself to swallow. "Are you upset to be going home so soon?" he asked. "Is that why you are so freezing today?"

"No, though it will be nice to see my little brothers again."

"Yes. " Diego hit the brakes abruptly and pulled the van over to the side of the road. Meg looked at him with wide eyes.

"*Lo siento*, but I cannot talk with you and drive at the same time. I cannot see your face when I must watch the road also."

Meg's jaw clenched but Diego didn't care if she was upset by his persistence. "Meg, tell me why you are so—" he searched for the words he wanted, but couldn't find them, "so *like* this." He turned the car off, tucked the key into his pocket, and sat on the edge of his seat so that he could see Meg clearly. At least she was paying attention to him now.

"Margareta," he said. He reached up and put his finger under her chin.

At his touch she finally looked him full in the eye.

His mouth went dry. *I don't think I'll be able to handle it when she leaves. Especially if...* "Meg... *por favor, necesito saber.*" (Please, I need to know.) His voice sounded a little choked even to his own ears. "Have you changed your mind about wanting to pursue a relationship?"

"Changed my mind...?" Meg's eyes widened. "No! Of course not... I thought that maybe you had, but I never even considered it." She frowned and appeared ready to question him about it, but he stopped her.

"Why have you been acting this way then?" He leaned against the seat back. "You ignore me, you do not want to talk to me, and you tell me that you do not want anyone to see us together. I thought you were trying to prepare for it to be easier on me when you tell me that you are not interested." He shook his head. "But why did you do that? I do not understand."

Meg scooted her legs around so that she could face Diego more easily. "Diego, I'm sorry. I wasn't even thinking about that....and I didn't realize..." She looked out the windshield, then back at him. Her cheeks were pink. "I was upset because you said you would only be gone until Tuesday, and you didn't send word or anything. I was mad—and am still a little frustrated—because you didn't do what you said you would. You didn't keep your word. And I assumed it meant that you didn't want to be around me. So I guess I was giving you the cold shoulder."

"Cold shoulder?"

"Freezing, like you said. Ignoring you. All those things you mentioned. I'm sorry, Diego, especially for scaring you like that. Will you forgive me?"

He traced a finger along her jaw and cupped her chin, then lifted her face gently until she was staring into his eyes. "Yes, I forgive you. But I must also ask you to cut me some rope. I did *not* keep my word—although I never was sure how long it would take exactly. I do not apologize for the length—the churches were all in great need of my services and I was doing God's work. But believe me, I did not want to leave you." He smiled faintly.

Chapter Twenty Five

Meg stared out the window of Gertrude and watched the drooping trees fly by. Inside the van it was shadowed and cool, thanks to the new air conditioner Diego had just installed. But she knew that hot and humid air awaited them outside.

No matter. They were finally visiting Horsetail Falls, the famous natural landmark located outside of Monterrey. Diego had been praising the beauty of the spot for weeks, and Jeff had planned to let the young people visit after the work was finished, on the last day. They had completed everything yesterday after a long day of hard, steady work, and had all fallen into bed a little after dinner, instead of hanging out in the sanctuary as usual. Meg had wanted to stay and talk with Diego but had known that they both needed the extra sleep. They had re-connected a little that morning in the van but there was so much more to say.

Today she hoped they would have the chance. *The last day.* Meg felt her chest begin to ache but chose to ignore it. She was going to live the remaining hours to the fullest. God would forgive her for filling the time with memories, wouldn't He?

She turned from the window and looked to the front, where Diego was driving. His eyes were already watching her, reflected in the rear-view mirror. She looked back without embarrassment.

What was going on in that head of his? In rare moments she could almost guess—but the curtain went down when his eyes were on her. He always looked so intently, yet she had no idea what he was seeing. He hadn't complimented her at all, and hadn't given her any verbal roses to savor after the night on the balcony. It was a bit disappointing but it was probably more beneficial in the long run.

And really, he didn't have to say it. She could simply appreciate the fact that he *was* looking at her.

Diego hit the brakes in his signature fashion and Meg steadied herself with the back of his seat. The road had led to a tiny village where a few souvenir shops were strategically placed. Hammocks, blankets, pots, and sombreros were for sale, while children ran in the clearing.

Diego pulled the key out of the ignition. "I'm going to go get us some Joyas. Jamie, are you up for more shopping?"

"No thanks." She spoke from the back seat where she sat with Teresa. They had been sticking tight together all week, probably due to the fact that neither of them were on good terms with the two young men in their group. Meg sighed. Sometimes she felt a little guilty, being as happy as she was and having everything going so smoothly with Diego. *But never too guilty.*

She laughed out loud when Will came back into view a few minutes later. He strode purposefully towards the car with a big grin on his face. All she could see of his face *was* the grin. The rest was obstructed by the flopping brim of a huge straw sombrero, which had to be at least three-and-a-half feet in diameter. The word MEXICO was stitched across the front in red yarn.

He maneuvered the hat through the passenger door opening and took his seat. Meg posed the first thing that had come to mind on viewing him. "How are you going to get that on the plane?"

"I'm going to wear it."

"I am *not* going to be seen in a group with you with that thing on your head!"

"You're going to have to deal with two of us." Will pointed out the window, where Pete had just rounded into view. Sure enough, he had one too.

Meg sighed. "You guys are crazy."

Diego followed Pete with a crate of pop in his arms. Will reached across the dash and opened Diego's door so that he could heft the crate in-between the front seats.

Diego scooted onto his seat. "Enjoy, my friends. It will be your last chance to have Joya for awhile." Meg began to distribute the pop to Pete & the girls in back.

Fifteen minutes later they reached the end of the road—a parking lot. Everyone hopped out, ready for the twenty-minute climb to the falls. Pete and Will were the most enthusiastic; they took off quickly after Diego gave short directions. Teresa and Jamie followed them at a more steady pace. Diego and Meg lagged behind.

Silence enveloped the two of them, a full silence. They walked slowly, only a few inches between them. Pete and Will were out of sight, and Teresa and Jamie were a good fifty feet ahead of Meg and Diego. They probably wouldn't be looking backwards, either.

Meg glanced quickly at Diego's hand. She wondered if he was thinking the same thing she was. It was tempting—and holding hands wasn't exactly kissing. But if by any chance Teresa and Jamie were to look back, Meg still didn't want to give the impression that they were a couple. Plus it wouldn't be good for keeping her head clear.

Their shoulders brushed a few times. They continued on for five minutes without words. It was a comfortable quiet, though Meg felt a small sense of urgency. They really didn't have much time. Should they be filling it with conversation?

The path bent up ahead. Teresa and Jamie had disappeared around it awhile before them.

The light sound of bubbling reached Meg's ears. When they rounded the bend, the first sight that met them was running water. Sunlight flashed off of it as it streamed over and around rocks and stones of every size. The slow river flowed until the hill dropped, creating a small series of rapids. A plush slope of grass to the left of the path ended in shallow pools of side-waters.

Though their pace had been slow, Meg was already quite warm, and the water looked invitingly cool. "Do you mind if I wade a little?"

"*En absoluto*. I will join you."

They slipped their sandals off into the grass and made their way down to the water. The bank was steep, and Meg kept a hand on Diego's arm for balance as she put a foot out to test the temperature of the water. "It's cool, but it feels great."

Suddenly Diego's arm was no longer supporting her, and she felt herself wobble. A quick look up showed his grin. Before she could realize what had happened he lifted a hand and nudged her lightly on the shoulder.

It was enough to ruin her precarious balance. She tripped backwards into the knee-deep water. Her feet landed in the soft mud but the rest of her body continued falling backwards. Her arms flailed and she was just about to seat herself in the water when Diego grabbed one of her wrists.

He laughed. "Margareta, you are clumsy. It is a good thing you have me around to catch you." He shook his head at her, his feet firmly planted in the grass, his fingers still wrapped securely around her wrist.

She decided to take advantage of the opportunity. "I'll show you clumsy." With a quick jerk of her wrist he was off the bank and tripping in the water, trying to find his own balance. When he reached a hand out to catch her shoulder for support, she tried to step back—but was hindered by her skirt, which was clinging to her shins. It was soaking wet almost up to her knees.

A second later he had his balance, and still had his arm on her shoulder. Sunlight surrounded them. Meg looked up at his face and smiled. *What a goof.*

He smiled back, lightly moving his hand up over the curve of her neck until he cupped her cheek. All silly gestures were gone. His other hand lifted so that his fingers rested on her hair. "*Eres muy hermosa.*" His tone was almost—reverent? "That God could have given you to me…"

Meg tilted her head and let his words sink in. *Hermosa*—beautiful. Yes, she felt beautiful when he was around. And he saw her, with all of her flaws, as a gift.

She squinted her eyes and allowed herself to look, *really* look at his face. No, she wasn't just attracted to him because of the flattery of his attention, as Teresa had warned her. She wanted to look back, to show him that she found him attractive, to somehow reveal just how weak her knees *did* feel when he was around. She wanted to belong to him. To spend time wrapped in his arms. Now was not the time for that—it would not be so for a few years. But that didn't stop her from thinking about it.

She wanted to kiss him. She knew that also wouldn't be coming for years, but when he was standing a foot away and the sun was lighting up his face—she couldn't help wondering what a brush of his lips on hers would feel like.

She closed her eyes for a moment. This refinement process was a bit tougher than she thought.

"We need to get going."

She opened them to see him a good three feet away. He wasn't making eye contact. Had he been feeling the same thing?

"Come on." He nodded towards the bank. "You are looking much too like you are ready for a kiss right now, and I am much too ready to give you one."

Meg almost tripped in the water. Well, that was an honest way of putting it. She felt a wide smile grow on her face. He sure didn't mince words. It was refreshing, and helpful to know what he was thinking.

Hee hee. I look kissable!

"We should keep going." He took a deep breath. "The others will wonder what is keeping us."

Meg nodded and followed him out of the water. She noticed he didn't offer her his hand.

The path that wound upward for the last few hundred feet eventually curved and ended in a metal bridge. The roar of falling water had been getting progressively louder; it was now steady and vibrating. Meg glanced up at the waterfall towering above them.

The impressive picture brought an analogy to mind. *My river of feelings—my great, wide river of feelings for Diego that deepen daily—have come to a cliff.* And it felt like there was a very small channel of output for them. No kissing, no hand-holding, very little romantic talk, no confidence in a future together. The rocks only allowed a little stream of her emotions to trickle through. But the weight of the rest was pushing from behind. She wanted to spill her heart, she wanted to kiss him, she wanted to let it all rush out over the rocks in a great surge of water. *But this wasn't about wants.*

No. It is *about wants*—but it was about channeling them to God and not Diego. Meg knew deep down that if she were to let the river flood over the rocks and down the cliff, the calm pool of her serenity below would be destroyed.

She felt his hand brush a hair away from her mouth—she hadn't even realized it was caught there—and even at that light touch she felt her neck tickle. "Diego, I need to tell you something." She turned to look at him. "I think it would be good if you didn't touch me, at all. I don't think it's wrong. It's just— it's just that I can't think straight." She felt her cheeks warm and pulled her hair off of her neck. "It feels to me like we have the commitment, the go-ahead from God. And it all feels so right—but we really don't." She kept forgetting that they didn't. "Well, *I* don't." She sighed. "I'm just so confused."

He put his hands in his pockets and spoke after a moment. "I understand, Meg—every time I feel your skin I focus on only that. Because I want you to listen for God's leading I will give you more physical distance. I have been trying, though—very hard. If I slip up, it's because I'm a naturally affectionate person."

Meg smiled. Yes, she had seen the big bear hugs he frequently surprised Yolanda with. She met his gaze. "You thanked me for my modesty, and I think I need return the thanks for your honoring me with your restraint."

Chapter Twenty Seven

Meg flopped back on her bunk with a sigh. What a wonderful day—and it wasn't over yet. Memories she had wanted, and memories she had made. It would be a long while before the details of that afternoon faded from her thoughts.

She rested her hand over her chest. It had been tight all day, though she had been ignoring it. There would be plenty of time to be depressed later. Her throat had caught a few times, too—had tightened in a way that she had only felt before when she was acutely homesick. She *wanted* to go home, but home was somehow divided between her family and wherever Diego was.

She sat up and ran her fingers through her hair. There was only half an hour for her to take a shower and get ready for the farewell dinner Jeff had planned. She reached up to the top bunk and fingered the four skirts that had been her wardrobe for the last five weeks. She didn't want to wear any of them—she wanted to look different and *special*. There was finally someone to dress up for. A man would notice and appreciate her, in a different way than her father always had.

Jamie appeared in the bathroom doorway, her body wrapped in a beach towel and her hair up Swahili-style in her bath towel. "Shower's free, Meg."

"Okay, thanks." Meg grabbed her own towel off of her bunk. "Hey, Jame?"

"Mmm-hm?" Jamie looked up from where she crouched next to her bunk.

"Do you think I could wear your full-length dress tonight? The blue one, with the roses on it?" It was a light cotton dress—practical enough to wear around the mission, but slightly more dressy than any of Meg's things. Jamie had worn it many times, so Diego had already seen it. *But never on me.* She knew she would feel prettier in something she hadn't worn before.

Jamie pulled the dress out of her suitcase. "Go ahead. I was thinking of borrowing Teresa's tulip skirt for a change. Not that I really care what I wear anymore, since no one's noticing."

Instead of feeling frustrated with Jamie's moping, as she would have been a week ago, Meg felt only sympathy. "Ah, Jamie-bananie." Meg reached her hand out and touched the tip of Jamie's fingers where they rested on her sheet. "Who cares who's noticing?" *Like I should talk, when I'm feeling like Cinderella.*

"Yeah." Jamie exhaled and handed the dress to Meg.

Meg was just about to take it when she remembered—*my market dress.* The one she had bought specifically with tonight in mind, the beautiful blue-embroidered Mexican gown that she had envisioned wearing as she danced with Diego. She didn't need Jamie's dress.

Meg looked across the bunks at Jamie's back, where her long black curls hid her face. The blue and white flowers of Meg's dress would look stunning with her hair.

Meg wanted to push the thought away, but it persisted. *I want to wear my dress.* She had spent her own money on it.

But Jamie would feel pretty in it, even if Pete *was* indifferent. Meg swallowed. "Hey, Jamie?" Jamie's blue eyes met hers as she turned around. "I've got something you can wear." Meg lowered herself to pull it out of its wrapping.

Jamie smiled when she saw it. "Wow, that's beautiful."

"Thanks. Here." She tossed it carefully across the beds.

"For real?"

"For real."

"Thanks!"

Meg picked up Jamie's rose dress and turned for the bathroom. Teresa was in the other shower stall and was singing at the top of her lungs. She seemed strangely happy, despite the tension that remained between herself and Will. Maybe she was just happy that the trip would be over soon and she wouldn't have to deal with being around him all the time.

Seven minutes later Meg was out of the shower and standing in front of one of the tiny cracked mirrors. She fingered her wet hair, which was a riot of half-waves around her face. It always curled right after the shower, then tamed down to a thick frizz with the help of a blow-dryer. But it never looked like she wanted it to.

Teresa whirled by looking like perfection, with her hair long and straight and shiny. Jamie walked into the bathroom and twirled around for Meg to see the dress. "This is so pretty. Are you sure you don't mind?"

"I want you to wear it. You make it look pretty."

"Thanks." She surprised Meg by giving her a quick hug. Then she reached up and tugged one of Meg's locks. "Want me to do your hair?"

"There's really not much you can do with it. It's too short for braids. About all I can do is blow dry it straight. If I don't, it just half-curls and half-hangs."

Jamie's eyebrows raised. "I've got an idea." She turned around and two seconds later was standing behind Meg with a bottle of mousse in hand. "Your hair sounds a lot like mine—half-wavy, half-curly. I use this stuff to make it *all* curl."

Meg had always admired Jamie's long, black curls—the exact opposite of her own hair. "I thought your hair was just naturally like that."

"Well, it is, halfway… This emphasizes the curls and tames the wispies at the same time."

Their eyes met in the mirror and Meg smiled. "Go ahead." She wished they could have been this comfortable with each other four weeks ago.

With a pop of the cap and a *whoosch* of the foam, Jamie set to work on her new creation. Fifteen minutes later, Meg took one long last look at herself in the mirror. The mousse had worked better than she had expected and now a handful of shiny spirals framed her face. It made her hair look considerably shorter, but she liked the results. Light touches of make-up here and there—applied by Jamie's experienced hand—only emphasized the glow of her features.

And the dress. It really was beautiful—sleeveless, with a high wide neckline that stretched from shoulder to shoulder. The material draped from her collarbone to her mid-calves, and it fit reasonably well considering the differences between Jamie's shape and her own.

She felt beautiful, and she knew it wasn't because of what she saw in the mirror—it was because of the look she hoped would be in Diego's eyes when he saw her.

Teresa and Jamie were waiting on the beds. Teresa stood and nudged her hair back over her shoulder. "Wow, Meg, you look great."

"Thanks." Meg deposited her hairbrush and makeup bag by her pillow and followed the girls out the door.

Cool night air brushed past her face as she took the stairs slowly. The guys were standing in a group underneath one of the lights, Kerryn playing amongst their legs. Her dad, Jeff, and Adela were talking near the sanctuary.

They all moved towards the van, and Diego came alongside Meg for a few feet. "Is that a new dress?"

"No." Meg couldn't keep back a smile. "It's Jamie's, and she wears it every Sunday."

"I never noticed it before." He looked down at her.

In the van Meg figured it would be better for her to stick by the girls, so she didn't get a chance to talk to Diego again until they were seated across from each other at the restaurant. A long table full of food was spread in front of them, yet Meg discovered she had no appetite.

The ache in her chest had grown. Diego was honoring her wishes by not touching her, but their eyes caught across the table about every minute and held for long moments. Every time, she found it harder and harder to keep her tears back. It didn't help that she was probably exhausted, underneath the excitement of the evening.

Meg picked at her napkin. Ever since Diego's proposal she had been acting like he was hers. Her actions had been a reflection of her emotions. But at the same time she knew that if she had distanced herself emotionally, she would not have to be sitting here so close to tears.

She was leaving him without really knowing if they would ever meet again. So many *ifs* that she didn't want to think about. All week she had been assuring herself that he was God's choice for her, that everything would work itself out. But she had not talked to God about it in-depth. Since the night of Diego's declaration and her prayers afterwards, her conversations with God had been sporadic at best. She did not have an answer to give Diego, and that was frustrating and scary. *Why don't I yet?* Tonight would be the opportune time to tell him.

I am afraid. A small suspicion was quickly growing into real fear. She didn't want to give him up. Jeff had read them a verse at worship time today. "*Fear not, for I am with you… Be not afraid, for I am your God. I will strengthen you and help you, I will uphold you with my righteous right hand.*" For some reason it failed to comfort her. She didn't feel strong. She didn't want help with anything—she wanted God to give her Diego.

Would God punish her for doing that? A sudden twinge of fear hit. Was He going to take Diego away because she had been slipping up?

No. God was perfect and good. He might not choose to give her Diego, but it wouldn't be because she wasn't good enough, or to punish her for mistakes she had made.

She had been foolish. She had not waited on His timing for everything. *I've dreamt about him every night, I've dwelt on him every minute of every day…* She felt tears coming again, tears of embarrassment. And despite her resolve she was still scared that God would take him away because of her unwise actions.

Meg looked over at her dad. She still hadn't told him anything about what had transpired in the last week. She just hadn't been able to find the right moment, or the right words.

Could Diego see her thoughts? He didn't know her that well yet, did he? And yet every time he looked at her he seemed so serious. Was he afraid, too? A glance at his plate showed that he hadn't eaten at all, either.

Conversation flowed around them. She needed to start nailing down her emotions, *now*. There was a whole week of disregarding them to mend.

A group of Mexican men dressed in bright crimson costumes entered the room, instruments in hand. They took their places at the end of the large wooden floor and began warming up quietly. It was time to dance.

Diego's gaze was waiting for hers. He opened his hand on the tabletop, asking with an action.

Meg motioned with her own in response. "In a little while. Why don't you ask someone else first?" She needed to compose herself before she was standing in his arms.

He nodded, and she watched through a blur as he scooted back in his chair. He approached Adela, bowed, and asked her to dance with him in Spanish. Meg watched them walk to the dance floor and position themselves. Soon Adela was being whirled around in Diego's arms.

She really is beautiful. Tonight her hair was hanging long and black down her back, and she wore a bright red shirt. Meg glanced at Jeff, who was leaning back in his chair, watching. From the way his eyes were following his wife's every move, he also seemed to be noticing her beauty. It probably wouldn't be long before he cut in.

Diego turned and all Meg could see was Adela's back. She was a small woman, and had to look up to see Diego's face.

Meg stopped fiddling with her napkin. *His Mexican wife.* Great time for a reminder. She had totally thrown that idea out the window. Seeing a short Mexican woman in his arms was a sobering sight when for the last two weeks she had pictured a tall, fair girl there.

The song ended and Jeff scooted back in his chair. Diego handed Adela over to him, then came back to the table. He once again held out his hand. "Dance with me."

She allowed him to slide her chair back, then she slipped her hand into his. They positioned themselves, his hand resting very lightly on her waist, her one hand on his shoulder, the fingers of her other entwined with his.

"Did I ever tell you that the first time you came, I thought you were eighteen or nineteen?" He stepped smoothly to the beat, an easy lead to follow.

She shook her head.

"Right now you look like you are fifteen." He must have seen her reaction, because he was quick to explain. "That is not bad. You just—look young. Your big eyes and your face." She felt his shoulder rise and fall in a shrug.

"I thought you would notice Teresa right away when we came." She kept it to a statement of observation.

Now his shoulders shook a little with laughter. "Why?"

"Well—because. Guys are always attracted to her." *Rather than me.* The end of her sentence remained unspoken, but Diego was quick to catch her meaning.

"Teresa was around me to speak Spanish and make a friend. I *noticed* you."

"Yeah, right." He was just saying that because he had to.

"You do not believe me."

"No, not really. I mean, you noticed me—" *the night of the tattoo?* "later. But you can't honestly tell me you thought, on first introduction, that I was prettier than her."

When he spoke his voice held confusion. "What do you mean? It is not that she is prettier than you, or you more than her. With me, I am more drawn to you. With another man, it is not the same. Different men like different flavors."

Meg laughed. "You mean different men have different tastes?"

"Yes."

"I knew *that*." She shifted her fingers so that they were cupped in his hand. "But isn't there—uh, a general measure or scale with you guys? Certain girls are just more attractive—they're put together nicer, or have more feminine features, or something?"

He tightened his hold on her hand. "That is what your American movies and magazines make you think. But it is not true. And you must simply hold my word on it."

They danced for a few more measures before he spoke again. "Which of you looks more like your mother?"

"Most people say that Teresa does, but my dad says I have her mouth and eyes."

"I bet she is beautiful."

Meg nodded. "When Teresa and her and I go out people sometimes think we're sisters."

He shifted his hand so that his palm rested on her waist and his fingers curved behind. "I would like to meet her."

Will looked up as their waiter once again neared the table. He had already come at least five times, asking if they needed more water, napkins, *etc. etc. etc.* But Will had seen the glances the twenty-something young man had cast towards Teresa.

Will shifted in his seat. She was two people down from him, and the waiter had specifically approached her chair. Will tipped back a little in his seat as he watched the handsome young man bow, then hold out his hand politely. "Will you dance with me?" His English was perfect, with an added hint of a dashing Spanish accent.

Will tipped back farther to see Teresa's reaction, but could only view the back of her hair, which was down tonight. He felt his balance over-compensating and realized just in time that he was about to fall flat on his back. He grabbed the back of Jamie's chair and pulled himself back up with a *thump*. Teresa's light laugh filled the air and he heard her say "*Sí.*"

Will turned to watch her put her hand in the waiter's and stand in one smooth motion. The awkward position of his head hurt his neck, so he turned to Jamie. "Wanna dance?"

"Ah, sure." She looked surprised, but stood and made her way out to the floor with him.

The Mariacci band had started a lively 4/4 tune, complete with trumpets, castanets, and spirited guitars. Will was a reasonably okay dancer—Rebekkah had forced him to learn—but Jamie was not so skilled. He didn't mind, though, because her concentration was kept on the steps and that way he didn't have to make casual conversation. He steered them towards where Teresa and the waiter were dancing.

Teresa had a beautiful smile on her face, and was laughing again at something the waiter had said. *She sure is giggly tonight.* He moved closer, trying to catch what they were talking about, but it was in Spanish.

By now the floor was filled with dancers. Will decided to tune out the couple and focus his attention on Jamie. He had done a terrible job of it so far, and Jamie needed this. She had been very quiet and depressed lately. It was probably because Pete had dumped her.

They danced for a good five minutes. Will gave her a few lessons in rhythm and steps, managing to get a few smiles and even a laugh out of her. The song sounded like it was drawing to a close when Diego tapped Will on the shoulder to cut in. "May I?"

"Sure." It was time for him to do some cutting in of his own.

He made his way through the crowded floor to where Teresa and the waiter were applauding the song. The band struck up another song, a slower waltz.

Will halted. *A slow song. Maybe I shouldn't...* It had been a week since that awful scene at Bishop's Palace, but he still didn't know if she would accept an invitation to dance. She had deliberately avoided him all week. He fingered the ring in his pocket. Was the timing right? He had prayed about it more every day, but the opportunity to make his case had never presented itself. The work week had been chaotic as they tried to finish their projects, and they were so tired by evening that they hadn't left the mission at all. So he hadn't had any time to be alone with her.

This was his last night before they went home, and he didn't want to face that long ride without things worked out between them. He wanted her to know where he stood—even if she did reject him.

No, he couldn't worry about that again. He would never get the nerve up to talk to her if he started thinking along those lines.

He took another look at her and noticed that the man's hand was holding firmly to her waist. There was a lot less space between them than there had been during the previous song. *That sleazeball.* Why was Teresa smiling at the guy? When Will caught sight of her face over the waiter's shoulder she was looking straight into the guy's eyes.

Will reached up and tapped decisively on his rival's arm. "May I?" The young man turned.

"Yes, of course." The waiter handed her over to Will with a polite smile.

Will had situated himself correctly, right hand in the air waiting for hers, left hand reaching towards her waist, when he looked back at her face. The smile had disappeared and she was looking everywhere but at him.

He hesitated, then placed his hand gently on her waist. She pulled away from his touch, her eyes on the floor. "Please, Will. I don't want—"

"Teresa, I need to talk to you." He started to draw her closer, expecting resistance—but it ended up being much less than he had planned on. She was very close to him. His stomach dropped and he swallowed hard. For the twenty-second time since he'd seen her at breakfast, he had the very strong urge to kiss his best friend's breath away. *Not yet, Will. If God is merciful, just a few more minutes…*

"Well, what?" Teresa broke the spell. Her voice sounded shaky, but from what he could tell she was totally oblivious to what he was feeling.

"Uh…" he stumbled. He tried to remember what he was going to say. He looked back into her face and was surprised to see her fighting for composure.

"Can we at least dance, instead of standing here?" she asked.

Will moved them into the waltz, but he couldn't concentrate on the steps. Twice he came close to knocking into other couples. How was he supposed to broach such a big topic? Teresa wasn't even looking at him. "Let's go outside." He managed to maneuver her towards the edge of the dance floor, past some potted palms, and out onto a balcony overlooking the city.

They had stopped dancing, but their hands were still linked, and he still had his arm around her waist. "Teresa, I love you."

That got her attention. "And I need to apologize. For the last five years

I haven't been serving you. I've been wasting time with Rebekkah that should have been spent preparing myself for you. And I probably shouldn't even try to offer you myself now, but I really need your help."

He pulled her close so that the distance between them disappeared and her face was nestled between his neck and shoulder. She was still rigid, but she didn't completely resist his nearness. Her hand was limp in his so he cupped it tighter, drawing their intertwined clasp close to his shoulder while his other arm circled her waist. He heard her let out a long breath.

"What about Rebekkah?" She spoke into his neck.

He pulled back so that he could see her face. "Rebekkah broke up with me the first week we were here. She sent me a Dear John letter."

He watched a range of emotions play across the face of his love. "What a chicken. I can't believe she waited till—a letter? What a despicable way—" Teresa pulled back from him. "*Why didn't you tell me?*" He saw her catch her breath as her eyes started to fill with tears. "Ah, I get it." Now she looked really angry. "She's probably met somebody else, so you have to get back at her by hooking up quick with me before we get home."

"*Teresa.*" He cupped her face in his hands. "That's why I didn't tell you earlier. At first I figured I'd keep it to myself because my pride was smarting, yes. But it didn't take long for me to finally wake up and see what I've been too immature and blinded to for the last ten years—that *you* are the one I was made for. I've been praying and watching and growing in my admiration of you for the last four weeks—and I know that doesn't sound long, but we've been with each other almost twenty-four hours a day, and I've already known you for twenty years." He smiled. "Once it starts, it really doesn't take long to fall completely in love with your best friend."

By this time she was really crying, but a smile had grown, too. He smoothed his thumbs over her cheeks. "We work so well together, Reeses. I think we'd be a dynamite partnership for Jesus. You balance me, and make me laugh harder than anyone, and we're both headed for the mission field. You aren't embarrassed to cry around me." He pulled her in and rested his cheek on the crown of her head, aware of her soft silk hair, aware of where her tears and breath warmed his skin through his shirt. "You're comfortable and exciting all at the same time. You remind me of my mother. I could talk to you for the rest of my life and still have words to share. Your wisdom astonishes me. And I don't think kissing you would ever be boring."

He stepped back, reached into his pocket, then lowered himself onto one knee. There—*now* she was smiling. He momentarily forgot the next part of his well-rehearsed speech. He had never seen her look at him like that before—respect and adoration and grace all evident in her expression.

"Teresa, will you spend the rest of your life with me?"

She nodded.

Yes! He took her hand in his and held the ring between his fingers, then paused as she drew it back.

"Wrong hand, Will. See? L is for left." She was shaking with laughter.

"Sorry." He grabbed the other and slid the band onto her ring finger. It felt good to have it out of his pocket and on her where it belonged.

Teresa looked down at his face in shock.

I'm engaged. What in the world—? She looked down at the ring on her finger, just the one she would have picked out. It looked familiar… "Did you get this at the marketplace?"

"Yeah, about two weeks ago. It's been burning a hole in my pocket ever since."

"It's perfect." She watched as he slowly stood up.

"*Querida…* May I kiss you?"

My goodness, he even asked this time! And where had he learned the Spanish for *beloved*?

"No." She watched his eyebrows draw together.

"Oh, okay. I understand. We need to be careful—"

"Darling, I was just kidding."

He reached up and cupped her face. "I don't like it when you tease me."

"You're going to have to learn to live with it."

"I think I can handle that." He brought his face closer and she closed her eyes. As he kissed her softly her hand reached up to rest on his cheek and his arms circled her waist. She felt more than a little lightheaded—at the way the events had suddenly unfolded, at the fact that she was engaged, and at the feeling of his kiss which, she could tell, was a giving one.

Will pulled his head back slightly and looked down into her eyes. "Whew." He seemed a little out of breath, too. "Now *that's* a kiss." It almost sounded like his voice was shaking. He dropped his arms to take her hand. "Come on."

He walked her back to the table, and as they neared it Teresa could see that everyone was oblivious to what had just transpired. Will cleared his throat.

"Can I have everyone's attention, please?" When all eyes were on them he turned to look at her. "My best friend has just agreed to become my wife."

The whole table broke into applause, Pete whistling loud over the din. Teresa immediately looked at her dad. He had a big smile on his face. *Good.* So Will had cleared everything with him. Then she looked at Meg, who simply stared. Diego and Pete didn't look at all surprised—Will must have schemed it all with them—and Jamie seemed to be looking at Teresa's hand to catch a glimpse of the ring.

"When's the date?" Jeff spoke up from the end of the table.

Will turned to Teresa. "Uh, we don't know. Didn't get that far yet."

Jeff grinned. "Well, it looks like we've got *two* new team members for Hermosillo!"

Chapter Twenty Nine

The soft material of Meg's now-thoroughly-worn skirts brushed against her hands as she gently laid them in her suitcase one by one. A small corner of the bag was reserved for souvenirs—a Joya bottle, an old film canister containing a small amount of dirt from the work site, a few bracelets for her brothers. And on top of all the clothes rested her journal, full of more mental souvenirs then she ever would have imagined it would collect when she had first packed it.

She let out her breath slowly in time with the zipper she pulled shut around it. She was completely packed, and there were still two hours before they left for the bus station. She checked her watch; it was past one in the morning. In the corner bunk Teresa slept in a tightly curled ball. Meg felt the old twinge of jealousy rise as she caught site of the ring on her sister's finger. Meg was ecstatically happy for her, but she also wished that she herself could have been leaving with at least an *invisible* engagement ring on her own finger.

As Meg pulled back the sheet in the doorway she caught sight of Jamie sleeping contentedly, curled up on a nearby bench. Meg looked around the mission, committing every detail to memory. The faraway lights, the dim shadow of Saddle Mountain, the mournful howls of a dog, the sound of the slight breeze whispering through the fronds of the palms. *This is home.* She looked up at a bright star above her. *I don't want to leave, God.* Even if there was no Diego, she probably wouldn't want to leave.

Diego had been foremost in her thoughts since she had entered the dorm half-an-hour ago. He was nowhere in sight, not even out with Pete and Will, who were playing some one-on-one basketball. Will was playing with an unusual intensity, Meg noticed. He probably had excess energy from the adrenaline boost Teresa's acceptance of his proposal had given him.

Perhaps Diego was in the sanctuary, or in the kitchen... No. He would probably be on their balcony. Meg felt her feet moving. She wanted to be with him. There were only two more hours.

Cease striving, and know that I am God. She looked up into the darkened sky again, but there were no falling stars to even misconstrue as being signs.

I need to stop. She'd been giving in to every feeling for the last week. *You have to obey in the small things if you're ever going to obey in the crucial things.*

Sometimes the small things *are* the crucial things.

She was now at the bottom of the steps, and had two directions to choose from. One lead to the balcony stairs, the other away from the lights under a secluded, scrubby palm tree where she could clearly see the stars.

Meg moved to the right.

Not five minutes later footsteps on the path alerted her to someone's presence.

"Margareta?" Diego's voice whispered to her from ten feet away; his form, framed in the moonlight, filled the sidewalk, his shadow approaching her ahead of him. "Can I join you?" He spoke in Spanish and she understood.

"No, *por favor.*" Her voice cracked.

Diego stepped back. "I will be back to say goodbye." She couldn't see his eyes in the shadows but knew from his tone that he would keep his promise.

She watched him walk away and put her arms tighter around herself, squeezing her eyes shut.

One and a half hours and a lifetime later she still felt no peace. She felt totally and completely alone. *Perhaps because I have left you alone this past week, is that it, God?*

She glanced at her watch. Two-forty-five. They could leave anytime now. She heard the sounds of voices and van doors opening. *I need to go help them.*

"Meg." Diego's voice sounded from the opposite direction and she turned. Now his face was totally illuminated in the moonlight so she could see every movement. "*Ven aquí.*" His voice broke as his words ended, and he held out his hand to her.

She approached him and slipped hers into his, swallowing to keep the tears in her throat. He hooked his thumb with hers, clenching the upper part of her palm firmly before slowly sliding his fingers down and around hers so they were fully enclosed in a warm grip. *The Mexican handshake.*

From behind his back he brought out his left hand, which held a small package. "I have had this for awhile now." He handed it to her, a small square box with plain brown-paper wrapping, a twine tie, and a small paper tag on which was written "*Para Margareta.*" Diego let go of the handshake so she could turn it around. On the bottom, slipped beneath the twine, was a folded envelope.

"Do not open this letter until you have made your decision," he said quietly. Meg looked at the little package.

Jeff's voice broke the quiet as it came to them on the night air. "All right, time to say our goodbyes!"

"My bags—" Meg turned to the sounds of activity.

Diego touched her arm. "I loaded them."

His fingers wrapped loosely around her wrist then. "I know we agreed not to touch, but can I give you a goodbye hug?"

At her nod he gently pulled her into his arms. Meg buried her face in the crook of his neck. Between the sound of his breathing and the closeness of his skin and the tightness of his arms, she could barely breathe. She held on tight.

I love you. She wanted to say it, but something stopped her. She pulled back and looked into his face. One small trail of a tear glistened on his cheek. He kept his arms around her as she reached up and wiped it away with the tips of her fingers, then brought them down to her lips, transferring their moisture to her own skin. Then she put her fingers on his lips. He caught her hand at his mouth and held it there. "I will miss you," he said, his breath warming her hand.

"*Vaya con Dios,*" she managed to whisper from her tight throat, and with those words she slipped out of his arms and ran down the path.

Everyone was hugging and saying their goodbyes. She joined in and a minute later Diego was there, also saying his farewells to the rest of the group.

As the van pulled out of the mission gate she turned in her seat and caught a last glimpse of him, waving under the light of the courtyard lamp. She lifted her hand in response but didn't know if he saw it.

Chapter Thirty

Jennifer Atwell sat at the kitchen countertop, sipping a cup of lemonade as she flipped through her daughters' Mexico pictures for the fifth time. *All these friendships they have formed, and people they know, that I have never met*—though she had heard second-hand stories from her daughters' many phone calls from Mexico, and knew a lot about the faces she was looking at now.

She flipped the page and Diego's was the next picture she saw. *Good-looking guy.*

Rick had mentioned the mild interest Diego seemed to have shown towards their Meg. Maybe that was why their second-eldest daughter had been an emotional firecracker since returning from Monterrey three nights before. The moment Meg had walked off the terminal Jen had seen it on her face—something was eating away at her. She had been crying quite a bit in the last seventy-some hours, and sleeping just as much. Jen knew it was a mixture of a bunch of things—reverse culture shock, home feeling foreign for the first time, missing Monterrey, coming off the high that mission trips always give you. But was there more to it? Surely it couldn't be jealousy of Teresa's happiness—Jen had watched Meg struggle with sister-comparisons throughout the last few years, but at newly seventeen Meg would know that marriage wasn't even a possibility at this point.

The younger kids had noticed it, too. Amos, at four, could tell that Meg was not happy. This morning when he woke up he had asked his mama why. Joel was the quiet one, and was usually always there with a hug, but the six-year-old had left Meg alone since she returned. And Jen had over-heard a conversation between Daniel and Nathan that had made her laugh. Daniel, her ten-year-old, had been confused as to why Meg had been crying so much lately. Nathan, at thirteen, had it figured out. "She's a girl. They cry about everything."

But Jen didn't have it figured out. Meg was her quiet girl, and was always harder to reach than Teresa. Teresa inevitably volunteered informa-tion and spilled her heart whether things were going bad or good. Meg, however, took a lot of careful prodding. Jen suspected that Meg's journal had received most of her deepest thoughts since the time she was eight years old.

"Okay folks! Time for family pick-up!" Her husband's voice sounded from the living room, where most of the family was occupied with various leisurely pursuits on this rainy day. Jen set down her cup and headed in to help.

Daniel was at the CD player and had apparently decided upon some work music for them. He popped in a CD and hit *Play*. Trumpets blared an opening intro, then Frank Sinatra began to croon from the speakers:

> *South of the border, down Mexico way*
> *That's where I fell in love when the stars above came out to play*
> *The mission bells told me that I must not stay*
> *South of the border, down Mexico way.*

Jen looked at Meg, whose composure was beginning to falter.

> *And she sighed as she whispered 'mañana'*
> *Never dreaming that we were parting*
> *And I lied as I whispered 'mañana'*
> *'Cause our tomorrow never came.*

Meg dropped her journal and pen and headed for the stairs to her room.

A knock sounded on the front door, and Teresa got up from her position on the couch to answer it. Jen watched as the door opened to reveal Will on their front deck.

Jen watched him watch her daughter. They stood there staring at each other as if they hadn't just eaten lunch together an hour earlier.

The sound of little feet came pattering up the basement stairs. Apparently her two youngest sons had been deaf to the pick-up-time command of their father, but had no problem sensing Will's presence. "Will! Come see! I just learned how to ride my bike!" Amos was clambering over Joel as both boys raced to make it to Will first.

Will reached down and scooped Amos up in his arms, then took hold of his ankles and let him hang out upside-down in front of him like a monkey. Will was their favorite wrestling partner, excepting only their own father. "Okay, guys. First I have to talk to Teresa a little bit, though. "

Joel looked up at Teresa. "Are you sick, Teresa? You look funny."

Jen decided it was time to break in. "I think she's okay. Honey, why don't you let Will and Teresa have some time alone?"

Joel turned with a grouchy look on his face. "They've been alone since they got back from Mexico."

Will swung Amos back up into his arms, then set him down firmly on the ground. Amos's face was red and round as a cherry as he grinned up at Will in adoration.

"How about we all go bike riding—all four of us," Will said.

"Yeah! Yeah!" Joel and Amos jumped up and down, then followed Teresa and Will out the front door.

Rick, Daniel, and Nathan were left. Rick sat back down on the couch. "Well, guys, I guess we can leave the mess till later."

Meg lay stretched out on her bed, a blank sheet of paper in front of her. She was going to write the letter.

First she addressed the envelope, carefully copying Diego's address in her best handwriting from within her journal to the paper. *Monterrey,*

Nuevo León, México.

Ten minutes later she had gone through four sheets of paper and still had only half a page written. It was not coming. *This can't be that hard. Just write yes.*

She smiled. "Yeah. Just write YES." She pulled out a clean sheet and, pressing firmly, wrote the one word out in large letters. *See, that wasn't so hard.*

She folded it in thirds, then slid it in the envelope. She was about to lick it shut when a knock sounded on her door. "Come in."

She turned to see her mother enter the room. Meg's stomach tightened.

Jen seated herself on the bed. "What're you writing?"

"Nothing." Meg tried to casually slide the envelope into her Bible so that the address was hidden.

Jen put a hand on Meg's leg. "You don't have to be defensive, honey. I was just curious."

Meg rolled over and put her hands behind her head. She stared up at the ceiling. *Do I tell her?* She didn't want to, but she knew that she probably should. Meg took a deep breath.

"I was writing a letter to Diego." Jen seemed to wait for her to continue—almost as if she knew there was something big coming. *She* always *knows.* Meg sighed. "We got to know each other pretty well while I was down there. He asked me if I wanted to keep up a correspondence with him once I got home.. . . and he goes to college at Wheaton so he would maybe come up and visit every once and awhile this fall once school is back in session. I told him I would give him an answer when I got home." She avoided looking her mom in the face. *Well, I'm not lying.*

"I see." Jen was silent for another few minutes that stretched out into what felt like a half-hour. "Do you think he's, well, serious?"

"I'm pretty sure he is."

"Did he say so?"

Meg nodded. "He said his intention was eventually marriage." She finally looked at her mom and watched as one eyebrow raised.

"Wow. That is serious." Jen shifted on the bed. "So, when were you planning on telling Daddy and me about it?"

Meg looked away again. "Uh, I don't know. I kept meaning to, but it was just—I don't know. I couldn't think of how to start the conversation, or when. I'm not like Teresa."

Jen leaned back against the post of Meg's canopy bed and looked pointedly at Meg's Bible where the envelope resided. "So what's your answer?"

Meg felt her face heat. "Well, yes, probably."

Another long pause. "How old is Diego?"

"Twenty-two."

"Do you think maybe he should have mentioned something to your dad about it?"

Meg felt her shoulders tense. "I thought about that—but he comes from a different culture. Plus he didn't even really have a dad himself, so I don't think he knows the traditional American protocol for that sort of thing. Plus, he's a guy. They're afraid of dads."

Jen smiled. "That all sounds legitimate. It's not that big of a deal— Daddy didn't ask Grandpa if he could marry me. I guess it's just an added bonus of courtesy that Daddy and I would appreciate. But it's not necessary." She took a deep breath. "Don't you think five years is a big age difference?"

"Nah. When I'm thirty he'll only be thirty-five."

"But it's a lot wider when the difference is barely seventeen and a full twenty-two."

Meg rolled her eyes. *I knew I shouldn't have told her.*

Jen lowered her chin. "Muggah, don't give me that look. Just hear me out. I'm not attacking you. The choice is yours to make—I can't force you to do anything. You could have corresponded with him via e-mail without Daddy and I even knowing. I just had hoped that we have a closer relationship than that."

Meg sat up and gave her mom a hug. "We do, Marmee."

"Do you realize how fast things can happen when you're visiting each other on the weekends?" Jen smoothed her daughter's hair back. "If he was a thousand miles away in Mexico, it might be a little different—although with the speediness of e-mail you would probably know each other very deeply in a very short time. But if he was only two-and-a-half hours away—and if you guys have already gotten to the point where you think you could be engaged soon—I don't know. It makes me a little uneasy, to be honest." Jen looked her in the eyes. "Have you prayed about it?"

"Of course." Meg twiddled her fingers. "Mama, are you uncomfortable because he's Mexican?"

Jen shook her head. "Meg, you know we would never judge based on that." Meg had known that was true before she asked the question, she was just feeling defensive.

Her mom continued. "You are seventeen. God may have many other things for you to do first, even if He does want you to marry Diego. Are you open to that?"

Meg was silent, and had turned her face into her pillow. Her mom let the silence sit over them for a minute before going on. "Another thing that you may not have realized, Meg, is that marriage changes things. I'm not saying that it's bad—it's a wonderful, wonderful thing. But there are some things that just can't be done once you get married. It takes energy and work to keep a marriage strong. That's the way it's supposed to be. Are you ready for that?"

Meg spoke with her face pressed into the bed, but the words were still clear. "I just don't understand why God would give me someone like Diego and seem to fill all of my dreams, and then take him away. Diego and I seem made for each other, Mama." The last sentence was forced out between teeth clenched to keep from crying.

"Meg." Jen laid her hand on her daughter's shoulder and massaged it gently. The touch loosened the rest of Meg's self-control.

"I don't want to lose him," she choked out. "I decided not to get involved in the dating scene because I knew that God had a much better plan for me. And now He's given me Diego. And I know he's not perfect, he's human like I am, but I love him, Mama." A sob cut off her voice for a moment.

Jen took a Kleenex from the dresser and wiped Meg's tears from her cheeks as they came down. She pulled her daughter into her arms.

Meg's voice was muffled against her mom's shirt. "What would be the purpose in taking him from me?"

Jen waited until Meg's sobs had calmed and then handed her another

Kleenex. "Meg, I *know* you think you love him, and I know you think he loves you. And I don't doubt that you have strong feelings for each other. But—honey—mission trips are usually highly emotionally-charged occasions. They're like summer camp, when all the counselors 'fall in love' and date each other for three months and then it trickles off once they all head back to school. When guys and girls are in very close, intense contact with each other for an extended amount of time, it gets the feelings going." She smiled.

"But you met dad at summer camp!" Meg threw a used Kleenex at her.

Jen sighed. "Well, here's another way of looking at it. It might be like your decision not to date. You were willing to sacrifice the fun of a short-term relationship with someone so that you could have a better relationship with the man you ended up marrying. Maybe you have to crucify the relationship with Diego now so that God can resurrect something better, later—maybe with Diego, maybe not."

Two more tears rolled down Meg's cheeks. "Why would he do that?"

"What's that Elisabeth Elliot quote you like so much? Something like 'it's not a sacrifice if it doesn't cost you anything?' Maybe God is testing you. Maybe Diego is your Isaac—you have to take him to the altar like Abraham took his son, and completely cut off contact with him, without knowing what God will do."

Jen tipped Meg's face up so she could look into it. "Maybe God is asking you to make a choice. He may be saying, 'Do you want Diego, or do you want Me?' Only you know for sure."

Meg looked beyond her mother's shoulder, staring out the window at the now-darkened sky.

"Do you think He's asking me to make that choice?" she finally whispered, her eyes coming back to Jen's and starting to fill with tears again.

Jen tightened her embrace. "I can't tell you that, honey. Only He can." She paused. "Do you want me to pray about it for you now?"

Meg nodded, unable to speak, and listened as her mother spoke quietly to God. When Jen finished the prayer she moved Meg over so that she could once again sit next to her. "Do you want some time alone to think and pray about it?"

"Yeah, I guess I'd better."

Jen stood up and turned to leave. Then she turned back, kneeling and taking Meg in another quick hug. "I love you, Muggah."

"I love you too." Meg clung to her, but only for a moment. "Thanks for coming in here."

"Sure."

Meg lay back across the bed, alone with her thoughts. *What do You want, Lord?* It had seemed too impossible that he would want anything other than for her to move ahead with Diego. In assuming that, she had blocked out anything that had hinted otherwise. Instead of *Show me what Your will is*, her prayers had been "There isn't any reason why Your will can't be this, is there?" It hadn't even really been a question. It had been a statement. "Lord," Meg said out loud, "I'm sorry about that. I should have listened."

A voice inside her was nagging. *Maybe now that you've acknowledged that God might want you to give Diego up, He will give him to you.* Meg pushed it away. She couldn't let her desires interfere with God's anymore.

She continued to pray silently, sometimes coherently, more often a disjointed train of thoughts and emotions directed towards her Maker. By the end of half-an-hour, she knew that she must write another letter to Diego.

Slowly she crossed over to her desk and sat down. She opened the drawer to draw out a fresh sheet of paper. Next to the stationery was the box and the letter Diego had given her before she climbed into the van in Monterrey. Meg picked the envelope up. *"Don't open this until you've made your decision."*

Well, she had made her decision...she could read it now, couldn't she? *No.* She put it down. She had to finish her letter first. Then she could read his without it influencing any part of what she wrote. She picked up a blank piece of paper and laid it on her desk.

August 2

Dear Diego,

After a lot of prayer and struggle I feel that I finally have some clarity about what my answer to you is supposed to be. I have a letter sitting next to me right now that says all that my heart wants to tell you. But I don't think it's what I'm really supposed to say.

My feelings for you run as deep as possible for a seventeen-year-old girl. They would mature into something even stronger and more secure if I gave them the chance to blossom. I think they are a gift from God. But sometimes He gives us gifts only to ask us to give them back to Him.

Meg stopped for a second, tears running down her cheeks.

What I am doing is giving a love offering back to God. It breaks me to do this, but that is the only way God will be able to use me—broken and poured out. If I accepted your offer my soul would be happy, but it would not be satisfied. Trust in the Lord with all your heart, and lean not on your own understanding. In all your ways acknowledge Him, and He will make your paths straight.

I am at a crossroads, Diego. I have come to a standstill. Your path has overlapped mine and I am standing in the middle looking down yours. I want to walk along your road with you. But when I turn the other way I am forced to see my path stretched out in front of me, separate from yours. I must follow it. I will not grow in my faith until I step past the crossing and continue my journey on the road God has chosen for me.

Perhaps our paths will meet again, later—perhaps mine will end in yours, and I will journey with you. But I also will never reach that merging unless I walk away from you now. And I can't consider that, either, because it would create false hope and I would not be able to focus wholeheartedly and joyfully on the tasks God has given me for the present.

I will continue to pray for you.

Meg

Meg dropped the pen from shaky fingers and tried to take a deep breath. Her chest was so tight she couldn't get more than a gulp of air. She pulled out the envelope already addressed to Diego and with trembling hands folded the letter without re-reading it and slid it in. She licked the edges of the flap and closed it, the bitter taste of the glue staying on her tongue. One finger firmly pressed along the "V", sealing her decision inside.

She pushed her chair back and stood, swaying for a moment as weariness came over her whole body. Her bed looked very tempting—she could curl up in a ball and cry herself to sleep. But she had something to do first. Envelope in hand, she left her room and made her way downstairs to her parents, who sat in the kitchen.

"I did it," she said, placing the envelope on the tabletop. "I said no." She looked up. Her parents were silent, but they both had tears in their eyes.

"Can you mail this for me?" Meg asked. Her mom nodded.

"Thank you for helping me." Meg went around the table and gave them both hugs, though she kept herself mentally distanced. If she didn't, she would end up not wanting to leave the circle of their arms. "I think I want to be alone for awhile."

Back in her room she opted for her bed, leaning against the headboard with her pillow to her back. She held Diego's envelope in her hands. *I've made my decision. It's out of my hands now. I can read this.*

She pulled out the single sheet of white paper and found two paragraphs written in Diego's block handwriting. The first paragraph was in Spanish, which she wasn't yet apt at translating. Diego knew that, for the second paragraph was the translation.

MARGARETA,
THIS BOX CARRIES NOTHING AND EVERYTHING. IT IS FILLED WITH AIR, BUT IT HOLDS MY LOVE FOR YOU. REMEMBER THE TALK AT THE GRENGA STAND.

Meg closed her eyes for a second, trying to remember. There had been many visits to the grenga stand. Her gaze fell on the small box laying beside her. "Para Margareta." The letters were thick and black. "*I don't want to go around unwrapping packages that belong to other women. I'm going to wait*

224

till God sends me someone that has 'For Meg' on the tag."

Meg felt her stomach drop. *What is he saying?* She returned to the letter.

I SIMPLY WANT YOU TO KNOW HOW SOLELY AND UNIQUELY SUITED TO YOU I
HAVE FOUND MYSELF. IF IT IS NOT GOD'S PLAN FOR ME TO MARRY YOU, I
WILL MARRY NO ONE.
    DIOS DE BENDIGA.

      DIEGO

By the time she had finished the letter a clenched fist was over her mouth and her body shook. *Why, God? Why did you make me go through this?*

Ten minutes later Jennifer knocked softly on Meg's bedroom door. Hearing no answer, she opened it a crack to find her daughter asleep, her cheeks pale with traces of tears. One hand was tightly clenched around a piece of paper.

If anyone would come after me, he must deny himself and take up his cross and follow me. For whoever wants to save his life will lose it, but whoever loses his life for me will find it ... For the Son of Man is going to come in His Father's glory with His angels, and then He will reward each person according to what he has done

Matthew 16:24, 26